Geoffrey Wines Series

THE FIXER

A Political Thriller
ANTIM STRAUS

Copyright © 2023 Antim Straus
Published by Tim Straus, LLC

This novel was originally published in 2022 under the title "Disorder – A Novel." While the original storyline has been maintained, numerous edits were made to better align this novel with the overall Geoffrey Wines Series.

This novel is a work of fiction. Any references to current or historical events, businesses, organizations, countries, governments, real people, or real places are used fictitiously. Other names, characters, places, and events are products of the author's imagination, and any resemblance to actual events or places or persons, living or dead, is entirely coincidental.

Cover Design by Steven Bassett

12092024

BACK COVER COPY

Geoffrey Wines and President Osbourne are back. Now twenty-four years later, Wines is a seasoned journalist, and the president is comfortably in retirement.

But strange events are rocking the presidential election, and an unlikely candidate is emerging. The president has learned this is the work of The Fixer, a mysterious operative he used in the past, and who is employing a new set of tools and cohorts to tilt the election.

Charged with connecting the dots and exposing the plot in the pages of *The Washington Post*, Geoffrey Wines seeks the help of a skillful colleague who has the moral compass and computing power to uncover practically any person, misdeed, or link to put the whole story together.

The question is whether their efforts to expose the mysterious Fixer and his plan will be too late.

All the world's a stage,

and all the men and women merely players.

They have their exits,

And their entrances.

And one man—in his time—plays many parts.

~

"As You Like It"

William Shakespeare

Prologue

The man sits at his computer, troubled, a glass of Eagle Rare Ten Year Old Bourbon neat in the heavy Waterford tumbler he holds. Day has now transformed into dusk, as snow falls outside the window of his ancient oak paneled library, awarding a view of the Swiss Alps most other Americans can only imagine. Touching his lips, he considers the words on the screen.

"Do I proceed, or not proceed?" he questions aloud, mimicking the syntax of his favorite author—though no one else is in the room.

Shifting forward in his seat, he carefully reads his communiqué, contemplating the consequences of its calculated deed, while relishing the brilliance of his crafted prose.

MY NAME IS JOHN BUCKLEY.
I AM CALLED "THE FIXER."
I COMPLETE LARGE PROJECTS, COLLECT EXORBITANT FEES,
AND PASS ALONG EVEN LARGER EXPENSES TO MY CLIENTS.

I DO NOT HAVE AN OFFICIAL OFFICE,
A LISTED PHONE NUMBER, WEB SITE, NOR STREET ADDRESS.
MY BUSINESS IS ALL REFERRAL,
YET NOT ONE CLIENT KNOWS MY NAME.

MY ASSIGNMENTS HAVE HIGHLY DEFINED GOALS.
I GUARANTEE RESULTS.
MY EFFORTS ARE NOT MEASURED IN SPENDING LEVELS,
SIZE OF ORGANIZATION,
MEDIA IMPRESSIONS, NOR SOCIAL MEDIA HITS.

I HAVE CHANGED NATIONAL BORDERS,
FORCED LEGISLATIVE ACTION,

THE FIXER

CREATED GEO-POLITICAL UPHEAVALS,
AND TANGIBLE SHIFTS IN PUBLIC ATTITUDES.

YOU HAVE WITNESSED MY WORK.
ONE OF MY PROJECTS LITERALLY ENDED THE COLD WAR.
YOU JUST DID NOT REALIZE
WHO ORCHESTRATED IT.
HOW IT HAPPENED.
AND WHY.

MY CLIENTS HAVE ONLY THE BEST INTENTIONS.
MY SOLUTIONS HAVE NO BOUNDARY.
EMPLOY NO SINGLE DISCIPLINE,
NOR RESTRAINED BY LAW.

WHEN MEN OF POWER
NEED HELP.
THEY HIRE ME.

I FIX THINGS.
I AM THE FIXER.

Chapter 1

Three former presidents of the United States waited for their guest to arrive.

"Are y'all sure y'all want to do this?" the Texan asked.

"I certainly do" answered the oldest, "Things have digressed for over forty years. We need to get more citizens involved. We must overcome our malaise."

"And to vote! We need to get the young'uns to vote," added the Texan.

"And to just understand this country cannot survive if no one cares," pontificated the middle president.

The other two agreed.

"Then we should follow our plan," he continued, "This Fixer comes highly recommended. We need his help. Our country needs *our* help."

Their openness with one another allowed them to admit they're distraught and regrettably understand their reality—they are viewed as partisan politicians. They know their personal pleas would be construed as opinionated banter by at least half of the citizenry. Therefore, unsuccessful.

Yes, they did need this outsider's help.

Their guest arrived and the four men sat in the comfortable seats of the plush hotel suite.

"You know my rules," the guest stated. "I meet only with the men who give me my assignment. This will be the only job I undertake from each of you. You provide your precise goal and I do the rest. There will be no discussion." He paused, before adding, "this gives you deniability."

The three presidents smiled and nodded in agreement.

"No negotiation on fees either. Nor expenses," the man instructed. "You will not know my strategy, my tactics, nor actions. But I do guarantee results." He looked each man in the eye. "Agree?"

The three former presidents approved and shared their desire to *reinvolve American citizens in American Democracy.* They had watched voter turn-out plunge and were eager to find a way for Democracy to survive. For the Republic to survive. For broad common understanding of the American Experiment and the civics which make it possible.

Their guest accepted the assignment and gave them the tools needed to wire $1.2 billion to a Swiss account. They were told the money would be withdrawn. Spent. No receipts provided. The presidents were prepared for the immensity of the tab.

Last, their guest told them they would never see him again.

They called him "Elvis" after he left the meeting.

And with the rest of the world, they too would wait to learn *The Fixer's Plan.*

A year later, they began to feel they had made a dreadful mistake.

Chapter 2

MEN WITH EGOS ARE EASY TO PLAY.
MEN WITH HUGE EGOS ARE EVEN EASIER.
THEY ALL WANT THE SAME THING.
FAME,
MONEY,
POWER.

BROKE MEN WITH HUGE EGOS ARE EASIEST TO MOTIVATE.
THEY WANT IT ALL.
NEED IT ALL.

I DIDN'T LOOK FAR FOR MY TARGET.
FOR THE CENTRAL CHARACTER TO MY PLAN.
A PATSY BEING OFFERED A NOT-SO-PATSY DEAL.

FEW COULD RESIST.
EVEN FEWER WOULD EMBRACE IT WITH SUCH ENERGY AND FLAIR.

ONE PRE-PLANNED TRAIN-WRECK IS ABOUT TO HAPPEN.
WITH THE MOST UNSUSPECTING ACCOMPLICES.

Chapter 3

Geoffrey Wines stood and stretched his now sixty-year-old frame at his bullpen desk in the sprawling *Washington Post* newsroom. Unlike the political reporters who were tied up reporting and interpreting the day-to-day machinations at the Capitol, Wines reported on everything else happening in DC. The mayor's office, police, arson, drugs, gangs, financial corruption, municipal waste, abuse of power, hanky-panky in the mayor's office—even a few public acts of kindness that needed telling.

His two Pulitzer certificates hung over his locked filing cabinet. The respect and admiration from his editors and other reporters were never far away either. In addition to his metro reporting, Geoff eagerly accepted assignments to train young reporters—and even interns. Many of these young reporters went on to successful careers as respected journalists; and in one way or another, thanked Geoffrey for their solid start.

Indeed, Wines liked his perch as a reporter's reporter. He shunned the political beat. It had too much baggage. A reporter's motivation was always questioned, and that dried up leads. He preferred the gritty drama of humanity. And tracking down a story.

"How do you find stories?" his fellow reporters would ask.

"Finding a story is never hard," he would simply reply "I'm curiously skeptical. When things happen that shouldn't be happening, I want to find out why."

Since breaking the tainted cocaine case twenty-five years earlier, his antenna continuously twitched. This time, he couldn't rationalize his way out of it. Too many coincidences were happening in the upcoming presidential election. Odd stuff.

"Time to go to work."

Chapter 4

Almost everyone in the country
knew his name.
Knew his face.
Watched him on television portraying
a successful businessman.
An entrepreneur.

He had written books.
Placed his name on buildings.
Opened casinos, resorts and golf courses.
His public persona—solid gold.

His bankers knew different.
His wealth—an illusion.
His business practices
suspect and bankrupt.

He would be the perfect tool to fulfill my assignment.
But my strategy
will doom my sponsors' own plans.

This will get interesting.
And difficult.

Chapter 5

Though Geoffrey Wines didn't report on the *Washington Post's* political beat, he found national politics interesting. As the pre-presidential debate season began, he couldn't believe the political carnage. Twenty candidates split between the top tier and the also rans.

These events are never a love fest. But this year seemed different: The front runner branded "Low Energy Jeb"; a top conservative "Lying Ted"; a likable young Senator "Little Marco"; a seasoned Midwest Governor "One for Thirty-Eight Kasich." And the opposition candidates dubbed "Crooked Hillary" and "Crazy Bernie."

All of this from a man who falsely claimed the current president was born in Kenya.

> *Seriously.*
> *How could this possibly be happening?*
> *Who talks this way?*
> *Who acts this way?*
> *Without severe retribution?*

Swagger or not, only someone with a guarantee. Political parties just do not allow candidates of this depravity to represent them. Never. Ever.

> *Yet it is happening.*
> *Is this a one-man game?*
> *Is this brash candidate working solo?*
> *Or is someone behind this?*
> *There would have to be someone high in the party supporting this candidate.*
> *Wines felt his antenna twittering.*
> *Once again.*

Chapter 6

Two's company.
Three's a crowd.
Twenty is a cluster fuck.
A bar fight.

The plan worked.
My man crawls from the pile.
Declares himself the winner.
Takes the Party hostage.
With only one-third the vote.

Crowd sourcing.
Well, yes and no.
But now "My Man"
Is "The Big Man."
Even with small hands.

Bullet proof on Park Avenue.
On to the Big Show.

Chapter 7

Today, four former presidents met for lunch as they did often since becoming good friends. Partisan politics behind them, they appreciated the ability to dive deep into their past experiences, decision making, and personal philosophies with men who shared the same office. The same responsibilities, stress, and security clearances. They trusted each other and spoke openly.

The big election was gathering steam. No incumbents were running. Just relatives. Really close relatives.

One—her party's front runner. The other—painfully losing out.

"You don't suppose Elvis had anything to do with this front-runner?" the oldest president started. "You all don't suppose Elvis is behind this. Do y'all?"

"Naw," drawled the Texan.

"Doubtful, I would say," added the third president.

"Who?" asked the fourth.

No one answered.

But today, alarm bells were ringing with three of them and they needed to discuss what they could have unleashed.

The fourth merely sat and listened.

He had used "Elvis" in the past and understood exactly how he worked.

"I sure hope Elvis' plan doesn't backfire," he thought to himself.

Chapter 8

THE MAN IS NOT SUBTLE.
AND HE TELLS THE TRUTH.
THIS ELECTION WILL BE THROWN.
JUST NOT TO HIS OPPONENT.
WAIT UNTIL MY FRIEND TURNS ON THE FAN.
STUFF WILL FLY EVERYWHERE.

Chapter 9

In 1991, the Soviet Union collapsed. Suddenly and unceremoniously. The Cold War ended. Geoffrey Wines thought about this often. After twenty-five years, he could never resolve how it happened. Tin-Pot Dictatorships nor World Powers don't just unilaterally surrender, disarm, and dissolve. Never in the history of the world. And today's Russia is not a superpower, but a powerful nation, nonetheless.

Still, the Soviet fall happened right under all our noses. And on President Robert S. Osbourne's watch.

Could President Osbourne's Operation Blueprint be a clue?
The Soviet's collapse just a few years later.
Did one lead to the other?
Same strategy. Different game.

Wines knew the complete "Operation Blueprint" story. He broke it. Provided front page stories in the *Washington Post*. The DOJ, FBI and DEA's entire anti-drug operation was highly successful, but a rogue operator destroyed the program when cocaine tainted with some lethal substance killed users.

Wines, and his intern Emmett Washington's investigation uncovered the story and Geoffrey Wines' later off-the-record interviews captured every unreported detail and player —including President Osbourne — in his still unpublished investigation, *"THE CAMP DAVID CONSPIRACY."*

The "Blueprint "story did not originate from the Capitol beat. It arrived through the pushers and pimps of his Metro news beat. A metro investigation. Gritty. Ugly. Unseemly. Yet by unraveling the complete story, including a one-on-one interview with the president at Camp David, he understood how President Robert "Bobby" Osbourne planned. And how he had prompted one of the most effective, yet suspicious "war on drugs" programs undertaken by any government.

Prompted.
He didn't do it himself.

Didn't order it himself.
He just assembled the right players . . .
In the right places . . .
Who found each other . . .
And it happened.

Yes, indeed, his program brought the drug cartels to their knees and reduced the consumption of cocaine by over fifty percent. *In just six weeks!* The president's team had accomplished this unbelievable feat. A masterful move. A Queen's Gambit. Yet not one federal department would take credit for it.

Not one.
Had Osbourne caused the Soviet Union to collapse, too?
Did he somehow assemble the right people in the right places to make it happen?

Wines pondered the thought. Yes, certainly, defeating the USSR had been the goal of every president since Truman. But Osbourne succeeded. Quietly.

And without Star Wars.

If Osbourne was the "what, when and who," he just needed to uncover the "how." It will be a hell of a story.

What am I waiting for?
No time like the present.
And who knows, it may even lead to another story.

Wines instinctively grabbed his legal pad and ruled three columns using his fat pencil.

"Start with something that is true and go from there"
Hemingway's mantra as a journalist and novelist.

Good advice for a modern-day investigative reporter, too.
What do I know is true?

Scribbling "President Osbourne" at the top of the left column; "USSR Falls" on the right-hand column, he left the center column blank. This column could reveal the how.

Thank goodness the *Washington Post* computerized archives were complete and easy to access.

This would have been a pain in the ass to microfiche.

Now he could scan all the past headlines and articles with just a key stroke.

Maybe some good will come from being owned by a tech giant.

First, begin with a scan of headlines—starting the day after Osbourne's first inauguration. All the headlines for each day of his tenure. Wines found the list surprising as he hand-wrote each key event in the middle column:

- Exxon Valdez Oil Spill
- Poland Holds Free Elections
- Suspicious Drug Deaths Across the US
- Tiananmen Square Massacre
- US Freezes Arm Sales to China
- Berlin Wall Falls
- Osbourne Meets with President of Russia
- US Invades Panama
- Feds Bring Down Drug Cartels with "Operation Blueprint"
- US – USSR Arms Reduction Agreement
- American with Disabilities Act Signed
- Iraq Invades Kuwait – Oil Fields Burn
- Build Up of US Troops in Saudi Arabia
- Clean Air Act Signed
- "Conventional Forces in Europe Act" Limits Military by NATO & Warsaw Pacts
- US Builds Force to Invade Iraq – Hussein Stands Strong

- Gulf War Begins with Operation Desert Storm
- 100 hours of "Shock and Awe" – Hussein Surrenders
- The New US Military – Leading Edge Technology
- Nothing Can Hide from US Smart Missiles
- START-I Signed reducing US and USSR Nuclear Warheads
- Soviet Union Dissolves
- President Raises Taxes
- Interviews Reveal Soviet Military Officials Feared US Weapons

Interviews Reveal Soviet Military Officials Feared US Weapons.

The last item on the list literally jumped off the page. Had Soviet military officials admitted they "feared US weapons?" With a grin, Wines then went back and added Star Wars to the top of the list, though not one bit of it had ever been implemented.

A pattern emerged. Connecting the dots from this premise, the headlines began to form a clear strategy. Osbourne consistently reduced the importance of nuclear superiority and emphasized the size of conventional forces.

But why?

Further, Osbourne worked to minimize oil imports and consumption via the Clean Air Act.

A shot across the bow of Soviet drilling revenue.

Wines kept staring and studying the list.

Osbourne utilized NATO and involved the alliance in his responses to both China and the USSR. And he continually supported new democracies in Poland, East Germany, and failed ones in China.

Then, the Gulf War and Saddam Hussein's invasion of Kuwait.

Defeat Iraq. Defeat Russia?
Were they connected somehow?

He continued to stare. Speaking the words. Searching for a connection.

Oh my god, the man is a genius.
A master manipulator.
Just like Operation Blueprint.
But how did he pull it off?

Had Osbourne convinced Saddam Hussein to invade Kuwait? And challenge the US to stop him while also standing down for six months while the US staged its fighting force with no interference?

Then the United States defeats a powerful Iraqi military using the most sophisticated arms ever seen. On live television no less. Afterwards, allowing Saddam to remain in office.

What else is related to this? Wines entered a few more keystrokes and his screen filled with a chronology of the Gulf War.

Saddam's army stood poised to enter Saudi Arabia. But never did, even though every military planner said it would have been a cake walk and would have thrown a wrench into the US invasion plans.

Most odd.
Especially considering Saddam's hate of the Saudis.

An American Ambassador had given confusing signals to Saddam, assuring him we would support an invasion of Kuwait. Very strange.

Our State Department does not make that type of mistake.

After Saddam's defeat, the US provides helicopters for Iraq's military to defeat the Kurds and other internal enemies.

Unheard of.

And Iraq never reimbursed Kuwait for damages to its oil fields.

Offending governments are never let off the hook.
Obviously, the US was not trying to defeat Iraq.
Nor even stop another Middle East border challenge.

If the objective of the Gulf War was not to save Kuwait or defeat Saddam Hussein, then why the shock and awe?

Who were we really wanting to defeat? A bigger prize? What could be an even bigger prize? What other major event happened in the man's presidency?

The shock and awe of the Gulf War.
Soviet military officers feared US weapons.
Shock and awe.
Soviet fear.

The answer now obvious, particularly with a little 20-20 hindsight. The ultimate prize for any president.

But how could Osbourne have pulled this off without a single whisper? There were no leaks, even after all this time. That would mean no departments within the Federal Government were used. Even the most top-secret schemes shed at least one confidential source. But not this one.

How? And who'd done it?
Maybe it's time to give the president another visit.
And collect on the man's promised fishing lesson.

Chapter 10

SECURING A THIRD OF THE VOTE WAS EASY.
STRENGTH IN SMALL NUMBERS.

WINNING FIFTY PERCENT WILL BE HARD.
GETTING TO FIFTY PERCENT PLUS ONE
WILL TAKE SOME UNUSUAL STRATEGIES.
AND UNCONVENTIONAL TACTICS.

EMBEDDED HELP WILL BE A MUST.
OUTSIDE ASSISTANCE REQUIRED.

IT IS TIME TO VISIT OLD FRIENDS?

Chapter 11

"President Osbourne's office. Pat Hayes speaking."

Geoffrey Wines paused for a moment. A familiar name from 25 years ago.

"Hello Ms. Hayes. This is Geoffrey Wines from the *Washington Post*."

"Well, hello Mr. Wines." She sounded surprised. "How long has it been since we last spoke? My goodness, over 20 years. How may I help you?"

"Ms. Hayes, I wanted to see if I could travel down to Greenville and meet with President Osbourne. Is he doing okay?"

"Yes sir, Mr. Wines. The president just celebrated his 90th birthday. Fit as a fiddle. Sharp as a tack. Stays active too. But only doing the stuff he loves."

Wines could envision Osbourne in retirement. Waking early. Fixing some "wood-fired coffee" and catching his breakfast.

Probably has a fishing pole permanently welded to his hand.

"In fact, Mr. Wines, he brought up your name just the other day. Seriously, he did! He said he suspected you would be calling him soon. Something about the current news, he felt sure would raise your suspicious mind. Don't know what or why. But he said if you call, to be sure to tell you he wanted to take you fishing at his and Clarence's favorite fishing hole. Said they told you about it at Camp David." Pat then paused; Geoff denoted a sigh. "Unfortunately, Clarence Robinson passed a few years ago, so, it will just be you and him. My, he misses that man."

Wines thought about the president and Clarence Robinson. Lifelong friends who would do literally anything for the other. *Anything.* Clarence played a key role in Operation Blueprint and in Wines' complete exposé, *"THE CAMP DAVID CONSPIRACY."*

"Ms. Hayes, that is most generous of the president." He also could not get over how loose and chatty Pat Hayes was with him. He also thought it isn't unusual to have former executive assistants follow out-of-office presidents into retirement. The president must have expressed some nice words regarding their past association. Maybe because he never reported on anything they discussed that day with Clarence and DEA Agent Chuck Harding.
> *But why is she being so open?*
> *So chatty?*

"When can you come down? The president will be here for the next four weeks. Late Springs are particularly nice in the Piedmont. Couldn't drag him away from here if you tried."

"Well, then Ms. Hayes, how about next week?

"That works. Let's plan dinner at the president's house on Tuesday night and then fishing bright and early Wednesday morning. Bring casual clothes only. Call me back with your air travel plans. We will reserve a hotel and one of our security details will pick you up. It makes things run a lot easier with the Secret Service folks here. Is that okay Mr. Wines?"

"What's not to like? Thank you, Ms. Hayes. I'll call you later today with my flight plans."

"My pleasure, Mr. Wines. My pleasure."

Wines placed his cell phone on his desk and thought for a minute. He did not expect such a warm reception. Pat Hayes addressed him like a long-lost friend.
> *That had to come from President Osbourne.*
> *The man wants to talk with me.*
> *Pat seemed to communicate he had wanted me to initiate the call.*
> *In fact, he was expecting it!*

It would be odd if he is even thinking about the first Gulf War. Especially after the debacle of the Second Gulf War.

Does he want to know why I hadn't written anything else about Operation Blueprint? Does he suspect I wrote a complete exposé? Probably guessed I would. But because I never published it, he wants to know when.

Possibly.
No, he's got something else on his mind he wants to share.

What's the lesson he said Clarence had taught him? "Don't enter a fight unless you must. But only on your own terms. And only when you are ready."

Which must be now!

Chapter 12

THE PROS GO WITH POLLS
FILL BUCKETS.
SPEND LOTS OF MONEY.
THIS WILL BE A MISTAKE.

FOR US, WE WILL:

SUPER MOTIVATE A FEW.
GOD. GUNS. BABIES.
AND IMMIGRATION SHOULD DO.

TARGET SOCIAL MEDIA MESSAGES
TO ENERGIZE MANY.
AND MANY MORE
TO DISCOURAGE A FEW.

CROWD THE FIELD WITH SPECIAL INTEREST CANDIDATES.
DIFFUSE THE OTHERS' VOTE.

NO LANDSLIDE NEEDED.
JUST A RAZOR THIN MAJORITY
IN A FEW KEY STATES.

TOTALING 270 ELECTORAL VOTES.

I'LL USE THE POWER OF TWO-SEVENTY.
THIS WILL PUT HIM IN OFFICE.

ALONG WITH A LITTLE HELP FROM MY FRIEND.

Chapter 13

A black GMC Yukon Denali pulled into the circle of the new Greenville Downtown Marriott at precisely 6:45 pm. One of the Secret Service agents detailed to protect the former president—President Robert S. Osbourne—quickly stepped around the car and welcomed Geoffrey Wines to Greenville.

Wines lifted himself into the right rear seat with the agent closing the door behind him. Soon they exited the hotel lot and proceeded toward the president's home.

"Everything in order at the hotel sir?" the agent inquired in a most friendly manner, meeting Wines' eyes in the rearview mirror.

"Yes sir, a very nice hotel. New?" Wines asked.

"Opened about a year ago. The Greenville downtown keeps expanding south and Marriott wanted to be a part of the extension. It's going to be quite nice on the other side of the falls, too."

This was not the sleepy town he'd imagined. Though he had heard how much it had grown, he didn't realize the city's business wealth: Michelin, BMW, Hitachi, and several other cash-rich international firms had replaced the textile industry. And along with it came a strong blue collar job base along with a large contingent of engineers and computer jockeys.

"Sir?" the agent interrupted his thoughts. "We're heading up Paris Mountain to where the president lives. He has his office suite in his home. Calls it his 'West Wing' as the house faces north and south atop the mountain, and he absolutely did not want to obscure the view down to the lake off to the east."

The man lives to fish.

"Also Mr. Wines, the president asked that I tell you to not be surprised when you arrive at his home. His personal secretary, Pat Hayes, also lives with him. Moved in about three years ago. A few years after her husband died. I will say, it has been very good for both of them."

> *Wow. Didn't see that coming.*
> *Pat is what, maybe ten years younger?*
> *Not a big deal.*
> *No wonder he asks the Agents to forewarn guests.*
> *It also puts a whole new spin on her friendliness and openness during my call.*

> *Am I the subject of pillow talk?*

The road up the mountain twisted with pines, a few oaks, and maples—all in full leaves. Flowering trees and bushes completed the landscape. Soon they were at the president's front gate and the agent pressed a series of buttons to open the high security barrier. They continued through a tight forest-lined drive that emptied onto a small turning circle and the president's rambling cedar wood home. A huge furnished front veranda with flower boxes on the railing, pots containing red and white geraniums hanging between the porch columns, and two mature magnolia trees, also in full bloom, guarding each side of the porch.

> *Very southern.*
> *Very pretty.*

As the car pulled up, President Osbourne and Pat Hayes gave a friendly wave. Both looked great. Fit. They almost glowed.

> *Thank goodness for Osbourne's wisdom.*
> *This scene without the president's forewarning would have been just weird.*

"Mr. Wines. Welcome to our home," the president proclaimed gesturing toward Pat Hayes and reaching out to shake Geoffrey's hand, followed by Pat extending her hand. "You remember Pat Hayes. She was my administrative assistant at the White House. Still is. But for the last few years, she has also become my roommate and, let's say, significant other. Long story. I can tell you later."

They are blushing.
Newlyweds?

"Well, sir. You certainly look like a *very* happy couple. I am so delighted for both of you. And Ms. Hayes, thank you for making my visit run so efficiently."

"My pleasure Mr. Wines. My pleasure. And please call me Pat. Why don't you and the president settle onto the veranda while I fix Mr. President a Makers. And you? What may I fix for you Mr. Wines?"

"A Makers would be perfect. Thank you."

"Mr. Wines," the president smiled, "I guess our living arrangement is driving you crazy. The old reporter's antenna is twittering, huh? It's a wonderful story. And a double blessing, too. Pat and I have worked together since I was a Senator. She followed me when I became the Vice President, and then eight years in the White House. She and her husband also followed me here when I left office, and she remained my executive assistant. Well, about five years ago, her husband John, a really great guy died, and about three years ago, we looked at one another and just decided to move in together. You know I had been a bachelor for almost thirty-five years since Emily Rose died."

"Yes sir. I remember."

"Well, anyway, we are both very happy. But she just can't seem to break away from calling me 'Mr. President.' But like any other relationship, there is no question who is really in charge," the president concluded with a wink.

"Are you married? I don't believe I saw an announcement."

"No Mr. Wines. We're not married. No need to. Just too many complications at this point. Both of us are certainly self-sufficient after lifelong, high level government positions. Nope. We're not married, but we are incredibly happy together. She fills the long void in my life after Emily Rose died. And I guess I do in hers after John passed."

"Well, like I said, I am very happy for both of you. And it certainly seems to be agreeing with you two."

Osbourne nodded. "Now Mr. Wines, I know you are itching to discuss something other than my love life. That's why you called. Right?"

I need to ease into this discussion.

Wines straightened in his seat. "No sir. I called because you owe me a fishing lesson. I've been holding onto an IOU for over twenty years."

"Excellent Mr. Wines. You will get that tomorrow. At Clarence's and my favorite fishing spot on the lake," Osbourne said, pointing down at the lake off to the east side of the house. "Come on now. We have about thirty minutes before dinner is served. Pat will be leaving us alone. What's on your mind?"

"Well, sir, ever since the day at Camp David with you, Clarence, and DEA Agent Chuck Harding, I've been thinking an awful lot about you, and if I may, the way you make things happen. You're not a puppet-master. Nor even a manipulator. But you do have an uncanny way of getting people into the right places to 'let things happen on their own,'" Wines said using actual finger-quotes.

"Thank you, Mr. Wines. I think."

Wines shook his head. "No seriously. It is quite masterful. You probably don't know I continued to investigate Operation Blueprint after our meeting and after the cartel trials were over. And you may have guessed I prepared a manuscript of the complete story, a complete exposé including corroborations we did not discuss that day."

"I would not have expected anything different from you, Mr. Wines," the president said with a smile. "In fact, I counted on it."

My goodness.
He is so open.

"That manuscript is on the shelf until I figure out what to do with it," Wines injected to let Osbourne know its publication was not imminent and not what he wanted to discuss during this visit. "But the story did make me look back at your time as president and wonder how some of the other major events came to happen."

Pat interrupted, placing two identical crystal tumblers with Makers and cracked ice onto two coasters with the Presidential Seal. "You boys look like you're already into it. I'm back in the study if you need anything. Take your time, Harriet will be serving dinner in about 25 minutes."

"Thanks hon." Osbourne smiled as he took his first sip.

"You know Mr. Wines," he continued, "at the end of each day, while in the White House, a steward would serve me this identical cocktail, and everyone left me alone. It was my scheduled thinking and contemplation time. You might interpret it as my 'conniving' time. But it is essential for a president to reflect on the events of the day and figure how they fit into the larger picture. Otherwise, a president is just jumping at the latest crisis to cross the desk, and no real forethought ever happens. No consequences are considered or even understood on past events and actions."

Wines nodded his head, careful to not interrupt the president's thoughts.

"Fishing helps too. But they never allowed me to stock and fish in the Basin. Had to wait for the weekends at Camp David. Anyway, here we are together, enjoying a Makers and reflecting on past deeds."

Wines sat silent for a bit, hoping President Osbourne would continue. He didn't.

"Sir?" Wines finally broke the silence, "Sounds like you want to tell me something. Am I reading you right, sir?"

Osbourne shifted in his stuffed porch chair, took another slow shallow sip of his Makers, then gently lowered the glass, and placed it back on the table.

"Mr. Wines, I want to tell you some things. About events and actions that took place during my administration. I want you to think overnight about what I am telling you, not so much because it is important you know, or that you will even want to report on those past events, but so you will better understand why what I will reveal to you tomorrow is so important."

Wines nodded.

Tomorrow?

"And Mr. Wines, I am not making tonight's conversation on the record, off the record, or no record. I invited you here because I trust your judgment on what should be done with what I will be telling you. I'm an old man, with not a whole lot of years left, but with a lifetime of experience and gained wisdom I hope can be somehow passed on."

Osbourne paused, looked Wines straight in the eye and smiled. "Hence, why Pat and I invited you here."

Confessions of a president?
Or something more?

"No, Mr. Wines. This is not a dying confession or even a clearing of my conscience," Osbourne smiled.

Is he reading my mind?

"But it is time for supper, and you, Pat, and I can talk over delicious stuffed pork chops, cooked kale, sweet potatoes au gratin, and if we're lucky, Pat's pecan pie for dessert."

Chapter 14

The supper was laid out on the dining room sideboard in warmed platters and bowls holding more than enough servings of each dish. The table elegantly set with President Osbourne on one end and Pat on the other. Wines sat on the side facing the food. The chandelier centered over the table fully illuminated the room with a warm glow.

"My goodness. Thank you, Pat. What a lovely meal," Wines gushed as he sat down with his full plate.

"Our pleasure Mr. Wines. Figured if you were traveling here to see us, we might as well give you a full stomach." Then she added, "Along with a full mind."

She really will be part of the president's story.

"Mr. Wines," the president interjected, once again reading Wines' mind, "The beauty of having your former admin as your mate is you don't need to worry about what she knows and what she doesn't know. She was there. She already knows everything anyway. And can probably remember it better too."

"Just like Nancy." Wines blurted almost before he had a chance to think.

Osbourne and Pat both leaned back in their chairs, holding back a laugh, then smiled at one another and almost in unison answered, "Yes, almost like Nancy."

Am I going to make it out of here alive?

"Okay, Mr. Wines, you came here on a mission. What do you want to talk about? Which event that happened on my watch do you want to discuss?

"Well, Mr. President, I want to learn more about the fall of the Soviet Union."

"What's to tell Mr. Wines, the presidents before me set them up, and I shot them. I merely showed the Soviets I would bring a gun to a knife fight."

His answer is uncanny.
Perfect fit with my Gulf War thesis.

Wines also noted an uneasiness between the president and Pat as they looked at one another seeking reassurance.
Do they want to go through with this?

Then they both paused, leaned forward in their seats, and nodded.

Finally, Pat interjected with a laugh. "Oh, Mr. Wines, you really are good."

"Ma'am?"

"The president always said you could figure out any story, put the dots together, and then seek confirmation. You did it on Operation Blueprint. You did it on your other Pulitzer story with the DC Mayor. I read the *Post* every single day. Even down here in South Carolina. And I do believe you may have figured out how Mr. President forced the collapse of the Soviet Union."

"Ma'am?" Wines politely exclaimed, surprised at her directness.

"Oh Mr. Wines. Just ask us what you want to ask us."

The president jumped in. "We'll tell you, but our answers will have the years of gained perspective we discussed out on the veranda."

"Sir? Ma'am?"

"Mr. Wines. Before reminiscing the collapse of the Soviet Union, I want to provide you with an overview to every problem a president tries to solve" the president explained, leaning forward in his chair. "It's simple physics, really. Every action has an equal reaction. Looking back, the problem we leaders who seek solutions make is we seldom consider or even recognize every action we take will have an equal reaction. And those reactions often set up problems that also need a solution. Often more complex."

"I think I understand, Mr. President." Wines confirmed, setting down his fork and leaning in to meet the president. "But why don't you, and Ms. Hayes, take me through it."

"You see Mr. Wines, the United States and the USSR evolved slowly over time. Yes, there were revolutions, but the changes that led to the consolidation of influence, power, and military might evolved. Even in places like Poland and Czechoslovakia, where the changes were gradual, though capped by a Soviet invasion. Unlike say Nazi Germany, who tried to change European borders and national allegiance in just a few years.

"Now since the end of World War II, the goal of the United States government had been to defeat the Soviet Union. To end their sphere of influence. To prove Democracy and Capitalism were stronger than Communism and a pure State-Owned financial system."

Wines slowly took a sip from his water glass, keeping eye contact, as Osbourne continued.

"For years we competed like two sports teams. Played on-going games. Races into space. Olympic hockey. Supported small countries to curry favor, and real estate, if needed. And built monstrous arsenals of rockets and nuclear weapons neither of us ever intended on using.

"We trashed-talked each other, but we never directly allowed ourselves to fight each other. We fought our Vietnam, and they, their Afghanistan. And today, we have our own Afghanistan. All miserable military failures. Those incursions failed because we tried to change national allegiances and borders in a short time. Longer term, they supported North Korea and we South Korea into a stalemate. We never directly confronted each other. Except in Cuba where both sides realized a real fight seemed too close for comfort and we both backed down pretty darn fast." Osbourne reached for his near empty tumbler of Makers and took a sip. "Are you with me so far Mr. Wines?"

"I believe so, but all you are stating is our history."

"No sir, Mr. Wines. No sir." Osbourne snapped. "You are falling into the same trap as me, and all the presidents who came before me in understanding actions and reactions. You see, in all the geo-political discussions—all the planning meetings, all the war scenarios—did we ever once ask ourselves what the breakup of the Soviet Union would mean? Actually mean? In what ways would it affect the world? The whole world. What would happen when there were no longer two centers of gravity, counterbalancing one another? Not to mention the psychological mindset of our citizens without a big common enemy. Sure, we talked about how to do it, but never the impact it would have in any granular or gravitational manner months, years, or decades later."

"But the Soviet collapsed, and you certainly had a major role in it happening."

"Yes sir, Mr. Wines, I did. And the way I did it, and the aftermath, were huge mistakes."

"Mistake? Mistakes? Are you serious Mr. President? Their collapse happened on your watch!"

Did he say, 'And the way I did it was a huge mistake?'
Stay cool Geoffrey.
He is going to tell you something big here!

"Not sure I know what you are referring to, Mr. President."

"Oh, Mr. Wines. Are you playing the wily possum? Of course, you know what I did. That's why you're here. You just can't figure out how I pulled it off."

Wines paused, thinking, contemplating where this would go.
Am I here?
Hearing this?

Pat interrupted his thinking. "Mr. Wines, let me forewarn you. Be careful what you hear, because once you hear it, you cannot unhear it, and your mind will explode."

Wines, once again reaching for his glass of ice water, turned to face Pat, "Excuse me, ma'am?"

Then she cautioned "Mr. Wines, after you and Mr. President speak, you will look at everything differently. What you thought is settled business, isn't." She then stood, "And gentlemen, I am thinking this is going to turn into a late night. Let me brew some coffee; let's retire to the living room and I'll serve my pecan pie in there. Between the caffeine and the sugar, you guys can go at it all night."

"Thanks hon. You're not going to join us?"
I need time to think.

Gather my thoughts.

"Ms. Hayes. Let me help you clear the table," Wines immediately volunteered as he stood and grabbed the closest dishes from the table.

"Sure, Mr. Wines. Just set them on the counter." Pat said with a quick amused glance over to her housemate.

The former president excused himself. "Since I am no longer allowed in her kitchen, I'll clear places in the living room. This is going to be interesting." Then laughing, "Interesting as hell."

● ● ●

The pie tasted delicious as promised.

I expected that.

But the story the president and Ms. Hayes told was even more delicious.

And dangerous.

● ● ●

Wines and Ms. Hayes joined Osbourne in the living room. A large coffee table surrounded three oxblood leather easy chairs; and a tidewater love seat anchored the room into a most non-contemporary conversation pit. Mahogany side tables each holding a shaded table lamp accompanied each chair. Ms. Hayes placed a tray with an insulated coffee urn, three mugs along with cream and sugar service on the table. A sliced pecan pie, dessert plates, and forks completed the setting.

"So, would you like to start with your questions or just state your theory on how I single handedly brought down the Soviet Union?" Osbourne started with just a bit of sarcasm in his voice.

"Sure, I'll begin" Wines began knowing this approach worked years ago, during their first face-to-face meeting at Camp David. "A few minutes ago, you said something like 'all I did was bring a gun to a knife fight. Is that correct sir?"

"Yes sir." Osbourne answered, looking over at Pat with a knowing smile. "Does that raise a certain suspicion, Mr. Wines?"

"Well, yes it does. And you referred to the trash talk between the US and Soviets, along with absolute avoidance of nuclear weapons."

"I did."

"So, my assumption is our conventional weaponry had progressed substantially beyond what most citizens or the Soviet leaders understood."

"Evolved into what Mr. Wines? What were those miraculous unknown weapons?

"Well, let's see. Laser guided cruise missiles. GPS. Real-time look down imaging. Stealth bombers."

"And . . . ?" Osbourne coaxed, while smiling over at Pat.

Wines cleared his throat as he prepared to put it all out on the table. "Somehow you convinced the Soviets we could win a conventional war, hands down. Somehow you convinced Mr. Gorbachev they didn't have a chance to defeat us in a conventional war. A knife fight as you called it."

"And how do you think President Osborne pulled this off?" Pat chimed in with amusement. "Called him on the phone? Showed him a video? Took him to a restricted site in Nevada? Or just said 'trust me Gorby.'"

"No. I don't believe any of those tactics would have worked," Wines laughed, "I think you put on a real live demonstration. Something Gorbachev, his generals, and the political hardliners could not deny."

Osbourne slowly nodded his head.

"See Bobby," Pat said using the president's pet name. "I told you he would connect the dots," Pat smiled as she rose and poured coffee into each mug. "Please continue Mr. Wines."

"Now I listed every major event that occurred during your administration. Dots if you will. Trying to figure how one thing logically connects to the next. And when you mentioned 'bringing a gun to a knife fight' my thesis gelled mighty quickly."

"Scary," Pat said, "He doesn't miss anything."

"So, you're thinking we just showed our new weaponry to Mr. Gorbachev and his generals?" Osbourne pitched in, sipping his coffee.

"Well, not exactly Mr. President. Not exactly a private showing. More of a spectacular public showing! A showing none of them could deny."

"Interesting Mr. Wines. Now how did I do that?"

"Well, Mr. President, I believe I know what you did. But I haven't any idea how you pulled it off," Wines answered while taking a bite of the pecan pie.

"What did I do, Mr. Wines?"

"You put on a real-life demonstration, a real war if you will, using our newest and most sophisticated weaponry in the deserts of Iraq. You soundly defeated the fourth largest military in the world in 100 hours— on their home turf no less. You ensured it was televised, the whole thing, on CNN. And when done, you simply pulled up stakes, exited the country, leaving it pretty much as it was prior to the demonstration. I mean engagement."

"Whew! That's quite a premise, Mr. Wines. And how did I make that happen?"

"That's the part I can't figure out. I know you set it up. Somehow. But I can't figure out how you convinced Saddam Hussein to cooperate."

Osbourne and Pat just laughed.

"And now you know why we invited you here, Mr. Wines." Pat chuckled.

Wines looked at each of them and saw their amusement.

"Is it true Mr. President?" Wines quizzed, "Did you somehow start the Gulf War to demonstrate to the Russians our superiority?"

"I did." Osbourne confidently replied.

This whole thing is unbelievable.

"But how?" Wines asked, his voice rising.

"Can't tell you how. I hired that out. But the plan became apparent to me once it was in motion. Here's my problem though. I need to know who I hired, because quite frankly, he is at it again."

Wines repeated Osbourne's last statement in his mind—*hired, and at it again.* "Wait a minute." Wines' head continuing to spin at the *two* revelations. "You don't know who you hired to convince Saddam Hussein to start a war in his own country, only to be defeated, so you could convince the Soviets they didn't have a chance against us in any sort of war!" Wines rubbed his temples at the revelation. "Is that right, sir?"

"That's right Mr. Wines. Pretty nuts when you think about it. Using an outside operator gave me complete deniability."

"That sounds familiar." Wines thought out loud.

Wines observed that Osbourne paused for a second. Then recovered his composure "All I did was brief him on my desire to end the cold war via the dissolution of the Soviet empire. Never anything about Iraq, Saddam, Kuwait. None of that. Just an objective. That's the way this man operates."

"A mystery man? You hired a mystery man to set it up? Wines probed, seeking confirmation.

"Yes. A mystery man. A 'Fixer' really. That's why we invited you to our home. This is a story of presidential over-reach, that, in retrospect, I am not very proud of. In fact, not proud at all. It let too many cows out of the barn. Created problems we are still trying to fix today. It humiliated the Russians in the process. And I hope no future president makes the same mistake."

"No future president? Is he still out there for hire?"

"Unfortunately, yes." Osbourne confessed. "Since I left office, I've seen him used in other bone-head mistakes. Even with Saddam again. Jeez." Osbourne confessed. "And regrettably, I am learning they are going to make an even larger mistake if you aren't successful."

"They? Me??"

Whoa. Am I getting enlisted?

"Sir? Am I being enlisted?"

"I believe so Mr. Wines. I believe so."

"For what?"

"Mr. Wines. It's getting late. And we're waking up pretty early tomorrow for your fishing lesson. Why don't you sleep on the possibilities, and we'll talk about it over our fresh catch breakfast?"

"But wait. Let's tie this up now!" Wines pleaded.

"Mr. Wines," Pat interceded, "We'll have the agent take you back to the hotel and then pick you back up around 5:15 am. Mr. President will meet you at his favorite fishing spot. I will say goodbye as you men will be fishing alone tomorrow morning without me. And my guess is you will be leaving directly for the airport from there."

Osbourne and Pat both stood.

Wines immediately followed, sorry they won't be continuing the discussion, but wanting to yield to his hosts wishes. "Well then Ms. Hayes. Until then, this has been an absolute delight. Surprising. Interesting. An honor. Delicious too. Thank you for your wonderful hospitality."

"My pleasure, Mr. Wines. My pleasure. I hope we see each other again."

Chapter 15

Geoffrey Wines did not sleep much. He could not figure out what President Osbourne and Ms. Hayes' were up to. Who their mystery man might be? He kept turning over what they had said. But more importantly, trying to understand where they were headed and the role, they were wanting him to play.

> *They have got to know some, or all of this will end up on our front page.*
> *But why?*
> *Who are they trying to influence?*
> *Who are they trying to defeat?*
> *Maybe today Osbourne's intent will become clear.*
> *And what on earth are his successors planning?*

• • •

Wines stepped into the cool morning air. The black Denali, and same agent who drove him back to the hotel, met him in the hotel driveway. Wines pulled his roller bag to the rear of the car and placed it in the back.

"Good morning, Mr. Wines. I hope you had a good night's sleep, albeit short."

"Thank you, I did. But I don't sleep all that much anyway." Wines replied.

"Right you are. Sleep is over-rated. But fishing isn't, and I am sure you and the president will have a wonderful time. He sure loves to fish. It's contagious. I fish with him often. Learn something new each time. He's waiting for you at the lake right now."

The drive from the hotel to the fishing lake seemed shorter than to Osbourne's home. No mountain to climb. They were there in fifteen minutes. No early morning traffic either. Plus, for some mysterious reason, every traffic signal switched to their favor.

> *Perks of a presidential security detail.*
> *Nice life if you can get it.*

They came to a small gravel cut-off and drove slowly along the rough road. Up ahead, the road descended toward the lake. Wines saw the shadow of another large SUV backlit by a small campfire near the water's edge. Two men stood near the fire.

"Morning Mr. Wines." The president softly hollered. "We're all set for catching our breakfast. Thanks men, for helping" he continued as the two agents dismissed themselves and took their positions about fifty yards from the fire. Close enough in case of danger. Clear views of land and lake. Secure for the president. But not close enough to eavesdrop on the president and his guest.

Wines noted the large granite-ware coffee pot sitting on the fire and several tightly wound *Washington Post* logs setting nearby.

"Oh, I always use your newspaper to start my fires," Osbourne mused. "Didn't need many today, summer wood is usually dry and starts pretty easily."

"That's good Mr. President. We successfully start fires each morning we publish. Rain or shine! Some stories smolder. Some flash and are gone. And some burn brightly for a very long time."

"Touché Mr. Wines. Nice line. I hear your warning. Speaking of lines, if we don't get ours in the water soon, breakfast will be mighty late."

• • •

"This lake is small, but quiet, especially early in the morning. And gets surprisingly deep in the middle. Perfect for bass and catfish. That's why Clarence and I loved it so." Osbourne lamented with a bit of melancholy in his voice.

Within a half hour, Osbourne had pulled in three nice bass and Wines felt delighted with his single catch. "Keep it moving ever so lightly," the president instructed, "No jerking until you feel a nibble. Don't over-react. Stay calm and cool. Think like a fish."

Think like a fish?
Does that mean 'follow the bait?'

Osbourne skinned and filleted the four fish, then placed them in a large cast iron skillet loaded with sizzling butter. "This is the secret of my longevity," the president explained, "Fresh butter, fresher fillets, and cool mornings. Who wouldn't live for the next day? And this is absolutely my favorite time of the year. Pre-summer. Cool mornings. Beautiful days. And not a lot of rain either."

"Understandable," Wines confirmed.

"Oh, and fire-brewed coffee too," Osbourne added as he poured and passed Wines a large steaming mug. Wines smiled as Clarence Robinson had told him about "Bobby's Fire-Brewed Coffee" during his Operation Blueprint investigation and follow-up. Clarence even thought of opening a coffee shop by that name.

"So, Mr. Wines. Let's pick up on the conversation we started last night. I'm deeply worried. I am worried we are about to make a huge mistake. This one may be irreversible."

Where we started last night?
There's enough there to sell millions of papers.

"Middle East?" Wines queried.

"No sir. Closer to home."

"Immigration? Drug cartels? Oil drilling. Oil pipelines? Climate change?" Wines started listing all the domestic issues he could think of.

Osbourne waved him off and flipped the fillets. Then looked up, "What's your take on the election?"

A dumpster fire.

Wines looked down and laughed, "Sir, quite frankly, I can't believe your party is allowing the front-runner to be in any way associated with your party."

Osbourne gave a concerned laugh, "And . . . ?"

"And it appears no one in your party is doing anything about it. Lots of squawking, name calling . . . hell, even the senior Senator from this great state said something to the effect 'it would be an utter, complete, and total disaster. If you're a xenophobic, race-baiting, religious bigot, you're going to have a hard time being president of the United States, and you're going to do irreparable damage to the party.'"

The president's head snapped up from looking at the sizzling skillet.

"Exactly, Mr. Wines. And I would add to the United States of America. So, what do you think is going on here?"

"Hard to say sir. I would say the man either has a guarantee of victory, or just doesn't give a damn."

"You're right. Let's say guarantee of victory." Osbourne proclaimed, then hesitated for several moments. "Now, Mr. Wines, we need to go off the record for the rest of this conversation. In fact, for everything we are discussing today."

Off the record?
Just for this morning's conversation?
Did last night not happen?

"Mr. President. What could we possibly discuss today that requires going off the record—that would not have been off the record last night?"

"Simply because what we discussed already happened. It's history. Nothing can change it. But what we will discuss today, will happen, and we need a way to stop it. Literally, the future of our country depends on it."

"Whew! You are serious. What could it be?" Wines replied, alert to the president's urgency.

"Mr. Wines. I need you. No, make that America needs you. You need to investigate, and expose, what is happening in this election. And I cannot be associated with your investigation. If you agree, I will tell you everything I know. Agree?"

Wines froze, gathering his thoughts, trying to anticipate the president's secret. What could it be? He says he needs *me*! *America needs me*. A secret big enough that last night's Iraq War confession would be deemed trivial.

"Yes sir. I agree."

I believe I have been enlisted.

Chapter 16

My Russian is perfect.
Time to call a friend.
Direct.
On a special line.

His phone is electronically answered.
I enter a special code.
Vladimir Putin answers fifteen seconds later.

"Hello Old Friend." He spoke.
"And to you." I reply.
"What can I help you with?"
"Need you to help in the American election."

"What's in it for me?"
I tell him who.

"Him? You must be joking."
"No. I'm not."

"What do you need?"

Chapter 17

Geoffrey Wines, Metro Reporter for the *Washington Post* now had one of the most explosive political stories he could ever imagine. Two stories! Not only were national politics not his beat, but he'd been personally given these news tips by a former president of the United States. Given an on-the-record account of the cause—and planned effect—of the first Gulf War.

And now, an off the record heads-up, on a soon-to-be-thrown presidential election.

> *Doesn't the mystery man understand what throwing a presidential election could do?*
> *Give me pimps and pushers anytime.*

President Osbourne had been careful to explain the three former presidents had no upfront idea or knowledge of The Fixer's—who they called "Elvis"— plan to throw the election. They just wanted to awaken the American citizenry to the importance of civics and participation in government. To vote. To care. To get involved. To understand issues. For the sake of democracy. For the sake of *our* democracy.

Then almost a year later, they figure out their mystery man would meet their objective by planting possibly the single-most-unqualified person into the race. And throw it so he wins the presidency! Our mystery man would put someone in office who had bankrupted numerous businesses; sued almost everyone he did business with; whose business most banks would no longer touch; an inability to manage people; and fired people who excelled on his game show, and probably his own business too. And who would most assuredly fail to manage the affairs of state or play well with other national leaders. This man's presidency would surely lead Americans to realize they MUST become involved and cast their votes for well-vetted, qualified persons.

> *Aren't the political parties supposed to do this?*

Wines then laughed. And the ironic kicker is this mystery man had already wrecked the candidacy of the brother to one of the former presidents who made the original request; and if the plan succeeds, will defeat another's wife.

Talk about ensuring deniability.
Talk about duty to Country, God, and Family,
In that order.
Whew!!

President Osbourne had laid out everything he knew about the pending election and his party's presumptive candidate. And it became crystal clear why he, and Pat Hayes, spent so much time the evening before discussing the Gulf War.

It's from the same playbook.

First, convince someone who is in a drastic financial position to act and play the part.

Two, guarantee financial security.

Three, give that person prestige and real power.

It worked with Saddam, though not in the long run.
Wonder how it will turn out for this guy?

And . . .
How do I track down the mystery man?
A man the sponsors do not know by name.

Wines realized he failed to ask Osbourne how he contacted the mystery man in the first place. He'd call the president after lunch. But now it's time for a little pinball and pizza at his favorite lunch spot a few blocks from the *Post* Building. Nothing clears the head better than a big slice of Meteor Pizza. And a bit of pinball.

Chapter 18

KNOWLEDGE IS POWER.
PERCEIVED KNOWLEDGE IS EVEN MORE POWERFUL.
CREDIBLE SOURCES FEEDING FAKE KNOWLEDGE BECOMES DISINFORMATION.
DISINFORMATION DISGUISED AS TRUSTED FACT IS POWERFULLY PERSUASIVE.

BUT WHO WOULD EVER BELIEVE THIS STUFF?

NEVER UNDERESTIMATE HOW FAST A LIE WILL TRAVEL.
WE SEE WHAT WE WANT TO SEE
AND DISREGARD THE REST.

Chapter 19

"Hello Mr. Wines. The usual?" The owner of Meteor Games & Pizza stood behind the counter. In the case were four large pizzas. Geoffrey Wines shifted his eyes to the center pie: Italian sausage, mushrooms, and cheese.

The man lifted a large slice and placed it into the brick oven behind the counter to bring it back to eating temperature. "Mr. Wines. Hoping you would come by today. This one's on the house. Not a free lunch, mind you. I got something I need to talk to you about. You going to be here for a while?"

"I can John. For you. Certainly."

"Good, grab a seat. I'll bring it over when its ready. Large Coke?"

"Sure. Thanks. Lots of ice, please."

"You got it."

● ● ●

"So, John, let me get this straight." Geoffrey Wines mused. "There are people who believe you are running a child trafficking business right here from the basement of Meteor Pizza?"

"Yes, they believe the game-room downstairs attracts kids, and we are kidnapping them." John then straightened his back with a look of bewilderment crossing his face, "And selling them!"

"Seriously?" Wines laughed at the preposterous charge.

"Mr. Wines, it's not funny. People are coming in here demanding I surrender to them. Others go downstairs to the game room, and tap on the walls, looking for hidden doors. One man, he sounded like an Ozarker—or someplace—came in, pointed a weapon at me, and demanded I stop. Somehow, I talked him down—gave him a large slice—and he left. Scary though."

"D'you call the cops?" Wines asked sipping on his Coke.

"No. He left with the slice. And thankfully, I haven't seen him since."

"Do you have any video of these events?"

"I do. Being in DC, we record everything. 24/7. Senators, Congressmen. Political pols. Reporters. Soft-drink thieves. Nut cases. All you guys. Got cameras everywhere. A Congressman comes in at 2:00 am, with someone he shouldn't, it's recorded. I don't hide them either." Pointing to the corners of the room where the cameras were securely mounted. "Between the video cameras, free pizza, and drinks for the cops, we never get robbed. But this insurgence of people looking for child trafficking in our game room is too much. What the fuck? How do these rumors get started?"

"Did you ask any of them where they heard about it . . . the 'child trafficking' at your restaurant?"

"Yeh, I got into an argument with one of the nuts. He accused me of trafficking children and passing the profits over to the Democratic Party. In fact, this nut insisted the Dem's candidate for president was running it and spinning the proceeds to her party. He demanded it was true. Said he had read it on the internet."

"Did he say where?" Geoffrey asked, wiping his hands, and pulling his notepad from his inside breast pocket.

John looked up thinking. "Couldn't exactly understand the man. Very thick southern accent. Something like 'Chin or Chan Four.' I don't know. Some Asian-sounding name. And Facebook! Kept seeing it on Facebook too. He said that was where he got all his election news. Election news? From Facebook? Geez, I pay Facebook to draw traffic here. But Jesus Christ, election news? What's wrong with NBC, CBS, *Washington Post*, *New York Times*, MSNBC, Fox, *Washington Times*? Or even Rush? All we see is election news. Who the fuck needs more?"

The restaurant owner then let out a long-defeated sigh, "Can you help me?"

"Maybe John. Let me investigate this. This does seem odd. And since so many are coming here from all around the country, it appears to be national—maybe orchestrated, not random." Wines paused and reached inside his top pocket, "Listen, if anyone comes in and starts asking about child trafficking, call me immediately. Maybe I can get over here and ask a few questions. Here's my card with my direct phone number."

"Thanks, Mr. Wines. Sure seems strange, doesn't it?"

"Strange? Yes sir, real strange. Somewhere, someone is screwing around and spreading some nasty rumors. Particularly accusing the Democratic candidate of running it."

> *I think I just got my metro-lead on Osbourne's powerful political story.*
> *My door just opened.*

Chapter 20

Shhh,
I got something to tell
It isn't right,
Nor completely wrong.
Just viable enough to be believed.

Especially when the reader wants to.
I can control who reads it.

And I've got just the girl to lead it.

Chapter 21

Katy Lynn Holloway had an earned reputation among political operators as a master of polling data. Her aging beauty queen looks often led her jealous competitors to call her the "Queen of the Poll." In any case, she could look at a spreadsheet, examine the demographic data, past election results, and immediately understand trend lines and probabilities. Candidates bid for her services. She always went to the highest GOP bidder.

One candidate admired her, but being cheap, wouldn't agree to her compensation requirements. So, out of nowhere, a special donor augmented her salary.

Now in front of her lay an entirely new set of criteria derived from deep analysis into Facebook data. It mysteriously appeared shortly after her arrival to the new campaign, forwarded via an Ivy League Poly-Sci professor. The opening screen of the Excel document clearly stated: "Not for Commercial Use – To Be Used Only for Academic Purposes."

This interactive spreadsheet embodied a polling person's dream come true! Astonished, this level of information and analysis existed. She had always compiled and understood demographics. But now, she also knew exactly what news media each person consumed, the search articles they googled, the actual articles they read, how they voted in past elections, the types and brands of products purchased, what groups they were affiliated with, their interests and hobbies, who they communicated with, and then everything about every single one of their Facebook friends. All this data identified 500 surrogate sets of voters she could pin-point target. Five *fucking* hundred!

Using the interactive and labeling sections of the document, she could also create her own surrogate groupings for pure political advantage.

Katy Lynn deeply understood polling data. Her model - "Birds of a Feather Flock Together" never failed her. In the past, she had tabulated data, compiled her own profiles sets, and then stratified every city block, zip code, Congressional district, state, region and finally the entire country. But who needed the last three? She could direct mail or canvass any area she liked.

But this tool would replace all that. She now had micro-targets. Amazing data on more people than there are mailboxes. And she could literally reach each one of them directly and discreetly, by simply tapping into their most trusted sources of information.

I collect.
I cluster.
I convince.

Close examination of the data allowed her to isolate deep fears, dislikes, political concerns, family discomforts, and trust in church, country, and God. The longer she studied the tables, the more convinced the full extent of its meaning could be used in a remarkable new way.

If I can convince, then can I also dissuade?
Can I dissuade people from voting for the candidate of their choice?

Yes, I can!
With the right messaging.
Through negative messaging!
And her boss' main opponent was ripe for negative messaging.

Boy was she!

Since coming on board, Katy Lynn finally felt she could win this thing. She believed she could realistically get her candidate elected!

"There is no way I can convince most people to vote for this guy," she screamed at her computer screen. "But I can target and convince some of his non-supporters to vote for a minor candidate instead, thereby leaving his main opponent short of votes in critical areas."

Short in critical areas!

She studied the screen and let her mind wonder about the possibilities. Then with a flash of inspiration, it hit her: "Or not vote at all! Totally shifting the electoral map!"

She then leaned back in her chair and laughed out loud, "That's it! I can't wait to put this theory to the ultimate test!"

Chapter 22

BOTS.
EVEN DISINFORMATION BLOGGERS LOSE THEIR JOBS TO MACHINES.
THOUSANDS OF BOTS CHURNING OUT FABRICATED LIES.
GIVEN THEIR EASTERN EUROPEAN SOURCE,
MY FRIEND IS BEHIND IT.

HE UNDERSTANDS SOMETHING WE DON'T.
NEWS TRAVELS FAST.
FAKE NEWS TRAVELS EVEN FASTER.

Chapter 23

Geoffrey Wines returned from Meteor, with a slushy Coke in hand and an excitement he couldn't contain. Since his visit with Osbourne, he had no idea how the three presidents' friend could fix an election.

Now he had a very good idea how it might be done.
Lies. Lies.
And more lies.

But he needed to compile more data than just a few nut-jobs showing up at Meteor Pizza. They claimed they read it on the internet. Something about "chin or chan." A lot about Facebook.

Grabbing his phone, and checking the internal *Washington Post* phone list, he dialed the four-digit number of the paper's "New Media Correspondent." A young reporter named Olsen, James Olsen. A self-proclaimed computer geek, hacker, and new media journalist. Internally, his rep assured he knew his stuff—inside and out. Knew about computers, understood how programming and systems worked, and had legitimate street cred as a master hacker. Quite a skill set for a reporter. But Wines had just one simple question in mind as he raised the phone's handset to his ear.

The other line was picked up on the second ring. "Olsen here."

"James, this is Geoffrey Wines in Metro."

"Yes sir, Mr. Wines. What's up?"

"James, please. Would you just call me Geoff?"

"Okay, Geoff. And please, call me Jimmy. What's up?"

Jimmy Olsen?

"Got something going, but in an area, I know nothing about. Perhaps you can help."

"Sure-thing Geoff. When we win a Pulitzer, will you share?"

Wines stopped—surprised by James Olsen's statement.

Am I perceived as a Pulitzer hog? He had won his first Pulitzer for stories he had single-handedly uncovered and reported. And his second

Pulitzer about Operation Blueprint, a DEA and FBI program designed to disrupt the Colombian drug cartels and local gangs. But he had needed to keep his young intern, Emmett Washington—now Managing Editor of *Time Magazine*—out of the news for fear his brother and mother would be implicated.

"Sir? Mr. Wines?" Jimmy caught himself, "Sir, that did not come out right. I did not mean to imply that you . . . well, that you . . . gosh darn, this is awkward."

"James, I mean Jimmy," Wines could feel the edge creeping into his own voice, "You are a journalist. Journalists aren't lost on words. Nor directness. Are they?"

"Sir. My thought was only respectful. You are what all of us young journalists aspire to. You find big stories. And report them. My thought was merely that if you are working on a story, it must be a big one! And big stories lead to big awards. That's all." Olsen eagerly confessed. "Yes sir, I would love to help you. What do you need?"

Wines wasn't sure who felt more relieved. He or Jimmy. He momentarily thought his colleagues thought ill of him. He would need to be mindful of it now.

From the mouths of babes.

"Okay, Jimmy, we're good. Look, I'm working on a lead. One of my sources mentioned an internet site. Something 'chin' or 'chan.'"

"In what context Geoff?"

Wines thought for a second before answering. Sources were dear and he in no way wanted to compromise any of his until he felt confident it would help. "Something about a restaurant being a front for a kidnapping and child trafficking ring," he slowly answered.

"Right up your Metro alley, huh Geoff?" Olsen quipped, then turned serious, "I believe you are referring to '4Chan.'"

"Four-Chan? F-O-U-R- C-H-A-N." Wines repeated and spelled out, writing the name in his reporter's pad next to his notes from the Meteor.

"Yes sir. It's a new breed of social media—well, really, it's a newsfeed. Far right stuff. They been pushing a story about the Meteor

Pizza restaurant here in DC being a front for child-trafficking and funneling money to the Democratic Party. Crazy stuff like that."

"You know about this?" Wines asked with surprise.

"Sure, it's my beat!" Olsen coolly and professionally responded, then continued, "Wait a minute. That's right. I've seen you there several times eating lunch at the Meteor. I love it too. Even go there for concerts at night. Are you specifically talking about the Meteor?"

"Yes," Wines confessed, "What else can you tell me?"

"Oh, sir. A whole lot more. And I can show you stuff you will not believe," Jimmy said, stringing out the last four words. "Stuff no one should believe. It will blow your mind," Olsen continued calmly. "But not from here. Not through the WaPo portal. I'll need to show you from my electronic home base."

Then Jimmy Olsen, a newbie correspondent for *The Washington Post* asked the senior reporter and two-time Pulitzer winner, "Can you keep your sources confidential?"

"Confidential sources?" Wines replied, then thought he heard a muffled laugh, "Nope. Blabber about them all the time." Wines continued with a smile.

This kid might be the real deal.

"Okay, Geoff, how about tonight? I'll take you to my home and show you on my system. How bout we meet in the parking garage, by Door B, at 5:15 pm? Work for you?"

• • •

Wines took the elevator down to the parking garage. He wondered if this Jimmy Olsen would look like Clark Kent's sidekick. Thin. Medium height, light brown hair, horn-rimmed glasses? Geeky. Camera around his neck?

Jimmy immediately walked up to Wines.

Yep, everything but the camera.

"Let me shake your hand, Mr. Wines. Geoff. I'm Jimmy Olsen. I cannot tell you how much I respect your work. Sorry about shooting off on the phone today," Jimmy spilled, "It is just that when you called for my help, I was overwhelmed."

"That's very kind of you . . . Jimmy" Wines accepted the compliment graciously, "Are we taking two cars?"

"Sir, prefer we don't. In fact, I prefer we visit my place via The Metro. Besides, where I live, you'll never find a place to park. DC. Quite a place! In fact, I live in one of your old stomping grounds." Olsen teased, "Yep, you'll feel right at home."

"Stomping grounds?" Wines retorted with a smile.

This should be interesting.

• • •

Geoffrey Wines and Jimmy Olsen exited the subway at the Benning Road Station. Jimmy looked at Geoffrey with amusement. "Look familiar? Any old friends you would like to look up?"

The boy does do his homework.

"I would, but they are all dead. A rather mysterious overdose as I recall. Neighborhood has changed a lot in 25 years." Wines answered, amazed at Jimmy's research.

Had he reviewed my past stories?
Does Jimmy know of the whole story?
My other sources from that story?
The ones I never reported.
Nor referenced in the WaPo stories.

"Yes sir, Mr. Wines. I mean Geoffrey, I moved into the neighborhood around four years ago, when I started receiving a regular paycheck from the *Post*. Found quite a deal too. A little bungalow on Steuben Street." Jimmy excitedly explained to Geoffrey as they walked. "Yep, the neighborhood is really changing. Gentrification. Out with the poor. In with the monied. This area is way too convenient to downtown to be poor."

"I see what you mean about not finding a parking spot. Haven't seen nary a one," Wines pointed out, "Nice cars too."

"Almost there Geoff," then Jimmy took an abrupt turn up the sidewalk of a wood framed single story bungalow with a porch that stretched across the entire front of the house.

"You live here?" Geoffrey asked with disbelief as they walked onto the porch. "You bought an old crack house?"

"Surprised?" Jimmy laughed, "In fact, I've been waiting for this moment since your call this morning."

"I thought the city had razed it," Wines said remembering the house where five Sons of Steuben gangbangers and a buffer died from an apparent overdose from a thought-to-be new brick of uncut cartel cocaine. "Hell, I remember it practically falling down the last time I saw it."

Jimmy smiled a wide smile and faced Geoff. "It was quite a find for me. Even in the biggest of gentrification frenzies, no one wants to buy an old crack house with a dubious past. Ghosts. Bad karma. Confusing cocaine with meth. Whatever you want to call it. Besides, no one knew who actually owned the place. So, it stayed unoccupied. Even the gangs and homeless left it alone. Couldn't be destroyed either." Jimmy laughed, "Even the old 'Sons of Steuben' banner still hung in the living room when I bought it. What? Twenty years later."

"How'd you know about . . ." then Wines corrected himself, "how'd you find the owner?"

"Ahh, Mr. Wines. Now you know the power of on-line investigations. Anything that has anything to do with legal documents, I can eventually track down, from the comfort of my Aeron chair." Then Jimmy added with pride, "And a little proprietary software."

Jimmy unlocked the door and they stepped into an immaculately clean and minimalist furnished living-dining space. "Welcome to my home, Mr. Wines."

"It looks like new construction," Wines said as he studied the room, while remembering what the place looked like so many years ago.

"Well Geoff, you are almost correct. When I bought the place, it was a cockroach infested, God-knows-what-lay-behind-the-walls mess. I knocked out all the walls, down to the studs. Like the houses in

THE FIXER

New Orleans after Katrina. This showed the wiring and plumbing needed replacing. As did the windows, kitchen appliances and everything else that *was* nailed down."

"Impressive," Wines countered, "You did all of the work yourself?"

"Thanks," Jimmy accepted. "Yes. Plus, as I will show you, it was imperative everything be replaced. Yet, despite years of neglect, underneath it all, this house is incredibly well built and sound. The foundation is solid stone. The structure is oak, not pine. Exterior siding is oak and cedar. Doesn't get better than that—typical of 1920 construction around here. But tearing out real plaster walls is a bitch. Dust and lattice splinters everywhere. Filled two giant dumpsters."

"Time and expense. How'd you swing it?" the not-so-subtle journalist in Geoffrey Wines asked.

Jimmy laughed, "A reporter's question, huh Mr. Wines?"

"Well, Jimmy. I need to understand my sources."

Jimmy walked over toward the duplex refrigerator. "Beer?"

"Sure," Wines answered.

"Like most millennial men, I got a wide assortment. What type? Pilsner? English Ale? IPA? Guinness? Porter? No malt liquor though."

"An IPA would be great Jimmy. Thanks."

Jimmy pulled a Lagunitas IPA from the fridge. "Glass?" he asked while opening the cabinet next to the refrigerator and grabbing a spotless pint beer glass.

"Please," Wines said, noting the efficiency of Olsen's layout.

Jimmy then continued his story. "Well, since I was sixteen, I worked on Habitat for Humanity crews. Mostly during the summer, but often during weekends the year round. My dad believed in getting folks into their own homes and started me working in that direction pretty early on."

"Plumbing. Electrical work. Sheet rock, and carpentry too?" Wines marveled, "And the time and money?"

"Oh, never let a question go unanswered, Mr. Wines." Jimmy laughed. "First, I got this place for a song once I tracked down the owner of the deed. Near impossible. He practically gave it to me since the back-taxes would have killed him. One of these inheritance-of-an-inheritance-of-an-inheritance deals. Hell, I bet the Sons of Steuben never paid rent. At least I could never find any record of them paying rent to the owner. Not sure how the taxes were avoided. No records exist they were ever paid. Interesting huh? I didn't need to pay any of the back taxes or anything. DC was delighted to have a tax paying owner who promised to refurbish the house."

"And cash flow, Jimmy? Rebuilding a house cannot be cheap. Especially on a young journalist's salary."

"Well Geoff, since you ask, building materials were pretty cheap coming out of the last recession. Remember? Few houses were being built. Since I knew exactly what I would need, I put it out for bid. Just like the big guys. And paid cash too."

"Cash?" Wines led, maintaining the game.

"Yep. Cash. Nothing seals a deal faster than cash. Besides, the house is small."

Wines looked around the room. The workmanship looked flawless. The walls a smooth gray. The paint even. White crown molding. Flawless. The floors were beautiful hardwood, too.

Jimmy continued, "Geoff, you look like I did the impossible. It's really not that hard. I didn't move any walls. And when you're putting up new sheetrock, ceilings, wiring and plumbing, it's easy to make stuff look good . . . if you've had enough practice. And after about fifty Habitat homes, I'm a reasonably accomplished tradesman. I even hold electrical and plumbing certification since I supervised about twenty of those homes."

"Amazing!"

"But" Jimmy grinned as he pointed Wines toward a closed door facing the living room. "this is what I really wanted to show you."

When Jimmy opened the door, Wines could not believe what he saw.

Chapter 24

E-MAILS, PRIVATE SERVERS, AND LEAKS, OH MY.
SOME "MISSING."
OTHERS EXPOSED "EVERYWHERE."
SOME QUITE DULL.
OTHERS STUPID AND EMBARRASSING.
NONE REALLY IMPORTANT.
BUT THEY CAUSE QUITE A RUCKUS.
WHO'D THOUGHT?
MY FRIEND DID.
MY FRIEND WHO UNDERSTANDS US BETTER THAN WE UNDERSTAND OURSELVES.

Chapter 25

Jimmy Olsen pushed open the door to presumably his home study and let Wines pass. Instead of an office, Geoffrey Wines found himself and Jimmy in a small four-by-five-foot hallway with a stainless-steel door on the opposite wall. The door behind him swung back and he heard it lock. Electronically! Then, next to the door, a keypad lit up and red laser beams could be seen scanning their presence.

"No way!" Wines exclaimed as Jimmy entered what seemed like a ten-digit code into the keypad. Olsen stepped back, forcing Wines against the locked door behind him. The steel door then swung out.

Out.
Not in?

Looking in, Wines could see the entire opposite wall of the room covered with huge monitors and equipment like what one would expect to see in FBI or CIA operations centers.

"Welcome to Planet Krypton, Mr. Wines."

One by one, the monitors came to life. Wines could feel the cool of a climate-controlled room. Two chairs with keyboards stood waiting.

Unbelievable.

"Seriously Jimmy?" Geoff finally responded, speechless about what he saw, but instantly recovering his surprise to react to the operation center's name. "Look, I get a man with your hacking credentials would have state-of-the-art tools. Even something as impressive as this setup" as he waved his hand across the room.

"Geoff. Yes, it is impressive. But what you don't see is what will amaze you." Jimmy confidently interrupted. "This room is totally self-sufficient. Powered by a Tesla Powerwall. Constant power. Ensures no surges. And keeps my power usage constant, and secret too."

"But isn't calling this Planet Krypton carrying it a bit far?" Wines interjected.

"Nope. This room is a digital fortress. It is steel fortified on all six sides. You would have to literally tear down the house to get into this room. Even fire can't touch it. It is also electronically shielded. No eavesdropping from the outside. No heat signatures. Digital air gap between components too, so it is totally hackproof. And any would-be robber or intruder would be in for the surprise of their life. Don't ask, Geoff." Jimmy laughed with a fiendish grin. "I won't tell you the how and why."

Wines knocked his knuckles on the wall. Tapped his foot on the floor. Solid. No clank. No give either. Hard as a rock.

Definitely solid.
Real solid.

Jimmy continued, answering Geoff's question.

"Mr. Wines. I guess you need to know my story. Yes, I was named 'Jimmy' by my dad who adored the *Superman* story. Yes 'Jimmy—not James.' He and my mom raised me in a small Iowa town. I was an only child. My dad was an old-style television and radio repairman. You know, big boxy tv's with tubes. Owned a little shop, stacked with old tv sets and racks of vacuum tubes. A cluttered workbench with soldering irons and electrical gauges and testers. He also had crates full of *Superman* comic books from childhood and always bought each new episode as soon as it hit the news-stands. Guess between the electronics and *Superman* comics, I didn't fall far from the tree. I built virtually all the computers and servers you see in this room. Saved a ton of money and made the systems undetectable. We're talking state-sponsored hacking security. Only better!"

"The cost? This must have cost you a bundle." Wines wondered aloud.

"Like I said, my dad had a near complete set of *Superman* comics. Including the rare early issues. Well, anyway, after he and mom passed,

I sold the collection. Used the money to remodel the house and build-out Planet Krypton."

"That explains the financial side of this place. Bet the collection brought a pretty penny." Then Wines interjected with a laugh. "So, as an adult you are living the part as Jimmy Olsen?"

"Yip. My bet is if *Superman* was conceived today, Jimmy Olsen would have been a hacker. Not a photojournalist."

Wines started to ask about his parents, but Jimmy continued, his eyes glued on one of the giant monitors on the wall. As he stared, he spoke slowly and earnestly.

"But to directly answer your question, Mr. Wines, the answer is a definite YES! My dad believed in 'TRUTH, JUSTICE, AND THE AMERICAN WAY.' Just like Superman! He repeated those words constantly. As a kid, I thought it was funny. But as I grew older, I learned it was actually his credo. That's why we built Habitat homes. That is why I became interested in journalism. To ferret out truth. And why I became a 'white hat hacker.' A hacker for good if you will. With a super system . . . the absolute most sophisticated and powerful system possible. It gives me super-powers!"

Jimmy paused for a second, cracking his neck and then motioning toward the electronic array before them. "Geoffrey. This is the closest thing a mortal man can come to being a Superman. You know, looking through solid steel walls . . . leaping tall buildings . . . disguised as a mild-mannered reporter working for a great metropolitan newspaper . . . fighting the never-ending battle for Truth, Justice, and the American Way."

Olsen then stopped and looked directly at Wines. "I know it sounds incredibly corny. But it's the truth. And . . . well . . . it's who I am."

Wines retreated from Jimmy's gaze for a moment. His mind racing.

> *Is this guy for real?*
> *I wonder how crusty old Ben Bradlee would have reacted to Jimmy's story.*
>
> *But I got to admit, this young man has a purpose and a goal.*

Got to admire a young man with purpose. And motivation!
Especially in journalism.

Finally, Wines looked up and grabbed Jimmy's hand, gave it a tight squeeze, and looked Jimmy in the eye. "Jimmy, maybe this world needs more people like you. And God knows, we need people like you in our profession and in the *Post's* newsroom. I look forward to seeing your work. I hope we can do a lot of great reporting together. And yes, share a Pulitzer or two."

Wines sat in front of the keyboard on the right. Mesmerized.

Look at this place!
We're going to get along just fine.
Beyond fine.

"Okay, Jimmy, please carry on. "Show me what you know about FOUR-CHAN." Wines asked, looking at the constantly changing screens in front of him.

"I will, but before I do, let me just demonstrate a few things about the Kryptonite System I created."

"Kryptonite?" Wines repeated.

This just keeps getting better and better.

"Yup. It's a system designed to find hidden things. Hidden things that when they come to light, could become deadly to the holder."

Deadly?

"For example. I have a near complete manuscript, by a Geoffrey Wines, of a story about an FBI and DEA operation that went terribly wrong." The wall screen in front of Geoff scrolled through several manuscript pages."

Geoff immediately recognized his own distinctive formatting.

Jimmy continued. "It's explosive. It implicates a wide number of important people. Yet, it was never published, even though the reporter won a Pulitzer on much narrower published stories."

Wines just stared at the monitor.

Is this a shake-down?
How'd he get this?

After a few moments Jimmy broke the tension. "Geoff, please, no worries. It's not going anywhere. But it is a nice way for me to explain my Kryptonite System. One you will immediately understand."

"Continue. Please continue." Wines directed tersely.

I'm not liking this.

"Okay, Geoff. You know us hackers can penetrate almost any system, right? We can enter giant data bases looking for stuff. Or even plant stuff we want others to find. But trying to find the right stuff in the mountain of data is difficult, inefficient, and renders a hacker's superpowers inadequate. But what if we can give the software a scent to follow, like a bloodhound to narrow things down."

"That seems reasonable. But doesn't Google already do that?" Wines answered, still unsure of Jimmy's game-plan.

My private manuscript god-dammit!

"Not really. Google can find sets of words or subjects. But it can't search styles, though the engineers at Alphabet are using AI to mimic famous writers. But this program compiles and then can discover documents based on how things are said, regardless of the topic.

"Let's take this manuscript as an example." Jimmy continued to explain. "I took your published *Washington Post* articles on Operation Blueprint and created a scent. An algorithm, actually. Then I set it loose across the internet to find anything similar. Obviously, it picked up the original *Washington Post* stories and other papers who reprinted the stories. It also found various publications, blogs, social media posts, professional and academic journals, plus broadcast transcriptions that referenced or used quotes from the articles. But I wasn't interested in those for obvious reasons. I knew they existed. The private emails were more telling, particularly the ones between South America and here! Man, were they pissed-off!"

"But how? I didn't send emails to South America."

"Ahh, that's right. But you did quote a cartel enforcer and I entered his speech pattern into the system. And voilà, my system ferrets out emails with his style."

"Emails? Cartel emails? Impressive!" Wines offered, thinking of Luther's scary presence when he visited the *Washington Post* boardroom.

Jesus Christ. Cartel emails.

"But then Kryptonite came across a deleted file from the *Washington Post* reporters' database." Jimmy said, looking squarely at Geoff. "Deleted from a supposedly secure system. A Bezos-Amazon Web Services secured system. A system holding culls of stories and perhaps confidential source information from *Post* reporters." Jimmy emphasized.

My sources.
They're in the manuscript.

"You mean you hacked your own company? Jesus Christ!" Wines incredulously asked.

"Well, yes. But to prove a point. Feel assured, I never shared your manuscript. That wasn't important. It still isn't."

"But my manuscript. You found it from a deleted whatever you call it file."

"That's right. Everyone, everywhere, believe they have secure files and even securely deleted or trashed stuff. Even Cartel email servers. And those guys are good. Better than most governments. But nothing is secure and absolutely nothing ever goes completely away. With the right tools, looking for specific patterns, we can find it. Or at least parts of it. And when we do, it's kryptonite for the creator of the data in the first place. For instance, those emails to and from South America would have absolutely indicted the cartels. Others too. And made your manuscript a whole lot more interesting."

Wines shifted, thinking about the value of confidential emails to a reporter.

Could a hacked email be considered a confidential source?

A named source?
An unnamed source?
Text-messages too?
Or an anonymous post on any social media platform?

"Interesting. But it can't be used in a court of law because it is stolen." Wines offered. "Reporting can use it as a source. But courts of law cannot. At least not without a warrant."

"Bingo sir. *Truth. Justice. And the American Way.* The power of the press. Guaranteed by our Constitution. At a great metropolitan newspaper, our job as journalists is to find it and report it. But we need to be wise in its application. Use good judgement. As I believe you did in your complete *'THE CAMP DAVID CONSPIRACY'* story. Full disclosure of every email someone writes is not reporting. It's not journalism. It's dumping garbage. And it's irresponsible.

"For instance, the full cocaine story you wrote would have destroyed the FBI and put other institutions in severe jeopardy. Probably would have tied up the courts for years on unrelated appeals too. Quite a story Mr. Wines. Whew. Quite a story. Better you let it lie. Good judgement sir. I approve."

Wines wanted to change the subject.

Now!

"So, in the case of Meteor Pizza and Games. And Four-Chan. You can track down the source of the outrageous child-kidnapping ring story?" Wines asked to change the subject and move things along.

"Yes sir, Mr. Wines."

"Call me Geoff."

"Yes sir, Geoff. We certainly can! And we will! I can find where the story originated. Who originated it. And then the exact path it made to that website and eventually others."

Wines paused. "Chain of possession?"

"Exactly. Chain of possession. With complete time-stamped documentation, if needed." Jimmy entered a few keystrokes and a screen filled with numerous Twitter posts. "Let me show you some real time outrageous stuff now appearing on the web. And explain to you how they got there and spread. Stuff that makes the Meteor Pizza child-napping look very tame. And, as you can see, it is spreading fast as more people click on sites or retweet sheer nonsense and lies . . . and people are believing it!"

Then Jimmy Olsen said something that struck Geoffrey Wines.

"You know, America's growing addiction to lies and disinformation will destroy 'the American Way' quicker than the spread of any of the opioids, cocaine, or any illegal drugs you tracked down. Much quicker! You know that don't you?"

Greater than the spread of drugs
in destroying the American Way?

Chapter 26

LENIN WAS RIGHT.
RELIGION IS A WEAPON.
WE'LL TURN POLITICAL RALLIES INTO RAPTUROUS EXPERIENCES.
WITH THE FERVOR OF REVIVALS.

SPEECHES WORSHIPPED AS SERMONS.
WHITE EVANGELICALS AS ACOLYTES.
POLITICAL CONTRIBUTIONS AS TITHING.

IS MY MAN THEIR NEW SAVIOR?
GOD, I HOPE NOT.
I JUST WANT HIM TO WIN.

I'LL HAVE THIS RELIGIOUS-RIGHT LEAD THE CRUSADE.
NEARLY 80 MILLION OF THEM.
25% OF THE COUNTRY.

THEY VOTE.
AND THEY'LL SUPPORT MY MAN.
IF HE STAYS ON SCRIPT.
AND HIS PAST BURIED.

Chapter 27

Katy Lynn Holloway now had her strategy. Her data supported what she was seeing on the news. Her boss had some sort of magical appeal to about thirty percent of the voting population. The GOP faithful who votes for anyone with an "R" after their name. This group won him the primary. A great starting point, but not enough to win a national presidential election with 270 Electoral Votes.

Even before switching to her current boss, it did seem odd to Katy Lynn how the "Religious R's" coalesced around her current candidate. It began long before she came on board. She remembered watching the live C-SPAN feed in January of her candidate speaking in front of the assembled students and faculty of a large Christian university.

Her candidate at the time, who she now referred to as "The Weasel" was a rather unlikable sort. He also spoke that day, pandering to the audience in his usual way, making religious references and closing his eyes in prayerful fashion when reciting verse. He knew them all. He had studied The New Testament like he had the Constitution of the United States. But he did not understand the true meaning of either, turning the words of St. Luke and James Madison to support his personal agenda. This weasel of a man was damaged goods. Many would stick with him, but she, herself, prayed for the day she could move along.

Her prayer was answered in a most unusual way.

The third presidential hopeful to speak—her current boss—had somehow wowed them. He stood in front of the assembled mass of conservative evangelicals like Jesus Christ; accepting their praise and acknowledging how they had turned out just for him; how only he could save them, their religion, their guns, their babies, and their Christian holidays from "those people" who wish to take it all away.

He too had pandered. Citing verse, though he didn't know a "Two" from a "Second"—he had somehow connected the University's credo to himself and cursed several times during the speech as the students snickered at his gaffs.

But in the end, the president of the university, the business minded son of its founder, went out of his way to endorse the man. She remembered thinking how unusual it was to have the university president bestow such praise on a single candidate. Unprecedented. To her, it sounded like a "paid political announcement."

> *Seriously.*
> *Someone must have paid the university president.*

He told the audience the 'business mogul candidate' reminded him of his late father, the famed televangelist, who founded the school. And while he noted neither he nor the school would endorse anyone for president, the long exhortation of praise sounded like a full-throated endorsement.

> *Business mogul?*
> *This man is the only casino owner in the history of the world to declare bankruptcy.*
> *This man had bankrupt projects around the world.*
> *This man withheld full payments to his suppliers.*
> *This man had over 3500 lawsuits, more than any single business in the world.*

She remembered the university president saying, "he is one of the greatest visionaries of our time" then adding, "in my opinion, he lives a life of loving and helping others as Jesus taught in the New Testament" and then listed ways the man had helped people who were struggling financially and in need.

She remembered thinking "WTF." None of her opposition research had revealed such generosity. In fact, there had been very little. His foundation was a fraud!

The university's president closing remarks also struck her: "As for Christians who might have misgivings about voting for a twice-divorced former casino mogul, my father had no problem voting for Ronald Reagan, a divorced Hollywood actor, over Democrat Jimmy

Carter, a Southern Baptist Sunday school teacher, in 1980. We are all sinners."

During the subsequent weeks, Katy Lynn had frequently wondered why the university president had gone so far out on a limb in supporting 'the business mogul' so early in the primary process. It was only January! Before Iowa.
Had he been tipped off?
Did he know something the rest of us didn't know?

Her skepticism only increased when the candidate later bragged to an Iowa audience, "I could stand in the middle of Park Avenue and shoot somebody, and I wouldn't lose voters."

Why does he believe he is invincible?
Does he know something we don't know?

Her blindside became reality. The man romped through the primaries, knocking off each seasoned competitor. Multiple senators. Two governors. And a very soft-spoken neurosurgeon.

Her candidate, "the weasel" was the last standing. An ego the size of Texas could not save him from defeat. He lost despite all her efforts. She thought she was finished in this presidential election.

But it wasn't over for her.

Katy Lynn was immediately asked to join the "business mogul's campaign." Not by the candidate himself. But by an unknown sponsor who picked up most of her fees.

Yet her boss, the candidate, came to love his "Brown Eyed-Brown Hair Queen of the Polls."

That was then.

Now she needed to grow the base of supporters for her candidate. To get him to 270 electoral votes.

Her sponsor suggested she continue to build his allegiance with the "values voter." The Evangelicals. The Southern Baptists. The

Catholics. And Orthodox Jews. They represented just over 50% of the electorate. "The Values Voters."

Values voters? They were unreliable. Yes, they turned out. And they only voted for GOP candidates. But if they weren't certain about the presidential candidate, they were also likely to not vote the top of the ticket, as they had with the previous three presidential elections.

Maybe that is why GOP voter turnout had been down in 2004, 2008 and 2012. The 2008 election was a GOP operatives' nightmare. Large turnouts, particularly among minority groups, created a tidal wave of Democratic support no GOP presidential candidate could overcome.

But now she had the tools,
And a plan to fix just that sort of problem.

Plus, her sponsor had promised "this year will be different. Any message you conceive will be augmented from beyond."

Beyond?

She delved into her database and immediately found three issues drove this group—*passionately* drove this group.

Abortion.
Same- sex marriage.
Transgender rights.

Using the data, she wrote an extensive position paper outlining the exact language to be used to convince the opposition's minority base NOT to vote for their candidate. These would be made into a juggernaut of Facebook ads and Twitter posts.

She won't know what hit her.

In the quest of 270, she also wrote out a strategy for convincing white, blue collar workers in Michigan, Wisconsin, and Minnesota to not vote for her either. She scribed the precise talking points to turn these bellwether states toward her candidate.

Imagine.
Eight years ago, the other party's president saved their jobs.
But today, we'll save their guns.

Campfires too.

Her custom messages would directly reach each intended audience: in their chat rooms; on their special interest sites; with likes and comments to their own posts. She would leverage the passion and energy of these issues to make her candidate and break the other. And with social media, she could have her new system up and running in mere days!

By next week, it will be at full steam.
Imagine.
Over 500 voter profiles.
With direct messages to each!

Chapter 28

"President Osbourne's office. Pat Hayes speaking." The friendly voice on the line brought a smile to Geoffrey Wines.

"Hello Pat. Ms. Hayes. Mrs. Osbourne? Geoffrey Wines here."

"Well, hello Geoffrey. Please, just call me Pat. So good to hear your voice. Mr. President and I have been wondering when you would be getting back to us."

"Sorry, past couple of weeks have been crazy. Is President Osbourne available?"

"Perfect timing Geoff. He is sitting right here."

Wines heard a muffled conversation.

"Mr. Wines?" she returned. "Mr. President asks if we can just put you on speaker phone. He said I would probably need to help him find what you are looking for anyway."

"Certainly. Pat. Please."

"Well, good morning, Mr. Wines." The president's voice sounded loud and clear for a speaker phone. "We were wondering when you would be calling us back. Haven't seen a thing in the paper about the old Gulf War story. Nor any pronouncements of an award-winning catch by a reporter visiting South Carolina."

"Nothing to report, sir. Still tracking down my sources." Wines laughed, then continued. with a serious tone. "On both stories, sir. On both stories."

"Yes sir, Mr. Wines." Osbourne started, with clear amusement in his voice. "We were wondering when you would be calling us back to ask about the mystery man. Something simple like, 'how did I contact him in the first place?'"

> *There he goes again.*
> *Knows my thoughts before I do.*

Pat interrupted. "Is that what you need Mr. Wines?"

Wines could almost see them winking to each other. What a couple! Almost like they know what the other wants without ever saying it.

"Yes ma'am. I'm working both stories the president mentioned," Wines answered quite seriously. "I need to know, does the president have any records from his contact, conversations, anything I can use to substantiate the source for both stories? Maybe even find the source."

"Oh Mr. Wines," Osbourne cut in, "You will never find this guy. He's as elusive as the fog over a lake. Here . . . then gone!"

"Yes sir, I gathered that from our discussions at your home. But the mystery man just didn't appear on your doorstep. You somehow summoned him. And the other three former presidents also summoned him for his current assignment. And I assume you spoke to him. In person. And then gave, sent, or wired money to him. And there may even be some updates he used to document his actions. Or at least, 'turn on your tv and watch what we did' kind of stuff."

"Hmmm. That rings a bell!" Pat suddenly offered. "Let me dig through a few of the president's personal papers and see what we can find."

"That would be great! Thanks."

Chapter 29

SOME MEN CAN'T HELP THEMSELVES.
AND THEIR SONS DON'T FALL FAR FROM THE TREE.
HE ACTUALLY AGREED!

SERIOUSLY, HE DID.
HOPE THIS DOESN'T EXPOSE THE WHOLE GIG.

Chapter 30

A FedEx arrived the next day. Early morning delivery. The *Washington Post* mail room had placed the package on Geoffrey Wines' desk.

Geoffrey wasn't expecting a package so soon, so he read the shipping label and smiled when he saw the Greenville South Carolina return address.

"I wonder if Pat had this ready before my call." Wines thought to himself.

Inside were three pieces of paper. Each a photocopy.
And a short, handwritten note.

> *G~*
> *This is what we could find.*
> *Hope it is helpful.*
> *All communications were outside archived channels, so all of this should be treated confidentially.*
> *P~*

One sheet had a phone number:

222-301-9876

The original looked like a page copied from a steno pad. That was all.

The second had an account number, but no identifying description. Also photocopied from a steno pad.

0090-4700-890003-2345

The third was a copy of a fax, with time and date, but no identifying sender information.

August 5, 1990. 0710 EDT

Pat had also scribbled a note:

> *This fax arrived on the president's personal fax machine located in the living quarters and listed the living quarter's fax number.*

Wines immediately understood why this fax never made it into the national archives.

Wines also knew this date well. Only three days after Saddam Hussein started his invasion of Kuwait and the date when Osbourne made his pronouncement to the World: "This invasion of Kuwait, it will not stand."

This note succinctly communicated the mystery man's strategy. It must have been his cryptic instructions to Osbourne on the steps he should take to make his plan work.

Correction. For *their* plan to work.

The communiqué was unique. A poem of sorts.

Weapons defeat armies.
Slings and arrows, the sword.
Missiles, the plane.
Bombs, the bunker.

You will amass the greatest ever witnessed.
Ever conceived.
For all to see.

Your target will perceive defeat.
And fold.
Without ever lifting a sling, an arrow, or stone.
Of their own.

Wines read and reread the passage several times.

Two thoughts immediately occurred to him.

One, Osbourne made no mention of this clue when they met. He claimed no knowledge of the mystery man's plans until the war started.

> *But then again, Saddam had started the war with his invasion of Kuwait.*
> *And Osbourne responded.*
> *Was Osbourne's "this invasion will not stand" pronouncement his way of communicating acceptance of the Fixer's plan?*

The United States of America had in fact amassed the single most sophisticated, lethal, and effective conventional force the world had ever witnessed. This technology instantly defeated Iraq. *And the USSR—though never firing nor receiving a shot—also surrendered.*

Wines' second thought marveled how uniquely succinct the writer's prose described the entirety of the Gulf War event. Not only poetic, but also exceedingly prophetic.

It told in a few unique words the strategy, events, and outcome of the Gulf War.

Do you think . . . ?

Wines picked up the phone and punched in the internal *Washington Post* extension for James Olsen.

The other line picked up on the second ring. "Olsen here."

"Jimmy, this is Geoffrey Wines."

"Good morning, sir. What's up?"

"Jimmy, I got something your comic book hero might be able to help us with. Can we get together tonight after work?"

"Sure thing Geoff."

A few moments later, Geoff's phone rang. It appeared to be a call from the outside as a 212-area code showed on the status panel.

Another technical improvement since Beez bought the paper.

"Wines." He answered.

"Mr. Wines?" a black male voice on the other end asked.

"Yes, this is Geoffrey Wines. May I help you?"

Geoffrey Wines always fielded outside calls with utmost delicacy. He never wanted to dissuade anyone calling his number.

The best leads come in unannounced.

"Mr. Wines. Th-This is Jacob Washington. Do you re-remember me?"

"Jacob? Emmett's brother?" Wines asked, remembering the time he met Jacob in his mother's apartment during his brother's internship. Interesting. Emmett's endless questions led Geoffrey to follow up on a lead that turned out to be his Pulitzer winning "Operation Blueprint" stories . . . and *THE CAMP DAVID CONSPIRACY* manuscript Jimmy Olsen had discovered.

"Yes sir, Mr. Wines." Answered the mature voice of now a fully grown black male. Wines smiled to himself. Of course, Jacob must be at least 35 years old now.

"Where are you, Jacob? A 212 number is showing on my caller ID."

"In Ne-New York City. Moved here after getting out of jail. Drug tr-trafficking. Live with Emmett. Made the parole move a lot faster. We have always looked out for one another. They figured an editor for Ti-TIME Magazine would be good for a convict who served his t-time."

"Well, that sounds good Jacob. I hope it is all working out well for you. And I hope Emmett is doing well too." Wines offered, genuinely interested in both brothers.

"Thank you, sir. Listen, I s-saw something the other day . . . uh, here in Ne-New York . . . and my brother Emmett thought I should sh-share it with you."

"Emmett didn't want the lead?" Wines asked.
Why would Emmett pass on a story lead?

"Guess not. When I told him what I saw, and heard, he t-told me I should give you a call. That you would know what t-to do with it."

"Okay, Jacob. Tell your brother thanks." Wines grabbed his pencil, "What'd you see?

"Well, sir, I've been working as an electrician's assistant since leaving jail. Was a t-trade they offered us in prison, and it hasn't been too bad. In fact, I kinds of like it. Union, so I make okay money. And full-up electricians make g-good money, le-legally!"

Wines just smiled. Jacob was one of those inner-city kids who got swept up in the cocaine business. Many end-up dead. Most find their way to jail. Some come out and pick up where they left off because prison is a grad school of sorts for these kids.

Guess Jacob chose a different path.

"Okay, Jacob. Please go on." Wines said as he reached for his note pad, "I'm going to take notes. Is that okay with you?"

"Yes sir. My brother said to t-tell you that I should remain an unnamed source. He assured me you would honor the request. Emmett said I don't need no t-trouble. But Emmett said what I saw could turn into something."

Wines' interest now piqued.

Intriguing.
Emmett Washington, former New York Times reporter and now Managing Editor of TIME Magazine passed on a story and asked his brother to tell me as an unnamed source.

"Please go on Jacob. What did you see and hear?"

"Well, we're in this high r-rise on Park Avenue. Doing some new office work. Nice place. Fucking marble and gold everywhere. Everything is t-trimmed in gold. Anyway, I'm bringing conduit up the service elevator. Got my Dre's on, so I can hear my boss if he needs anything else while I'm in the t-truck.

"Well anyway, a man and a lady, white, rich, she was carrying a handbag that must have cost what I earn a year, force their way onto the elevator right before the door closes. I looks up at them, but they ignore me like most rich white people do around us poor people. They start t-talking, th-thinking I can't hear them because of my earphones. But I did."

"They were talking?" Wines interjected.

"Yeah. That's what makes it so odd. No one talks on an elevator. Odd that they were riding the service elevator and speaking with these th-thick accents. Russian accents. Like this Russian dude in prison. Th-They must have been wanting to be unseen by the regular people in the lobby. Was talking about meeting with some campaign people. Th-that they gots something to share. 'To show, they said.' Th-that they could help some guy if he agrees to their help."

Wines immediately sensing the magnitude of the story, asked again, "What was the address of the building?"

"My brother told me you would asks that. 277 Park Ave. My boss does a lot of work in the building."

Bingo!

"What else did you see or hear?"

"Well, their meeting must not have lasted very long. On my way back down, maybe half an hour later, th-there they were again. Ignored me just like before. But this time I heard them say they got a nod from the big guy's son and would soon be doing stuff all over the internet for them. Don't know what. Th-then they just started laughing and she said her big boss would make love to her! I think she meant her big boss would love her for it. Makes me laugh. Dude in prison screwed up when t-talking too."

"Can you describe what they looked like?" Wines asked, not expecting very much.

"Nope. I can always remember faces. But I can't describe any of th-them. Never could. Nope. Sorry. Can't either of th-them."

Wines breathed out a sigh of disappointment.

Damn.

"But I do have th-their picture, Mr. Wines."

"Photo?" Wines blurted, absolutely flabbergasted. "You took their photo?"

"Sure. I hads my phone in my hand and th-they were just standing there ignoring me. So, I t-took it. Do you want it?"

"Jacob, you're a chip off the old block. Just like your mother. YES! I would like it!"

"I'll send it now. What's your email?"

"Geoffrey dot Wines at W-A-S-H-P-O-S-T dot Com."

Jacob paused, then asked. "Got it. Did it come th-through?"

Wines checked his desktop. Nothing.

Then, a moment later he saw the notification from a JWASH78 at Gmail dot Com on the top right of his monitor.

"JWASH78?"

"Yes sir."

Wines clicked on the WaPo system-sanitized attachment, and the photo file opened.

> *Damn. I know the woman.*
> *Odd connection, though.*
> *Why would these Russians be visiting the candidate's office?*

"Got it Jacob. Anything else? Wines asked. His heart almost ready to jump right out of his chest.

"No sir." Jacob then paused, "Oh wait a minute! Th-the woman said she had stepped out of the room to use the r-rest room. She asked if the s-son and her friend t-talked about anything. He said, 'no, not really, he just asked about the w-weather in Moscow.' But, if you ask me, it s-sounded more like he was t-trying to dodge the question."

"Hmm. Interesting." Wines thought about the last bit of information. "Hey, thank you, Jacob. And thank your brother too."

"Will do s-sir."

Wines hung up. Added the date and time to his notes and stared at the photo on his monitor.

> *I'm sure there is more to this story.*
> *A whole lot more!*

Chapter 31

Son tells Russians.
He's eager to engage.
Provides family's tacit approval.

But old hands suspect something.
Hope nothing is left smoldering.

That boy must be kept bay.

Chapter 32

Geoffrey Wines and Jimmy Olsen met at their usual spot in the *Washington Post* parking garage. The summer heat permeated the city and their walk to the Metro Station brought out the sweat after being in the air-conditioned news building all day.

Throughout the commute, Olsen stayed unusually quiet. While they seldom talked on the Metro, the walks to and from the stations were usually filled with banter, takes on the news, and a few jabs at Wines articles. Wines had become use to his chatter and boundless enthusiasm, but today Jimmy seemed somber.

Wines decided he would hold back and see if Jimmy opened up once they arrived at his home-base, Planet Krypton. Wines did not have to wait very long.

Immediately upon entering his front living area, Jimmy went to the refrigerator, grabbed two bottles of Lagunitas, poured them into pint glasses and handed one to Wines. Wines could sense the steam rising.

Jimmy plopped himself on the couch and right away started. "I cannot believe the paper is ignoring what is going on."

Wines let him continue without a word or acknowledgement.

"The web is covered with disinformation." He nearly shouted, continuing to emphasize his points using air quotes. "'Fake News.' And they refuse to let me 'report on it.' I have shown it to them. Have 'traced' exactly where it originated, 'how it spreads.' 'Quantified' how many times it has been 'viewed.' In a few cases, how it 'ended up' on Fox and in a few newspapers."

He then knotted left hand into a fist and pounded his right palm. "This is fucking disinformation . . . being left alone . . . left to spread without any light of day."

Wines moved forward in his seat, setting his beer on the coffee table separating the couch and chair. He nodded his head to let Jimmy know he was listening.

"Some of the stuff I am picking up is organic. But suddenly, an incredible amount is being bot-driven. That means, no real person is reading it, but the web crawlers and social media algorithms see it as traffic and give much of the stuff higher rankings—spreading it even faster on Facebook and even in Google searches. This radically increases the numbers of people who *actually will see it and* read it. Then it spreads even faster!"

Jimmy paused and took another long draw from his glass. "They don't see it as news." Then imitating the voice of his editor, "We can't spread 'these lies' even more by reporting it . . . Besides, no one is believing it . . . The American people are smart enough to know truth from fiction. They are just reading it for entertainment. Laughing at it. Not believing it. Like reading a conspiracy thriller."

Wines remained silent, waiting for Jimmy to continue unloading.

"Lies? These aren't lies." Jimmy continued, with rage in his voice. "These stories aren't about some guy fibbing about how much money he has, or how big a fish he caught. This is deliberate, commercialized, *industrialized* disinformation. Making up deliberate stories; fabricated without any basis of fact and then telling it and retelling it until the public perceives it as truth. Can't our editors see the difference?"

Jimmy buried his face in his hands, shaking his head.

Finally looking up, he stared directly at Wines. "Don't they see how dangerous this is? Don't they understand how it can distort everything good newspapers—the *Washington Post*, *The New York Times,* even *The Wall Street Journal* are trying to accomplish. Don't they know this is NOT just election year noise . . . but disinformation can and will become a permanent fixture in American life unless we—the free press, journalists—somehow expose it and stop it in its tracks."

Olsen then added physical emotion to his words by pounding his clinched fists on top of each other. "*Real news* will be fake news and *fake news* will be real news. Each competing for the public's attention. There's even a site claiming to be Denver's oldest newspaper. It is cited as the source for some misinformation being spread across the web. And the paper doesn't even exist! And no one has exposed them. No one! The confounding of real news and fake news is so great there is even a news site that says all their news is fake, yet people are believing it and sending it along as real. This is out of hand. Out of control! This is a genie that cannot be put back in the bottle."

Jimmy then looked directly across the table at Wines, his face flush, and eyes wide. "And we're not fucking reporting it!"

Wines' mind raced.

> *Obama born in Kenya was a lie perpetrated by one man.*
> *Swift boats against Kerry was a smear perpetrated by a known political organization.*
> *Rumors that Clinton killed Deputy White House Counsel Vince Foster was a conspiracy theory based on reassembling the facts of the case.*
>
> *But a child trafficking scheme?*
> *By Democrats at Meteor Pizza?*
>
> *A completely fabricated story that has been anonymously reported, spread, and then repeated and repeated until several someone's actually travel across the country to rescue the kids.*
>
> *If misinformation is that believable, it's dangerous!*

He finally spoke up, looking sympathetically at Olsen. "Jimmy, are you sure the editors understood what you were showing them? Like me, they may not understand all the machinations of the web like you. The extent of the web. Did they know what you were showing them was not from some discrete corner of the web? Or reaching just a few fringe subscribers? Did you show them that many of these stories have many more readers than anything we publish in the *Washington Post*?"

"Geoff. The answer is 'yes.' I detailed all of it. Showed it to them." Jimmy's voice rising with each revelation. "Wrote sample stories explaining it. They just don't want to report it. They want no part in spreading unsubstantiated stories. And without the stories themselves, there is not a story anyone will understand. It will be just a lot of 'bots'

- 'clicks' - 'things going viral' and 'fake newspapers'— but no 'who, what, where.' Just 'how.'"

Wines nodded.

"And they are reluctant to report on stuff that didn't happen. Isn't happening. And won't ever happen. Except, for those who are reading these fake stories believe these events . . . these mistruths are reality, have happened, are happening, and will continue to happen. This disinformation could change the dynamics of our elections and the way we think about each other."

Jimmy shook his head and collapsed back on the couch.

Wines slowly lifted his beer taking slow, short sips, buying time for Jimmy to cool down before sharing Jacob's story and President Osbourne's correspondence. In the silence, Wines too understood Jimmy's fears. Lies travel fast. Lies that promote fear travel even faster. Yet, he also understood the predicament of the editors.

The Washington Post and other papers can't spread lies.
Even in the context of a larger story.

And the larger story cannot be properly told without repeating the lies. Knowingly printing something that is stated to be a mistruth, could still leave the paper open to libel or lawsuits.

Click.
That's it!

"Jimmy." Wines broke the silence. "Jimmy, I got something to show you."

"What's that Geoff?" Jimmy responded with rejection still in his voice.

"Jimmy, you mentioned the 'bots' had kicked in and were causing the disinformation to spread even faster."

"Yeah. Last week. Almost like someone threw a switch. It was sudden and the traffic picked up—suddenly and immediately."

"And are you, are we, able to see 'who' is controlling the bots?"

"More than likely. Why do you ask?" Jimmy responded. Wines could see Jimmy coming out of his funk and becoming interested.

"Jimmy, if we go onto your system, right now, could you show me where the bots are originating?" Wines asked, being sure not to lead his witness. He wanted to see if Jimmy could confirm his hunch.

"Oh Mr. Wines, you are treating me like a confidential informant aren't you. You 'wascically wabbit.' But on the internet, bots don't come from anywhere, they come from everywhere. Especially if someone is trying to keep their presence a secret. But we can see if they have some sort of signature, then we can track down to see who is doing it."

"And how long would that take?" Wines said, hoping he might have an answer tonight.

"Oh, I don't know. Might have a pretty good clue before Wong's can deliver dinner. Is that fast enough for you?" Jimmy said, rising from the couch, his spirits lifting. "To the Bat Cave."

"To the Bat Cave!" Geoff joined in, delighted he had recaptured Jimmy's enthusiasm.

• • •

They entered Jimmy Olsen's computer room through the keylock procedure.

Immediately, the entire wall of monitors came to life. On the bottom right-hand side, Wines noticed a screen with the front door of the house and another screen looking outward toward the street. A title popped up on the screens: "Wong Cam."

Jimmy laughed as he saw Geoff's eyes focus on the front door monitors. "Movement activated. We'll know when dinner arrives. You buying tonight?"

"Sure Jimmy. Actually 'Mister Bezos' will be paying for this meal. This is a working dinner."

Jimmy leaned down and entered a short burst of strokes. "Geoff, do you want to handicap this race? Bot source or dinner? Which will appear on our wall first?" Jimmy offered waving his hand toward the screen in front of him, then the Wong Cam monitor, and a new window with a digital clock.

Jimmy Olsen positioned himself in the left-hand chair. His fingers flew across the keyboard and the screens started flashing a mirage of numbers, characters, and code. It scrolled faster than Geoff could comprehend its content. Jimmy glanced up every few moments, but never hesitated in his typing. This went on for a few minutes.

"My brain says to bet on you. But my stomach is hoping for dinner first." Wines laughed. "I'm betting dinner arrives first."

Suddenly Jimmy's typing became staccato. A few rapid fires, followed by stillness. Jimmy studied the giant monitor. Then entered a few more characters. Again silence. Another scan of the screen. More rapid-fire typing. Then calm.

Jimmy stood, carefully analyzing the code. Returned to his seat and entered a few more hasty keystrokes. Followed by a prolonged silence, and a final look at the large monitor in front. Half the characters started flashing red.

Jimmy gave the screen one final look and jubilantly slid his chair back, thrust his arms in the air and shouted "Winner. Winner. We beat the cashew dinner!"

Then spinning his chair to face Geoffrey. "Would the Jeopardy question be 'Why are Russian bots spreading fake news in America?'"

Wines smiled at Jimmy and nodded.

"Whoa, that was close." Jimmy gestured toward the Wong Cam monitor showing the delivery boy approaching the front door. Planet Krypton's doorbell chimed. "Stay here Geoff. I'll be right back."

● ● ●

Jimmy returned a few minutes later pushing a small cart with the food, plates, chop sticks, and two beers. Wines noticed the efficiency.

"Even Superman has only two hands. Hard to punch in a pass code while holding food, beer, and stuff. Makes clean up easier too." Jimmy mused. Then added, "Plus it keeps the food off the workstation" as he wheeled the cart between the two work chairs, a safe three feet from the computer consoles.

Wines got the message, using only the cart to set his beer and food cartons.

"Okay, Geoff." Jimmy becoming serious. "What gives? You knew the answer would be Russian bots. Why the dance?"

"Simple reason, Jimmy. I needed to verify another source."

"Another source? Did I?"

"You did!" Wines said standing and reaching into the small leather pouch he brought with him. He opened a folder and pulled out a laser printed copy of the photo Jacob Washington had sent him and handed it to Jimmy. "Do you know who these people are?"

Jimmy studied the photo for a moment. "No. Strange shot though. Service elevator? Odd place for a photo. Certainly not Instagram worthy. And I would say the subjects had no idea their photo was being taken. Yet, the person who took the photo had to be on the elevator with them. This looks like a smartphone's photo. But this is just a laser print of a photo." Looking up. "Geoff, do you happen to have the actual photo file? Or would it expose your confidential source?"

"No problem, I'll just email it to you." Wines responded.

"Sorry Geoff, your email won't work in here. Just Airdrop it to me. You should see 'JOS' on your drop screen."

From his iPhone, Wines forwarded the photo file.

"Did this photo file go through the WaPo server?" Jimmy asked.

"Through the email server." Geoff nodded.

"Good, it's safe. I set up the server to weed out any bad stuff." Jimmy said with a smile.

Jimmy swung around in his chair, opened his internal server, and clicked on the photo file. "Beautiful. It's all there." He mumbled and entered a few more keystrokes. Moments later, he started scrolling through the data appearing on the monitor in front of him. "New York? Park Avenue. 277 Park Avenue. Thursday, June 9 at 1:47 p.m. Why do I know that address? Phone belongs to Emmett Washington." Turning in his chair to face Geoffrey, "Your source is the Managing Editor of TIME Magazine?"

Wines continued to concentrate on the monitor, giving no answer to Jimmy's question.

Jimmy returned to his work. "Let me run this photo through facial rec."

Wines looked away as thousands of photos dizzyingly flashed by.

"Say thank you to the federal database." Jimmy mused. "Not a hack. I do have permission. But I also add my own layer, so they won't know what photo I am looking to match. Or whose photo or photos we land on."

Wines started to say something, but Jimmy cut him off. "Better not to ask. Trust me. We're good."

The computer pinged. Two photos froze on the screen with ID photos identifying both the man and the woman.

Jimmy read the screen again and slowly looked up and faced Wines. "You have a photo of these two Russians, taken a week ago in the service elevator of the building where the GOP candidate for the United States presidency has offices; shot using a new iPhone X registered to the managing editor of TIME Magazine???"

Wines silently nodded.

Let's see what else he knows.

"And the person accompanying the women is a back-room computer geek like me, and a little-known confidant to a Mr. Putin who I believe is pretty high up in the Russian government." Jimmy revealed before adding, "Though most journalists would never find this man's photo, much less this little piece of trivia."

Wines slowly nodded his head, his eyes never leaving the ID photos.

Jimmy then spun around in his chair and studied Wines' face. "And Geoff, because of this photo, you guessed the bots boosting the fake news stories were probably going to be found to be Russian. Do I have the scenario right, Mr. Wines?"

"Mostly, but not completely."

Jimmy took the bait and started typing again.

"Hmmm, interesting. Seems Emmett Washington, Managing Editor of TIME Magazine has a younger brother named Jacob who was released from prison for drug trafficking fourteen months ago and is currently employed by a New Jersey based electrical contractor. And . . ." Jimmy paused, hitting a few more keys, "They must be sharing the Friends and Family Phone Plan as well as the same residence in Manhattan. Nice address too."

Wines just nodded.

"Let's see what else I can find." His fingers flew once again across the keyboard. "Yep. AT&T. There it is. This cell phone number matches the photo's metadata. Well, look here, he sent an email to you from the email address JWASH78 at GMAIL just a few hours ago. Interesting, right after you called me to show me something . . . and, he sent the photo while you two were talking on the phone."

Jimmy once again spun his chair and looked up at Geoffrey, now standing in front of the wall monitors.

"Okay, Geoff. What am I missing?"

"Just what the couple on the elevator were talking about."

"Aha! And what might that be from Mr. Jacob Washington, brother of TIME Magazine's managing editor and source of your hunch?"

Wines pulled out his notes and read the conversation and observations made by Jacob to him earlier that day.

Jimmy hesitated, slowly shook his head, and looked up at Geoff. "Why didn't TIME Magazine want the lead? That seems odd."

"I don't know. Still trying to figure that out."

"Uhm, that is a bit more interesting." Jimmy reacted. "Let's see something. We know the exact time the photo was taken. And the exact GPS coordinates. I wonder if we can find the mobile phone numbers for the two Russians standing next to Jacob in the elevator.

"And if we can, then I should be able to track down who they might have called after leaving the elevator. And who will be making love to the woman!" Jimmy laughed. "And maybe even where."

Jimmy paused before confiding, "And if our new Russian friends have Droid or iPhones, with a few of my tricks, I might be able to learn a whole lot more. A whole lot more!"

"Exactly Jimmy." Wines encouraged. "And then, you might have a much more interesting story to take to our Editors."

"Okay, Geoff. I get it now. The story isn't the disinformation itself, it's the reason the disinformation is being disseminated . . . who is behind it . . . and why."

"Exactly."

If Jimmy only knew who is behind all of this . . .

Jimmy suddenly turned and faced Geoff. "Wait a minute Geoff. You and Jacob talked after you called me this afternoon. There must be something else you wanted to show me."

"There is Jimmy. But let's concentrate on this story first. Something tells me this is only going to get bigger."

Then Wines offered. "And probably more complicated."

Chapter 33

Geoffrey Wines left Jimmy Olsen's house with a feeling they were on the verge of a very big story. As he walked along the street toward the Metro Stop, he considered the things he had learned since President Osbourne gave him the heads-up about the three former presidents' effort to get people more involved in government and to start voting again. And with that knowledge, opening his reporter's eyes to some of the most unusual things happening in this year's presidential election.

The most unlikely candidate winning the GOP primaries.
The odd events at Meteor Pizza.
Russians in elevators.
Social media disinformation.
Russian Bots hyping fake news stories.
And to think, it's only June!

Looking at his watch, Wines took a detour to the Metro.
Yes, Jimmy, this is my old stomping ground.

I'll stop by The Sixteenth Avenue Baptist Church. My friend, the Reverend Dr. Derrick Brooks should be ending Wednesday night services soon. That is, unless "the Lord has grabbed me, and the fount of His word extends beyond our Earthly hour."

As Wines approached the front of the church, he could see his friend standing on the steps, shaking hands with the members as they left. A warm smile, pat on the back, tight hug, big laugh, or a serious look of concern animated from his face as his flock left the building. "Jesus loves, and I love each and every one of my flock" he would say to Geoffrey when talking about his church. You could read on his face this was completely true.

Reverend Dr. Derrick Brooks is the real deal.

Geoffrey held back, waiting for the Reverend to wish every member a good night before approaching his friend.

"Well good evening, Geoffrey. I didn't see you in Church. Were you here for the service?"

"No sir. Just got here. In the area working on a story and noticed the time. Thought I would come by to see you."

"Thank you, my friend. Come in. Come in. The Lord works in strange ways. I got something I want to ask you about."

They passed through the door. Dr. Derrick pulled the door tight to ensure it locked. "I hate doing this," he proclaimed, "but unfortunately, there are just a few too many who would vandalize the church rather than find it as a place of rest or refuge."

"I understand Reverend. My stories reveal things no one should be doing."

"Well, I guess we're in the same business. You report them and I save them." Reverend Brooks smiled. "Come back with me, Geoffrey, to my office."

They strode past the pews, across the altar, and entered a door cut into the paneling. Beyond the door, a short hallway with two small offices. The sanctuary was the only way in or out of the offices.

"Water?" the Reverend asked, reaching into a small refrigerator, "Mighty warm out tonight. Believe this summer is going to be a scorcher."

"Yes please." Wines answered as Brooks handed him a cold bottle of water. "Thanks Reverend."

The small office was arranged so the Reverend's desk faced the door; a large window filled the left-hand wall, narrow credenza behind the desk and bookshelves covering the other wall. Only one guest chair sat in the cramped space in front of the desk where Wines took a seat.

"The Sanctuary is my reception area and conference room" he told Geoffrey. "Keeps my mind on the real reason I am here."

Yep. The real deal.

"Geoffrey, I'm glad you came by tonight. I need to talk to you." Reverend Brooks leaned forward. Wines noted the concern in his somber eyes and uncharacteristically sad face. "There are some things happening in the church that just don't feel right."

"In your membership here at Sixteenth?"

"No, no. I believe all is good here. Group enjoys each other's company. Members bring their friends and neighbors, and they keep coming. With the neighborhood change, we are getting folks here who look like you. They seem to really like it here. And the older members have welcomed them. I like that. The spirit of the Lord welcomes all strangers, and people who look different from us."

"So, what's up Reverend?" Geoffrey asked, taking a sip of water.

"It's the conference folks. Just got back from our national convention. Seems the leaders of our church feel we should be taking a more active part in politics. Particularly, this presidential election."

"Well, Reverend. That's not new. Your convention has always been active in politics. They are traditionally Republican and were big proponents of Ronald Reagan and George W. Bush."

"Oh Geoffrey, I know. But this time it's different. It is not casual and subtle. This time we are being urged to support certain candidates. Particularly, the current Republican front-runner. And if we choose not to, or oppose such outward politicking, we are shunned by the conference and many of the members."

"Shunned? In what way, Reverend?"

"To put it bluntly, told to 'sit down, shut up and keep our opinions to ourselves.' Non-supporters are removed from key committees. Not recognized to speak." Pausing to look toward the heavens, the Reverend continued, "Biblically, those who speak out against the politicization of our church have become lepers, without the mercy of the Christians."

"When did this start?"

"It started moving in that direction during the 0-8 election. Seemed to grow with Obama as president. Many feared he represented the apocalypse to a Christian nation. You know, it's rumored he's a Muslim, born in Kenya and somehow snuck into this country." Reverend Brooks paused and reflected. "Man, all he is, is a Black man who became president. And all he has been trying to do is make life easier for poor people to get along."

"Okay. But Obama won two elections and has served for nearly eight years." Wines interjected.

"Yes, but during those years, the convention membership became much more conservative. And I will say, it has become a bit more racist in attitude, but not actions. They believe Obama, and all the Democrats and liberals are destroying the country by allowing gay marriage; any sort of abortion for any reason, including rape and incest; blasting contraception and birth control pills; and recently a rather peculiar fear that people whose gender identity is different from their birth identity will use our restrooms to attack our children. And . . . the convention seems to be supporting a man who doesn't like people like me very much."

Reverend Dr. Derrick Brooks then added in his full pastoral voice, "I fully understand the position on abortion. The Lord Jesus knows I do. But why would anyone make it easier, rather than harder, for some woman or girl to get pregnant by denying them contraceptives? How did birth control pills get so wrapped up in abortion? Why?" He ended shaking his head. "Make some sense out of that? Particularly if you are poor, and under-educated, like many in my flock."

Silence followed before either spoke. Then Reverend Brooks continued.

"Religious conservatives believe this is a Christian nation. But the ultraconservative wing believes they have a responsibility to save America by taking a hardened political stance. Forget the spirit and teachings of Jesus Christ, our Savior. Using scripture to justify any partisan stance is just wrong."

Wines remained silent, keeping eye contact with his Reverend friend.

"Look Geoff. You know Black people are typically Democrats. Especially here in DC. But it's my job to lead my flock to good decisions. To use the Lord's message to inspire these good decisions.

If I'm using scripture to coerce, rather than inspire, then I as a preacher am not doing my job. It's that simple. And if my church convention is trying to coerce politically, rather than inspire, then why are we even here?"

Reverend Dr. Brooks then made these final words loud and clear.

"When a group of self-righteous people get involved in politics, nothing good can come from it. Our job is to lead people into making the best decisions for themselves and their neighbor, not to cram our choice down everyone else's throats. If we stay on this path of cashing-in on our own morality—for political expediency—then this is going to turn out bad for everyone."

Wines paused for a moment and took in everything the pastor had said.

Surely Reverend Dr. Derrick Brooks didn't ask me to step into his office to vent.
There must be something else on his mind.

"Reverend. I personally agree with your opinions here. But is there something else you want to talk about?"

"Oh," Brooks said, shaking his head, "I'm sorry Geoff. Didn't mean to get so wrapped up." Then leaning across his desk and whispering, "The convention is my problem. Not yours. Nor even the publics. We're a big church. We need to resolve it ourselves. But I am hearing concerns from my flock the Democrats are killing babies, kidnapping children, and the illusion most abortions are late term for no good reason."

"That's nonsense." Wines offered. "Why are they saying this? Where are they hearing this?

"Facebook. Emails. News reports from the web. And they are all telling me they started getting floods of this during the past week, or so. Surely this information can't be right. Lord, I hope it isn't true." The Reverend then sighed, leaned back, and asked in a normal voice, "What's going on? Why is this happening, Geoffrey?"

Wines looked into Derrick Brooks' sad eyes. "Uhm, Reverend. I don't know."

Unfortunately, I know exactly what is happening.
Exactly as Jimmy predicted.
This is coming down awfully fast.

What would Jimmy need to track it down?

"Reverend, could you provide me with the names of the folks who are receiving these messages? Maybe I can track something down."

"I'll try Geoffrey. Why?"

"Well, sir, it's what us reporters do for *our* jobs. We track stuff down."

"Bless you Geoffrey. I was hoping you would say that."

Chapter 34

The three former presidents met on a three-way call. They purposely kept their conversation vague. But they needed to talk as they were distraught over the direction of the election. Even their secure line was not ready for this discussion.

"We need to put a stop to this," one of the presidents opined. "This man must not win."

"But what can we do?" replied the second.

"Wonder if my nephew can help?" ventured the third. "He traveled with the pageant for several years. He may have some stories. Embarrassing stories."

"I heard he brags about watching the girls getting dressed and undressed," offered the first. "Sounds pretty juicy!"

"You can't ask him. Don't bring your nephew into this" the second president warned. "It could expose our plan."

"Naw. Blood is thicker than water. He'll keep it quiet," assured the third.

"Yeah, but he can't know our plan. You need to keep him out of it," the second president nervously responded.

"Okay. I'll wait," answered the third.

"Keep us posted," asked the first.

None of them liked how any of this was going. They knew from their own collective experience this candidate would doom the country.

And put things on a path no single election could cure.

Chapter 35

Jimmy Olsen sat at his console in the control room of Planet Krypton, finally ready to view a confidential video the paper's Executive Editor had personally given him. He was asked to "use some of his 'Spidey' tools" to analyze a flash drive the *Washington Post* had received from an anonymous source. The editor told him nothing more and asked he speak to no one about it.

Before leaving the *Post* offices, the Executive Editor assured Jimmy this was the actual drive the paper had received. In fact, given the unknown source, no one had inserted or opened the jump drive on any computer at the paper—all they knew was the device purportedly contained one video file "*the paper would find amazingly titillating.*"

This was good news to Jimmy as he knew he could perform a complete forensic analysis of the file itself and any *signatures* the jump drive presented. To assure this likelihood, he implemented his special protocol to ensure the drive and any files on the drive were kept virgin and untouched. *And there would be no chance of any viral transmission from the device into his "Universe."*

He began by wrapping the drive with aluminum foil to create a Faraday cage prior to leaving the *Post* building. This ensured no transmission from the drive could track him to Planet Krypton. Of course, Jimmy had constructed his home's computer room to be one large Faraday via its metal sheathing and electronics.

Once inside Planet Krypton, he inserted the drive into one of the "virgin" computers he had built for just such a situation—which he also placed in its own "security box" to eliminate any wired or wireless signal from being transmitted when he activated the drive to read its contents.

Using this highly secure system and protocol, he then made a complete duplicate of the flash drive and all its data, including the video file and the meta data that would show the device number used to transfer the video file onto the flash drive. Finally, the device and all its contents were scanned for any encryption or viral presence.

After ensuring the safety and integrity of the file, he transferred the data from the box to the outside world where he used a second set of filters to once again ensure the only file on the drive, a video file, was completely safe and free of any viral infection. This final screening also performed the preliminary step he would use to ensure the video file had not been altered to create a "deep fake" or plant malware into his system.

When all these steps were completed, he then transferred the data onto his Planet Krypton system to watch and analyze.

Here goes.
Wonder what all the fuss is about?

The video had no soundtrack. It immediately appeared it have been taken by pointing a smart phone camera at a Samsung SUHD Television screen. The person taking the video must not have been concerned revealing this was a video of a video playing on another screen. The ultra hi def of the tv screen, coupled with the 1080 video capability of the smart phone, resulted in an amazingly clear video picture.

This wrecks any chance to see if the footage has been digitally altered.
Maybe I can track down the smartphone used.

The video ran for about seven minutes.

On the screen appeared a tight focus of a full king-sized bed with two women, fully clothed, romping and playing for the obvious amusement of an on-looker. After a minute, the two women begin to undress each other, ensuring each new erotic area exposed is met with kisses, licks, and intimate fondling. The camera then abruptly pulls back to reveal a plush hotel suite and a rotund blond man sitting in a chair observing the young lusty women. The camera remained fixed with all three appearing in the frame. The two women continuing their intimacy while the man simply watches. At one point, the man motions to the blonde woman to straddle the darker woman still lying on the bed. The light in the room picks up a faint glisten of what appears to be the standing blonde woman urinating on the darker woman under her. The man watches the two women for another minute, then rises and leaves the room, but not before his full face appears on camera.

"Oh my god!" Jimmy exclaimed out loud.

Jimmy reran the video, somewhat in shock. He carefully watched the man to see if there were any glitches in the sequence as the camera pulled back and once the man's presence appeared on the screen. He could not determine any. The full frame of the man's face was the same person sitting in the chair. And because this video had been recorded off the screen of another video, there would be no forensic evidence to confirm the veracity of the tape. He had only what appeared on the screen before him.

To ensure what he saw on the screen, Jimmy checked the analyzer to see if the file itself had been edited. None detected. Within the limitations of the material received, the video seemed to be real and quite revealing.

> *Wonder what the paper is going to do with this?*
> *Better give the Executive Editor a call.*
> *Maybe text him first.*

Jimmy rose from the chair, with the video still frozen on the rotund man's face to text his boss.

Suddenly . . .

Ping. Ping.

Ping. Ping. Ping.

Ping. Ping. Ping. Ping. Ping. Ping. Ping. Ping.

Jimmy snapped his head toward the wall of screens. His web monitors lit up like Christmas Trees. The ping alerts continued non-stop, filling all the monitors.

"What the heck? Oh . . . Oh my, the motherlode!"

He turned down the sound and grabbed his cell phone, switched it on, typed in a code, then waited for a tone. A moment later he entered Geoffrey Wines' direct dial number.

"Wines." The line answered.

"Geoff. Jimmy here. How fast can you get over here? I'm in Planet Krypton!"

"Taking the day off?"

"No sir, the Executive Editor asked I investigate something. We'll discuss it later. You need to see what's happening on the web right now! We've hit the jackpot!"

Chapter 36

Geoffrey Wines arrived at Jimmy Olsen's home thirty-five minutes later. This was an important story and Geoffrey knew Jimmy must be on to something.

Jimmy saw him approaching the front door on his "Wong Cam" and went to meet him, passing through the secure hallway, ensuring the door to Planet Krypton automatically locked behind him.

"What's up Jimmy?" Wines said as Jimmy opened the front door.

"Later" answered Jimmy as he motioned toward the back of the house.

Wines followed him through the security hallway and unlocking process into the Planet. Three large monitors were blasting images of Twitter feeds, Facebook posts and Google searches in a continuous and accelerated dance of cyber-America. With each post, he could hear a muffled PING alarm.

"Do you see that!" Jimmy proclaimed breathlessly.

"I see it. But what is it, Jimmy?" Geoffrey answered, his eyes transfixed on the large, agitated monitors over Jimmy's workstation.

"That sir are Russian bots at work. And a few domestic bots just doing their job."

"Huh?" Geoff returned, completely confused.

"Okay, Geoff. Let's back up.

"Remember a few weeks ago when you gave me the names of Pastor Brook's congregants who had been receiving the Facebook posts that were, let's say, unflattering to one of the political parties and its candidates. Disseminating untrue articles from some dubious sources. Disinformation about practically everything political."

"Sure. Reverend Brooks was concerned and asked if I, well actually we, could help."

"Well, Geoff we haven't helped anyone yet because we haven't reported anything. But I did lay a few traps and today, let's just say, today, we caught a herd of elephants and an equal number of bears!"

"Love the analogy Jimmy, but what the hell are you talking about?"

Jimmy sat in his seat in front of his keyboard. "Okay, Geoff. I better slow down so you can get a firm grasp on what we are seeing. And what it may represent. The posts will be the smoking gun *we* will take to our editors so *we* can expose this whole disinformation thing!"

"Okay. Shoot!" Geoff encouraged, seeing Jimmy's obvious excitement.

"Okay, Geoff. You gave me the names and Facebook account names from Reverend Brook's church. Right?"

Wines nodded.

"Well, Geoff, you and the good Reverend gave me the Rosetta Stone, no make that the Palantír, the crystal ball Saruman and Sauron used to spy on Frodo Baggins' fellowship as they tried to save Middle Earth. You might say we are going to do the same thing!"

Wines smiled and remained standing, perplexed, shifting his gaze between the screens and Jimmy.

"Okay. Okay. When you gave me the names and Facebook accounts of the church members, it dawned on me who these folks were and what they represented. And from there I did a few things."

"Did a few things?" Geoff asked, hoping Jimmy answer would be the right answer. "You didn't hack them, did you? I promised Reverend Brooks nothing would happen to the folks who volunteered their names."

"No worries, Geoff. But yes, as a matter of fact, I did hack them! And duplicated them. And then created new Facebook accounts that look like them, under new names, of course. Then activated those accounts to create their own dialogue and to click on certain things. In fact, I created a whole community of folks to find out some stuff."

Jimmy then leaned back in his chair, away from where Geoff stood, and gave a big know-all grin. "And today, those traps all captured what I suspected! And a whole lot I wasn't expecting! Behold my friend." Jimmy excitedly proclaimed, rising from his seat, waving his hand across the screen like a wizard.

Jimmy seeing Geoff's persistent confusion, proceeded. "So let me put this together for you. The posts the church members were receiving were clearly disinformation. And these congregants are all black. And they were all stories that would make them less likely to vote for a Democratic candidate."

Wines interrupted. "Right. It looked like the posts were designed to persuade people to NOT vote for someone, as opposed to FOR someone. Right?"

"Exactly. Somewhere, someone has concluded there is no way on 'god's green earth' an urban black citizen would ever vote for any GOP candidate, much less the current one for president. So, they start feeding disinformation to dissuade them from voting for the Democratic one."

"Interesting. An amazing twist of strategy." Wines observed.

Wonder what President Osbourne would think of that?

Jimmy continued slowly. "Okay Geoff. I did some stuff. I created multiple Facebook, Twitter, Instagram, and Google accounts that mimic black urban voters. Male and female. Varying levels of education and income. Some active posters. Some infrequent. Some dormant. And I also monitored the actual activity of the congregants' accounts. Didn't change or send anything from their accounts, just monitored the activity as kind of a fact check on my new surrogate accounts. With me Geoff?"

"Think so Jimmy. Keep going."

"Almost immediately upon establishing the new Facebook accounts, these new accounts started getting the same materials as Reverend Brooks' group."

"What's that mean?" Wines asked, wondering what Jimmy's take of it would be.

"Oh Geoff, it's amazingly clear. Whoever is pulling the strings at the campaign, has determined black urban voters can be dissuaded from voting by deluging them with false narratives about their presumed to be favorite candidate, and her party."

"Do you think it will work?" Wines wondered aloud.

"My guess is 'yes' – after all, isn't that precisely what all the negative political television ads are doing. Telling voters all the bad stuff about the other candidate – stretching the truth, but still staying within the guard rails of the FEC—Federal Election Commission—and the FCC who regulates broadcast media."

Jimmy continued. "But Geoff, social media is a completely different animal. Few people are seeing what I am seeing, and what I can track. So, if you want to tell people a candidate is a child molester, then you can direct that message to a very tight target, like, say, black urban voters. Or even tighter, black urban voters who are members of a Baptist church. Even black urban grandmothers who are raising a grandchild or grandchildren."

Geoff hesitated to let the information soak in, then asked, "And no one else can see the message?"

"Right Geoff. The public and the safeguards put in place are unaware this is going on. Unless someone reports it, but the remedial process is stupidly slow. Besides, these messages are here today and gone tomorrow."

"What about Facebook? Aren't they policing their own platform?"

"Jesus, Geoff. NO!" Jimmy practically yelled. "And Facebook really doesn't give a shit either. All they want is for people to stay on their platform. I even question whether they care that I set up all these fake surrogate accounts. Just as the bots 'read' and pass along stories. They seem more interested in touting numbers, not content, nor even people."

"Then Jimmy, how does this work with white suburban voters, who are educated and should know the difference?"

"Ahh, Geoff, you are really good! Just as addition is used as a way of confirming subtraction in arithmetic, my use of various surrogate groups led me right to the source of all this junk. Sources, I mean."

"How?"

"Let's say you are a Michigan or Wisconsin resident who is a member of an automotive union. You are also a deer hunter. Of course, your Facebook profile, group memberships, and readings would reveal this. You may even be reading the on-line edition of your newspaper, the *Grand Rapids Press* or *Milwaukee Journal Sentinel* by signing in through Facebook or Google—or maybe even use Facebook to verify a comment on a story you have written to the editor."

Wines nodded. He believed he was tracking with Jimmy.

"So, here's how this seems to be working. You may start getting hit with a barrage of stories about how one party will take away your hunting rifles and outlaw the purchase of ammunition. Or how they are planning to have all the auto plants move to Canada in the name of globalization. These are easy arguments to mis-state because some democratic politicians support similar things. Or, they might say their stand on environmental issues will result in all BBQ grills and campfires being outlawed."

"Seriously. Someone says that 'they might take away your bar-be-que grill?'" Geoff doubted.

"Yep. Pretty unbelievable. Now obviously, Midwest union members would normally vote for one party over another. After all, the Dems saved the industry in 0-8. But if I learn the party I have always voted for, will take away my guns, my ammo, AND my campfire, then I'm probably switching. At least, that is what the other party is betting on. And it may not take a lot of votes to swing a state where you have alienated the black vote and switched a small minority of the white union vote," Jimmy quietly concluded and started to enter something on his keyboard.

"That's a serious charge Jimmy. Can we prove it?"

"We can prove it, yes, but it also means you must believe and understand the hocus-pocus of computer algorithms. That will give a few, including our editors, some headaches. But believe me Geoff, this is real."

"I'm braced and ready, Jimmy. Let's hear it."

"Geoff, remember on your first visit here I told you about my Kryptonite program that can track down who has written or posted stuff on the web? Or anywhere?"

"Sure."

"Pay close attention here, Geoff. I took the posts that appeared on the churchgoers' feeds. Then using my Kryptonite program, I scoured the web and guess what?

"Can't imagine Jimmy. Did you find Jimmy Hoffa's body?" Then Geoff added with a laugh. "Or Hillary's emails?"

Jimmy paused, studied Geoff's face for a moment, then continued.
That's an interesting reaction.

"Nope. Something even better! I found the emails of a campaign official who laid out the strategy of dissuading voters via specific disinformation spread on social media. I got the emails!" Jimmy boasted. "They include specific topics and specific language to use. And it matches verbatim the Facebook posts sent to Reverend Brook's congregants. Ver-ba-tim." Jimmy repeated slowly.

"Go on, Jimmy. What else?"

"Further, I entered that email's language into Krypton and guess what, it identifies several other posts made across the web, mostly on Facebook. In fact, many of Reverend Brook's parishioners received those exact messages too."

"Meaning?" Geoff coaxed, wanting to hear Jimmy's complete thinking.

"Meaning . . . I established a direct link from the campaign to a voter's mailbox. Of lies! Out-and-out lies!"

"Don't tell me it is that easy?"

"Hardly Geoff. But through tracking tools, we can see the exact pathway a given message made from one GOP operative's office to Facebook and beyond."

"That sounds pretty straightforward, Jimmy."

"But it doesn't end there Geoff. We then find other websites and groups pick up the subject matter, use it verbatim or rewrite it, and post it as original content. And then it spreads like a wildfire across the web," Jimmy added, spreading his arms wide. "First organically. Then, Russian bots pour gasoline on the fake story, sometimes rewriting it, and within days, we may have over one hundred million reads through all the various postings, retweets and Facebook likes. But the initial readers—the urban blacks or Midwest union members—are the originally intended targets. All the rest of the viral activity simply adds to the authenticity of these purely fabricated stories."

Jimmy is breathless!

"How is this possible?" Wines wondered aloud.

"How is this possible Geoff? Because Facebook and Twitter are the sole news source for over half of this country! Didn't you hear, city papers are folding everywhere due to lack of readership. And people only read what they are interested in. They set their accounts to only send that kind of stuff. No damn perspective. Just endless mounds of crap. Delivered right to their smartphone! Multiple times a day! And if they read one story, they get lots more of the same thing!"

Better give Jimmy a moment to cool down.
This next question could be dicey.

"Got-it Jimmy. But how did you get the GOP campaign emails in the first place?

With a smile, Jimmy retorted, "Geoff, there are just some things you don't need to know."

Wines suddenly became deadly serious, stepping closer to Jimmy, his eyes penetrating the young reporter.

"Wrong Jimmy." Wines said firmly. "If my name is going on the story, I need to know and understand all the sources, AND how we got the information. Then and only then will *I* choose to maintain it as a confidential source."

"Okay Geoff. Okay. Cool down." Jimmy calmed, motioning his palms downward and stepping away from Geoff. "The source is the NSA. And Ed Snowden."

"NSA . . . and Snowden? Seriously Jimmy?" Wines exclaimed, staring down Jimmy like he was holding a gun pointed directly at his head.

"Let's just say Snowden and I have crossed paths." Jimmy confessed. "He's just a few years older than I am. And when the

Washington Post reviewed Snowden's leaked manuscripts, I was part of the WaPo team to ensure they were for real."

"You've been here that long?"

"Well, not officially. Now it gets sticky Geoff. Yes, I was part of that team. In fact, it's why I was hired, by Ben Bradlee no less— eighteen months before he died. He was intrigued with my story too, Mr. Wines." Jimmy smiled at the irony. "It is also why I have access to the photo data base we looked at before. Yes sir, with my tools, I also can read emails, from virtually anyone to anyone else; from anywhere, if they are not encrypted. And some that are encrypted, I can decipher."

"Even domestically? I thought the NSA only scoured foreign traffic?? Wines asked, innocently.

Jimmy threw his head back in laughter. "Mercy sakes Geoff. All internet traffic is essentially international. Remember, it's the 'World Wide Web?' Traffic bounces around the world, and beyond I guess, at the speed of light. IP's change by the second. So, until a piece of data is analyzed, no one knows exactly where it came from or where it is going."

"Geoff. You don't believe everything the government tells you, do you? Jimmy then added in a more serious tone, "Ironically, the NSA made it easy for me. They conveniently parked everything in one huge server farm in Utah. All I needed to do was find a way in! So no, I did not directly hack the GOP's email server, not this time. But I have hacked the NSA server farm that contains everything on their server."

"And you look like such a mild-mannered reporter." Wines said with a concerned grin. "But that doesn't get you off the hook. However, it does explain Management's reluctance to publish disinformation stories."

"Right Geoff. the *Washington Post* hired me to confirm the veracity of the Snowden leaks to avoid any planted disinformation. They were afraid the paper would be discredited. They bit the bullet once and won. Guess they don't want to chance it a second time. Especially when there is an election on the line." Then Jimmy continued in almost a whisper, "And because of our new owner, I guess. But we still need to report on the use of disinformation. It's vital. It's important. And if we don't, we as a nation are sunk."

Wines took a moment to gather his thoughts and consider the entire situation.

Could this work?
Would the Washington Post editors allow it?

"But for the current disinformation stories, maybe we have another angle we can use."

"How's that Geoff?"

"Maybe just a good old fashioned metro story. A church congregation caught in a conundrum." Geoff said and started to leave. "Let me ponder it a bit."

"Oh Geoff, but before you leave, aren't you going to ask me why I am working at home today at the request of our Executive Editor?"

"No time for it now. Later perhaps." Geoff said, grabbing his leather pouch and turning toward the door.

● ● ●

Jimmy accompanied Geoff to the front door of the house and returned to Planet Krypton.

He decided it would be smarter to finish his analysis of the video before tending his internet traps. His Executive Editor must be going crazy waiting to hear about the mysterious video.

Boy will he be surprised.
Two incredible stories in one afternoon.
From one mild mannered reporter.
With incredible powers.

Jimmy carefully watched the video one more time and then flipped through it frame by frame. Again, there were no jumps or anything to indicate the video of the video had been edited or altered.

His next step would determine where and when the video was taken. Who took it? Who sent it to *The Post*? And given its nature, who made it in the first place. Though it seemed obvious why it was shot. And distributed to the newspaper.

A few keystrokes quickly revealed the video's location. A data base of room decors showed the room matched the walls, carpeting and wall sconces of The Ritz Carlton Hotel in Moscow.

A search of another database also showed the male star of the video had stayed there during a beauty pageant in 2013.

Okay, I know the "where" and "when."

Now, let's see if I can get a handle on "who" sent this video and handled the jump drive?

Jimmy entered a few more keystrokes, then slid his chair back expecting a long response time before identifying the owner of the phone who recorded the video. These things usually take hours, if not days—particularly if the phone is from the other side of the world.

PING.

"Already? That was fast." Jimmy swung around in his chair and faced the monitors.

Up on the screen appeared a very familiar phone number and face.

I guess embedded metadata was the last thing the sender thought about.

Chapter 37

The strategy is now viral
My girl is doing her job.

Targeting
Then sending stories
no one should believe.
Inhaling its "truth"
Infecting themselves
And then spewing forth its contagion
To family and friends.

All unsuspecting
Yet willing partners
Whom my scheme
Expertly plays.

Chapter 38

Well, there he is. The face of one of the two Russians whose photo Jacob Washington had taken on the elevator. The man's identity. The man who Jimmy questioned why he had visited the candidate for the highest office in our land.

Yep, my Spidey Tools work.

Jimmy Olsen had, in fact, been able to track down the iPhone from the stored Bluetooth recognition data from Jacob Washington's phone. He also confirmed its identity by reading the cell tower traffic at precisely the same moment using the same basic NSA tools—Snowden had exposed—to gather information from Jacob's phone. The tools Jimmy had custom honed into a seamless system of eavesdropping, monitoring, and confirming. All at his disposal, if needed.

"Let's see if I can get the fuller picture here." Jimmy said aloud as he typed.

The Russian's phone is on.

Interesting . . . he's in New York.

Voilà. I now had access to the Russian's phone.

A few more keystrokes.

The video had been rerecorded in Moscow.

GPS map location.

Hmm, this precise location might be of some use later.

One more bit of information might close the deal and give the paper more important information to report than merely the movie's star liked to see women pee on each other.

Then again, it is rumored the man has his own golden shower.

Jimmy entered a few more keystrokes to probe in real time the metadata inside the Russian man's phone.

Yip. My hunch is right.

Jimmy scrolled through the phone's data and reviewed each time that specific video had been viewed on the phone. Not many. But the latest time and date stand out!

My editors are going to love this.
Geoff is really going to love this too.

Jimmy now had undisputable electronic evidence the pee vid had been viewed approximately ten minutes before Jacob snapped the photo of the man and the woman on the elevator. Right location. Exact time. Collaborating discussion. Could it prove the man's son had been shown the video?

No way to determine for sure unless I hack a bunch more phones.

To think none of this would be available without Jacob Washington's elevator photo.

It opens a kettle of fish.
For someone!

"Who needs to fabricate disinformation when you have real stuff like this?" Jimmy Olsen, New Media Correspondent for the *Washington Post* said to himself.

"And I got this! All of this!"

Chapter 39

Geoffrey Wines slid his chair back, stood, and stretched his back. The newsroom buzzed as the 4:00 p.m. deadline approached for the next morning's print edition. Over the partitions he could see reporters peering into their monitors to put the finishing touches on their stories. His screen revealed nothing but confusion, deleted names, and incomplete facts detailing untruths—a complete debacle of journalism.

Wines read his story again.

```
Washington D.C. - Every presidential election
since John Adams has had whisper campaigns and
this year is no different. Over the years,
citizens have been bombarded with pamphlets,
politically oriented newspapers, television
ads, direct mail, ROBO-calls, and recently
emails, texts and forwarded social media posts.
   In all these cases, the messages are open for
most people to see; the opposition political
parties to critique; and for the Federal
Election Commission and Federal Communications
Commission to regulate. But this year's election
cycle has taken on a new and more secret way of
directly communicating with the electorate. And
the secrets being shared are often false and
fabricated.
   Via social media platforms, particularly
Facebook and Twitter, highly targeted messages
can pin-point demographic clusters down to
precise locations and specific individuals.
These targeted groups receive social media feeds
others will never see and that by-pass the eyes
```

of fact-checkers, credible news organizations, and regulators.

Through a tip received by this reporter from the pastor of a Washington D.C. church, the *Washington Post* has uncovered a range of messages and posts that appear to be news related but are in fact total fabrications—designed to harm the election support of the Democratic presidential candidate.

Below are examples of the Facebook posts received by the Washington D.C. congregants. Due to the precise targeting, relatively few people saw these messages. Through our own protocol, we have found these messages are directed to these recipients based on their race, religious affiliation, urban domiciles, political party preferences, and membership in certain social media groups.

Likewise, the *Washington Post* has uncovered a totally different stream of misinformation targeting white union members in upper midwestern states.

In the Washington D.C. area, the posts are from a news organization called the "The Liberator." The Washington Post has not been able to find any newspaper or news organization by that name, though it once existed as a weekly abolitionist newspaper from 1839 through 1865. Further, on-line searches show the only place "The Liberator" name is used is through postings on Facebook and Twitter.

The *Washington Post* also checked the veracity of specific social media posts which have garnered large numbers of views, likes and retweets. No evidence is found to confirm any of their content.

Due to the misinformation contained in these feeds, the *Washington Post* has deleted actual names as not to spread the falsehoods, but to highlight social media's continual spreading of misinformation.

> THE LIBERATOR – (date withheld)
> Sources reporting (name deleted) is holding children caged in the basement of a pizza and amusement center.
>
> THE LIBERATOR – (date withheld)
> Update: Kids being held at the (name withheld) pizza and amusement center are forced to play act in sexual situations. More to come as facts emerge.
>
> THE LIBERATOR – (date withheld)
> Breaking News: Sources confirm the business (name deleted) has twenty-five children trapped. Videos of these kids involved in "sex-play." Accounting records confirm the (name withheld) is funding this operation.
>
> THE LIBERATOR – (date withheld)
> Leaked emails confirm the child trafficking at the (name withheld) was encouraged by (name withheld).
>
> THE LIBERATOR – (date withheld)

> Just in: (Name withheld) is seen on video tape with trapped children at DC pizza restaurant (name withheld). (Name withheld) is not joining them for lunch. (Name withheld) is having the kids for lunch. Cannibalism?

In the Midwest, Facebook posts proclaiming the Democratic candidate's desire to ban the sale of all ammunition for hunting rifles; export auto plants to Canada in the name of globalization; and abolish the use of campfires and BBQ grills to counter climate change. These charges were posted on a deer hunting site called "The Herd." As with "The Liberator", no news organization by that name exists and no public statements by anyone associated with the Democratic party have made the pronouncements reflected in "The Herd's" posts.

The *Washington Post* reached out to the Facebook and Twitter organizations for comment. Both platforms told the *Washington Post* they do not discuss the use of their platform by individual users. Facebook added "we do not believe it is our responsibility to monitor the content of users."

Wines stopped. "Damn." Frustrated and mumbling under his breath, "This isn't working. I now understand Jimmy's frustration. We're hog-tied. How can I—or anyone else—write a news story without including the facts? Sources? Linking the information to actual political sources. And how does anyone write a news story about fake news without spreading the untruths in the first place?"

Wines picked up his phone and called his City Editor.

"Terry." The line answered on the first ring. Wines knew Terry would be swamped at deadline and needed to give him a heads up prior to closing the paper.

"Terry. Wines here. I want you to know I won't have the church story for tomorrow's paper. It's not worth publishing. Seven hundred words of nothing worth reading." Geoff paused, then took a deep exasperated breath for Terry's benefit. "In fact, I would like to set a meeting with you, Marty, Cam, Fred, and Jimmy, I mean James Olsen, tomorrow, if possible."

The other end of the line went silent. A full ten seconds passed before Terry answered in his normal cantankerous demeanor.

"Geoff. Let me see if I have this right. It's 3:20 p.m. and you are leaving me with a 700-word hole in tomorrow's paper and you want to talk about it with me, my bosses, God, and young James Olsen. Right? Do you want Beez there too?"

He's pissed.

"Sorry Terry. You know I wouldn't leave you dangling without a very good reason. Please trust me on this. I think when I send you the story to read, you'll see immediately our problem and we'll need to figure something out. We have lots of information on a huge, WATERGATE BIG STORY, and we're not telling it! We need to figure it out Terry. And soon!"

Wines took a long pause and could sense Terry's discomfort. Though Terry was gruff, sarcastic, and a total pain in the ass, he is exactly what a City Editor should be. Experienced, skeptical, and demanding. Journalism needs more 'Terry's'– not fewer. Besides, he knew Terry would always have his back because Geoff always had his.

"Geoff, I know you know I'm not happy. Not happy at all. But hey, we go back too far for me not to trust your instincts. Let me see what I can do about a meeting with the brass. You know it will cost you. Cost you big! Really big!"

"Yeah, thanks Terry. I'll owe you big."

Big means the premium tippy top shelf 25-year-old.
Well worth the Benjamin at The Willard.

Bet Terry is already savoring it.

Wines hung up and immediately called Jimmy to give him a heads up. "Jimmy. We're going to have your meeting with all the brass. Probably tomorrow morning. Get ready."

Geoff also needed to determine how many assets he wanted to reveal during this meeting.

Chapter 40

Silence is golden.
But worrisome.

No suspicions.
No Times.
No Post.
No Journal.
No Today.
No Trib.
No Sixty Minutes.

No one even speculating.
Connecting dots.
Questioning what they most assuredly see.

What a false web we can weave.
When all the gatekeepers fail to perceive.

But then,
Will anyone notice?

Chapter 41

Terry set the meeting as Geoffrey Wines—two-time Pulitzer Prize winning journalist—requested. It was scheduled after the next morning's budget meeting where the following day's paper is laid out and stories slotted. Each of the section editors attend so they know the content of the entire paper. Cam Barr, the paper's managing editor and Marty Baron, the executive editor run the meeting.

Fred Ryan, the *Washington Post's* CEO and Publisher, along with Geoffrey and Jimmy joined at the end of the regular budget meeting as requested. Only Terry stayed as the other section editors were dismissed.

That will get the newsroom buzzing.
Must be something big.
"But what is James Olsen doing there???"

• • •

Cam, Fred, and Marty looked over to Geoffrey Wines signifying this was his meeting. Timeframes are short in the newsroom, so casual conversation is nearly nonexistent.

Wines leaned forward in his seat and nodded to each participant, then began.

"Gentlemen, we may be on the cusp of the biggest story this paper has encountered since The Pentagon Papers and Watergate. But it is sticky. And as dangerous as smuggling the Pentagon Papers into our newsroom. It will also open us to more scrutiny than Watergate. But sirs, this story is substantially more important than any of these, because it is happening right now."

The paper's executive editor, Marty Baron spoke up. "Well, well Mr. Wines. That sure got our attention. We like big stories."

Be careful what you wish for.

"Okay, let Jimmy—sorry James and I take you through in chronological detail what we have found unfolding during the last few weeks. Are we good?" Wines scanned his audience, getting only affirmative nods.

Marty spoke up again. "Before we get into this" then looking at James Olsen "I want everyone to know all of this, and I mean all of this, will be off the record until we decide to publish it. We discuss none of this with no one except those of us in this room. Am I clear?"

Interesting.
Does Marty already know where this is going?

All nodded in agreement, including Fred Ryan—the *Post's* publisher, a lawyer, and formerly founder of POLITICO—whom Beez had personally hand-picked to represent his interests at the paper.

Then with a smile, Marty continued, "Oh, let me add one additional point. Young Mr. Olsen here is in fact legally named 'Jimmy Olsen.' Our esteemed Mr. Wines, once again, has his facts correct. He uses the name 'James' for his by-line for obvious reasons. My guess is in a few minutes you will find out more about Jimmy Olsen than any of you had ever imagined."

The intrigue is building, and I haven't even started.
But what does Marty know that I don't know?

"Thanks Marty. Again, let 'Jimmy' and I take you through in chronological order what we have uncovered." Wines began, pausing again to let the thought set. "Since March, I am sure all of us have been scratching our heads regarding how successfully the current front runner in the GOP has ascended to the top. And we all know the truth about the guy and have wondered how our trusty, conservative 'old GOP' would let such a candidate survive."

"We could fill the Metro Section with just post-office stories from stilted contractors." Terry chimed in. "My phone rings every day with tradesmen wanting journalistic justice for all the 'revised contracts' incurred on the project."

"And our political reporters are all chaffing at the bit wanting to reveal more about the man's personal life." Cameron Barr, the paper's Managing Editor added. "But we have refrained since we tend to leave a politician's personal life out of the news unless it has relevance to politics. Especially since Monica-Gate."

"And the way the man treats the press during his rallies is totally unacceptable. I'm not sure he believes in the First Amendment. It's dangerous." Fred added, drawing on his experience in journalism, law and as a close associate to a former president.

Wines stood and wrote the word "Meteor" on the left side of the white board. "This is where the story began for me. The owner stopped me while I was there for lunch to tell me an incredible story of how a man from Arkansas came into the restaurant, armed, looking for the kidnapped children being held in the restaurant's basement. Said he had read it on 'FourChan,' some sort of internet news site." Wines then paused and looked at each person in the room, before continuing. "We didn't print this story, even after Mr. Olsen here found the site on the internet. We didn't want to spread false news."

Looking over to Jimmy, Wines wrote the word "FourChan" on the white board and sat down.

Jimmy stood and wrote "Denver Guardian" on the board. "You guys ever hear about this esteemed newspaper? Claims to be the oldest source of news in Colorado. No? Good call. It doesn't exist. But it does publish fake stories we tag 'right-wing conspiracy' and about the Democratic presidential candidate. It attracts about half a million readers via retweets and likes on Facebook." To the right of the words "Denver Guardian" he drew a megaphone with the words "Twitter" and "Facebook."

Jimmy then continued. "We chose not to report on this fake news site and the way it promotes itself because we 'didn't want to help in the spread of fake news.'"

Cam and Terry had seen Geoff's held news-story and nodded in agreement. Marty leaned back waiting for more, while Fred started scribbling notes on his pad.

Wines then took the floor, stumbling with his thoughts. "Okay. Here is where it gets serious. Pentagon Papers serious. A motive . . . the motive . . . I have a source, an impeccable *confidential source,* who I will not reveal to this group or to anyone, who gave me a heads up this presidential election is being fixed . . . and the GOP candidate is bullet proof . . . and will win at the end of the day. A Guaranteed Win." Geoffrey Wines then turned and wrote "CI-Guaranteed Win" on the white board and drew a star around it.

"Guaranteed to win" he pronounced, tapping the words as he spoke so the men in the room understood the gravity of the situation.

The men in the room froze at Geoff's statement. No one said a word as they pondered who could be possibly the source, and then the sources' prediction.

Jimmy reacted first, thrusting himself forward in his seat with a look of betrayal on his face. A couple of seconds later, his look changed to a big smile.

Jimmy just figured me out.

Geoffrey remained standing, not saying a word. He gave Jimmy a slight nod to acknowledge his feelings.

The brass in the room all looked at Wines, with uneasy expressions as they processed Wines declaration. Wines could see them wrestling with the decades of accumulated journalistic experience bouncing through their minds—being tested—pitting "need-to-know" with "want-to-know" to "how come you didn't tell us" to "the importance of maintaining confidential sources."

Finally, Marty, the paper's Executive Editor spoke up. "Geoffrey, while we absolutely respect your source's anonymity, we must ask you to rate their certainty of this claim. Would you stake this paper's financial survival on your sources' claim?"

"Marty, Cam, Fred . . . Terry. Yes. One hundred percent. I met with this source in person. We were sober. And the source wanted me to know. Plus, the source has absolutely nothing to gain by telling me.

And, under the circumstances, this source is in the position to absolutely know and make the charge."

Marty then looked over to Fred, the highest paygrade in the room. "Fred. Your thoughts?"

Fred leaned back in his chair. Then waved his hand across the five markings on the white board and laughed—a nervous laugh: "Gentlemen, we're not even close to a story here. But I suspect Mr. Wines and Mr. Olsen have a whole lot more to tell us." Then looking directly at Geoffrey Wines and Jimmy Olsen, asked, "Do we?"

> *I can't figure Marty out here.*
> *Is he in a power play with Fred?*
> *Or does Marty know something we don't know?*

"You're right sir. There is plenty more." Jimmy answered as he moved toward the white board. "I've been tracking 4chan and other web activity about the election and the presidential candidates for several months. It's what I do as the New Media Correspondent for this paper. You know we have had several internal discussions about how far we should go in reporting the fake news Geoffrey mentioned. The Meteor Pizza kidnapping story and pedophile rumors appearing on 4chan and the Denver Guardian are just a tip of the iceberg." Jimmy recited as he stepped over to the board, erasing the "Four-Chan" Geoffrey had scribbled and replaced it with "4chan."

Jimmy then listed "Anon" and "FBIAnon" under "4chan."

"These sirs are merchants of not misinformation, but disinformation. Blatant lies being posted on this far right web site. FBIAnon purports to be deep inside the FBI, providing details about how the Democratic front-runner's personal email server is a Russian trojan horse into the State Department; and her husband's foundation is a money laundering scheme with ties to Russia and North Korea. As you know, the *Post* has spent a good deal of time investigating their foundation and has not uncovered any issues with its giving or unsavory ties."

Jimmy paused and looked around the room of his bosses to ensure he had their attention before continuing. "And I have had the opportunity to peek into the stuff on the private server you have heard so much about and have not found anything that remotely confirms FBIAnon's claims."

Jimmy has seen their emails?
Does he have any other surprises?

Fred jumped from his chair. "You what? We can't do that!" Fred snapped. "We can't be reading people's emails without their permission. And we sure as hell are not going to publish stories about it."

Jimmy smiled, a confident smile and answered his boss' boss boss' charge. "Well sir, I have everything that was on the server when it was revealed during the Benghazi investigation. Figured it would come into play sometime and wanted to get to it before it was locked down or confiscated by the GOP investigators."

Marty interrupted. "Jimmy, are you saying you have every missing email, every shred of data everyone is scrambling for today?"

"Yes sir, I do. Lots of yoga class and grandparenting emails; plus a few unsavory jokes by the man of the house. But nothing that looked like true confidential State Department correspondence. Some things appear to be confidential—but, after checking, it's the same stuff any acute reader of the *Washington Post* or *New York Times* sees daily. Maybe some State Department social meeting stuff, but nothing even close to 'highly confidential' as we saw in the Snowden papers."

Fred repeated. "We can't publish or reference any of this. We will not! This paper will not be charged with illegally hacking private property."

At this point Marty stepped in. "Fred, in many ways I agree, and, in many ways, I don't. Fundamentally, is reading and reporting a public person's emails any different than stealing forty-seven volumes of the US Government's Pentagon Papers? Ignoring that it was marked top secret? And then reading, analyzing, and reporting its content. Or in this case, reporting the emails lack any nefarious content?"

Jimmy then held his hand up, motioning the group to stop.

The brass in the room turned their attention back to Jimmy, by far the most junior person in the room.

"Sirs, can we hold this discussion for now? This is not the important part. The real story here is the disinformation going wild across the web and how do we report it. And if I may continue, Geoffrey and I can tell you how the GOP campaign is behind a lot of the disinformation, and we can prove it."

Marty leaned back and placed his hands on the table.

Fred furiously scribbled more notes on his legal pad.

Jimmy turned to the white board and wrote: "GOP Strategy and Talking Points." He then motioned to Geoff and wrote "Black Metro Churches" with a blank bullet point under it.

Wines stood. "This is where good journalistic connections come to play. About three weeks ago, I visited a pastor friend of mine after his Wednesday night services. He told me a couple of things that seemed to mesh with my confidential source's claim of the election being fixed. He told me several members of his congregation were alarmed at things they were reading on their Facebook accounts. More stuff about the Democratic party being flesh eating pedophiles—led by their front runner for president. I met with the congregants the following Sunday after services. They gave me their Facebook account names and I asked Jimmy to investigate it."

Jimmy began to stand up when Marty interrupted.

"May I intrude for a moment?" Marty said, nodding toward Jimmy and looking over to Cam, Terry, and Fred. "I am not sure what Mr. Olsen is going to show us, but as you may have just gathered, Jimmy is an extremely talented computer hacker with top-notch skills." Then added, "And he has tools outside of this building that probably rival the NSA or CIA."

Chapter 42

The City Editor, Managing Editor and CEO/Publisher all looked at The Executive Editor with surprise. They thought they knew James Olsen talents. They knew of his winning several "white hat" hacking competitions, but nowhere in his bio appeared anything about a government class facility.

Marty Baron, the *Washington Post's* Executive Editor continued. "We hired Jimmy Olsen when Edward Snowden leaked the NSA and Homeland Security secrets in 2013. We wanted to ensure we didn't step in it and needed someone who could verify the leaks. It was probably the last *Post* thing Bradlee did before he died. He loved this kid. He loved his ability to uncover things people thought were hidden. Bradlee thought a hacker was exactly what the *Washington Post* needed."

Wines looked at Jimmy with a smile. And then over at Fred Ryan, the Washington Post's CEO and Publisher. He wasn't smiling. Concerns were written all over his face.

> *This is going to get interesting.*
> *Real fast!*
> *Hard core investigative journalism versus corporate interests.*
> *And inside secrets being revealed too.*

Fred spoke up, perhaps after reading the room. "Guys let's see what Jimmy Olsen and Geoffrey Wines have. Then we will figure the best way to handle it. Okay?"

Jimmy went back to the white board. He circled Geoff's words "Black Metro Churches" and drew another circle under it, leaving it empty. Then to the side he wrote the words "Surrogate Accounts" and explained.

"Geoff gave me the Facebook account names of the congregants who received the political disinformation. I then accessed the metadata from those accounts." Jimmy again looked at his audience and smiled. "Don't be alarmed. I did not touch any of their accounts. I did what

Facebook, and every Facebook advertiser does invisibly inside Facebook when they target an individual person. Facebook does it for them. Which means I did not hack those congregants, but I did hack into Facebook's database and downloaded the information any Facebook user could download about themselves. But I can read and understand the data. And then reassemble their targeting based on the data."

Jimmy paused again, looking at the deadpan expressions around the room. "Are you guys tracking with me?"

Cam asked. "Does Facebook know you accessed the data?"

"Not completely. No. But I did nothing they don't do themselves in selling their services to advertisers and directing things of interest to individual accounts. You might say I used the data these congregants should rightfully own and applied my own algorithm to it." Then he added, "You will have a much better understanding in just a second."

Cam nodded and leaned back in his chair.

"Okay, I reassembled the congregants' metadata and found the expected stuff. They are black; live in the inner city; attend a Baptist church; read certain publications like the *Washington Afro;* and generally, vote Democratic. They also use Facebook for hobbies—such as knitting, quilting, gardening—schooling for their grandchildren, and getting coupons for restaurants. They tend to read the crime sections of the *Post,*" Jimmy said nodding toward Terry. "And care deeply about things happening in their neighborhood and church. So, if I were wanting to divert this target from voting for the Democratic candidate, I would plant disinformation about her moral character into their feeds. Are you with me?"

All confirmed with a head nod.

"So, I laid traps to see what I would get if I set up a bunch of 'accounts' having the same profile and interests as the congregants."

"How many?" Terry asked.

"About one hundred. One hundred and thirteen to be exact. Okay, this is where the miracle—or bane—of social media happens. If you click on a gardening story once, they will feed you more gardening stories. If you click on another one, they feed you even more. If you downloaded a coupon for Bojangles, you may be fed one for Church's Fried Chicken. And . . . and if you clicked on one story about child trafficking at the Meteor Pizza restaurant, you will be fed another and another from different sources giving the Facebook user the impression it is a widely reported and presumably true story. And then other child molestation stories."

All nodded, presumably understanding how social media worked.

Jimmy then added, to ensure his bosses understood the gravity of the situation. "Sirs, this means if I click on one story about child molesters, I will get another from another source. If I click on it, I will get even more from multiple sources. Because of this activity, I might figure this is a widely reported, *and therefore*, a true story. Do you understand?"

Jimmy then added, with an edge in his voice. "And gentlemen, if a real newspaper like the *Washington Post* doesn't correct it, well then, to many, it is accepted as being real. There is nothing to counter the falsehood. Understand?"

Geoffrey added. "This is what alarmed Pastor Brooks. His congregants were receiving multiple stories about child trafficking and child imprisonment by the Democratic party. Stuff that certainly isn't true—but the constant stream of the stories convinces many in his flock it is true."

"Exactly." Jimmy added. "But now it gets even more interesting." Turning he wrote "Russian Bots" on the white board. Tapping these words with his marker he continued. "The food that feeds the Facebook beast are clicks. The more a particular story is clicked by a Facebook user, the higher it moves up in ranking and the more it is spread."

Then Jimmy added for clarification, "So, if I were a party—or government—who wanted to spread a certain story, I would create a whole bunch of accounts to 'click and read' certain stories. These are called 'bots' – short for robots."

"Damn!" Terry chimed in. "I now understand Geoff's concerns that we weren't reporting the whole story. But these bots? Are they real?"

"Nope. Neither were my surrogate accounts. They were computer driven accounts without a specific human behind them. They just work the system by clicking on preprogrammed content. And no one, not even Facebook knows how many of these fake-bot accounts there are. Looking at what I analyzed for this story, I would say at least twenty percent of the traffic is fake-bot accounts. All the same, these fake bots fool the social media algorithms, particularly Facebook, into believing there is considerable interest in the story and their algorithms keep moving the story up so more and more people get it—it's trending. And then it starts elevating similar stories so suddenly the Facebook user believes the story is true and being widely reported. When this happens, it's called 'going viral.' Reported by seemingly credible sources like The Denver Guardian. Or in this case, 'The Washington Liberator.'" He said adding "Washington Liberator" under the words "Denver Guardian" on the white board.

Jimmy then wrote "Deer Hunters" in the empty circle under "Black Metro Churches" and continued. "It doesn't end here in DC. Upper mid-west deer hunters get it too. Men in Michigan, Wisconsin, even Pennsylvania. White union members. Deer hunters. About as different as you can get from the black metro church goers. They get feeds too. But with a different set of "news articles" to create outrage against the Democratic candidates. In this case, the disinformation stories were their auto plants and jobs would be shipped off to Canada in the name of globalization; gun ammunition outlawed; and campfires and even barbeque grills would be banned for 'global warming' reasons."

"And these men believed this?" Fred asked in disbelief, his head shaking.

"Well sir, that I don't know. What I do know, as a quantifiable fact, is these men clicked and read numerous stories covering these topics. And continue to read them today. So, we could surmise they are seeing some truth in them. And let me add these Russian bots are pushing these stories as well."

"Does this mean our big story is: 'Russia is pushing fake stories that could impact our election?'" Fred asked spreading his hands to mimic the opening of a newspaper.

"Fred." Geoff answered. "The BIG story we're foretelling is one of mechanized disinformation and how these stories get started in the first place. And how all parties are knowingly participating. Let me repeat, how all parties are knowingly participating." Wines then paused for this thought to sink in. "But in the timeline, we are just a bit ahead of ourselves. Remember now, look at this whole story as an unfolding, because the Russian bots are just the 'Watergate break-in.' Not the 'cover-up.'"

Wines then looked squarely over to his Publisher. "Mr. Ryan, there is so much more."

Everyone in the room looked around, eyes meeting, heads nodding. Marty smiling.

Marty won't know what will hit him either.

Chapter 43

Geoffrey Wines stood in front of the boardroom white board and resumed the presentation. "We have 'fake news' – no, let's call it misinformation – no, correction, let's call it disinformation—spreading on the internet targeting certain groups of people."

Geoff purposely wanted to make the distinction between the cutesy term *fake news* and *misinformation*—the unfortunate errors the paper makes and corrects every day; and *disinformation*—out and out fabrications and lies."

Then he continued. "And we have a bunch of Russian bots pushing these stories across the internet. But gentlemen, how did these fabrications start in the first place? Who originated the first child-molestation and child trafficking story? Who originated the first auto plant globalization story? Who forwarded the first story about ammunition and campfires being outlawed in the upper Midwest?"

Wines paused and looked each of his bosses' square in the eye. "Now it is going to get very interesting. It's where 'gumshoe journalistic investigation' meets 'cyber investigative reporting.' This is the BIG STORY—the Watergate and Pentagon Papers' coverup stories."

Jimmy started to stand, but Geoffrey Wines subtly gestured for him to stay seated.

"Investigative reporters get stories from tips, overhearing conversations, stealing printed documents, or merely observing things happening. Cyber investigators operate exactly the same way. Remember that." Then motioning to Jimmy, Geoffrey Wines took his seat.

"Gentlemen, as Marty alluded to, I have cyber tools I personally want to keep secret and this newspaper should want to keep confidential. These are powerful investigative tools in the hands of good—or dangerous in the hands of evil."

Fred and Cam, aware of Jimmy's talents but not his tools, looked over toward Marty. Marty smiled and motioned Jimmy to continue.

"Geoff asked me 'Where did the first child trafficking story originate? Where did the first campfire and auto plant story originate?'"

Jimmy, learning from Geoff, paused for effect, and continued. "Thank goodness there were both these stories for me to investigate. It made my search so much more robust."

Then pausing again for effect, before adding, "And exact."

Jimmy has them on the edge of their seats.

"Well sirs. I found them on the web. Not through a Google search. But through a tool I designed and built called 'Kryptonite.'"

Even Marty is leaning forward on that one.

"Superman could only be harmed by Kryptonite. He kept it secret; but it was accidently exposed, and then Lex Luthor tried to destroy Superman with it. Everyone who records anything—except by maybe chisel and stone—has Kryptonite somewhere in their digital life, just waiting to be found to bring them down."

Wines noticed each man shifted in their seat.

Wonder what my colleagues are thinking now?

"First, let Geoff tell you about a tip he received and then I'll take you through how I discovered the origin of these stories."

Wines walked up to the white board and wrote "NYC Tip." He tapped the word with the back of the marker and continued. "My phone rings and the brother of an old friend is calling. He is a tradesman whose name and profession I am keeping confidential as requested. He was working inside a certain building in New York City when two Russians forced their way onto the freight elevator, he was riding with construction materials. They got off on the floor where the GOP front-runner has his suite of offices. About 45 minutes later, my informant said they were once again on the same freight elevator and talked about meeting 'the son, and how they thought the son would cooperate.'"

"Okay. What does this have to do with Russian bots?" Fred asked, looking very skeptical.

"As it turns out. A lot. A lot more than anyone would or could imagine." Wines smiled, answering the CEO's question. "Now . . . the brother of my friend thought it odd such a well-dressed couple would be on the service elevator, instead of the main elevators. He suspected something was amiss. And since he had his headphones on, they must have figured he could not hear them talking. And since he was being ignored, he snapped their photo, without them knowing it."

Terry laughed. "Who is this guy? We need a new metro photographer."

Wines continued. "My source then emailed me the photo and Jimmy ran the photo through facial rec software."

With this Marty leaned back in his chair and just laughed. Then straightened up and motioned for Geoffrey to continue. The others in the room shifted their gaze from Marty, then back to Geoff.

"And as it turns out," Wines continued, "the man in the photo is a little known, but close associate to Vladimir Putin. His background is in developing cyber systems."

"Are you kidding me?" Marty laughed again, shaking his head, and looking around the room at the other editors. "And the woman?"

"Oh, just some sexy, good-looking Russian lawyer type always poking around in American business." Wines smugly answered. "Prior to this, she seemed to be spending a lot of time with the National Rifle Association."

"Interesting." Marty quipped, wiping a few tears from his eyes.

"Keep going Mr. Wines." Fred instructed. "I want to know more about the facial rec software James—Jimmy used."

Wines turned to the white board and wrote "Russians visit GOP Candidate HQ." Underneath he writes, "Cyber expert" and "Lawyer." And under that he writes "Talks to Son."

Jimmy looked over to Fred, then to Marty, then back to Fred.

"Sir. It's Homeland Security's data base. Pulls from FBI, CIA, and a few places I am not sure I am supposed to know about. We have an understanding going back to 2013 when we were working on the Snowden leaks."

"Snowden . . . again. This gets more interesting by the minute." Fred acknowledged. "Please continue."

Wines interceded to let his bosses know his confidential source in the elevator who took the photo also heard one Russian say to the other that the candidate's son would play ball. He then signaled to Jimmy to resume.

"Well sir," Jimmy continued, "the next day, the very next day, the Russian bots started spreading these stories in huge numbers. Hundreds of bots taking the stories that had started elsewhere on the web and spreading them like wildfire. It was like someone merely pushed a button. Coincidence? Possibly. But wait!"

"So, you are thinking the sudden increase in Russian bot activity stemmed from this meeting and the candidate's son purportedly saying they would play along with the Russians? Am I following you Mr. Olsen?" Fred followed up while scribbling more notes on his legal pad.

Wines turned to face Fred. "Does seem more than just a coincidence. Right sir?"

Fred Ryan gave a slight nod, not looking up from scribbling more notes.

Jimmy then looked squarely at Marty Baron, the executive editor and mouthed the words "Video?"

Marty nodded, waved his hand for a pause, and turned to address Fred, Cam, Terry, and Geoffrey. Fred looked up and over to his ex-ed.

"Gentlemen, I need to let you know about something only Jimmy and I have been privileged to until now."

All attention now focused on Marty.

"The *Washington Post* received an anonymous package last week. Addressed to me. Marked confidential. It contained a single jump drive. Since Jimmy's little demonstration a few years ago, I did not open it, or place it into any computer. I gave it to Jimmy to securely open and let me know what he found."

Wonder if my book was part of that demo.

"He took it to his facility and safely opened and secured the file. It contained a single seven-minute video, shot in a Moscow luxury hotel room. There is no sound. The video focuses on two women on a king size bed frolicking, taking off each other's clothes and performing sexual acts on one another. A man is watching them from a chair pulled up next to the bed. After about five minutes, he apparently instructs one of the female participants to stand up and pee on the other. She does. After about another minute, the man then stands and walks through the frame—revealing his identity."

"And . . ." Fred asked. "Who is the man?"

Marty answered slowly with a touch of intrigue in his voice. "The man—in the video—is the GOP's—presumptive candidate—for president."

Geoff snapped his head over to Jimmy who was looking straight at him. Jimmy mouthed, "Sorry, I'll explain later."

"Is it real?" Fred asked, looking at both Marty, and then toward Jimmy Olsen, the paper's new media correspondent and computer wizard.

Jimmy fielded the question. "Sir, we can confirm the recording is real, but we cannot confirm it is absolutely authentic. It was a video recording taken off the screen of a recording. I ran every forensic I could and found no detection of alteration, but a true analysis cannot be completed without the original video."

Jimmy waited while Fred scribbled more onto his pad. Then continued. "But over the past week, I have learned a few other things."

Marty looked surprised. "More?" Shifting in his seat. "Go ahead Jimmy."

Jimmy now looked only at Marty. "Sir, I tracked down the Russian man's phone using the metadata from Geoffrey's source's photo. The Russian man's Bluetooth was on—surprising given his credentials. I was able to trace time and place pings off nearby cell towers too. Yes, even in New York. And then sir, I hacked the man's phone. Examined all its contents, including an exact copy of the video file you received."

"Holy shit!" Marty gasped. "You found the video's source?"

"And . . ." Jimmy continued. "Using the metadata from his phone, I found the video was played on the phone about ten minutes prior to Geoff's source shooting their photo on the freight elevator. We can only surmise . . . "

"The video was shown to the candidate's son?" Marty jumped in, his voice rising. "He saw the same video we saw?? Wow!"

Not knowing about the video or the other forensic work Jimmy completed, Geoffrey's mind clicked to something Jacob Washington had told him about the conversation between the two Russians.

> *The woman asked the man about any conversation he had with the son while she was in the restroom and the man seemed cagey about his answer.*

Geoff looked up at Jimmy and repeated Jacob's statement for the benefit of the room. He then walked up to the white board and wrote "Son views pee video."

The room went quiet as each member of the *Post's* management considered what they just heard. Fred scribbled more notes, looking at the white board and then touching the point of his pencil to specific places on his pad. He then looked up at Wines and Olsen.

"Geoffrey. Jimmy. There is still a gap here. The Russian bots started spreading the disinformation after the Russian visit. Where did the disinformation start in the first place?"

Jimmy immediately answered, "We believe—no correct that—we know it started with the campaign. Specifically, from the campaign manager."

"And how do we know this?" Fred asked, while adding yet another note on his legal pad.

> *Guess the lawyer in Fred is coming out.*
> *Jimmy is being cross-examined.*

"Sir, remember a few minutes ago when you asked the same question, and I mentioned my Kryptonite system."

Fred nodded, looking down at his notes.

"Sir, the language used in the original disinformation posts share certain linguistic elements. Both the black church goers and the white union members. I then asked my system to go out and seek the similarities that may be hidden in documents, emails, and other on-line files."

"Public files? Previously leaked files?" Fred probed.

Jimmy answered, "No sir, WikiLeaks files." Then added with a laugh, "Or should I say secured NSA copies of server emails."

"Where?" Fred blurted.

"Via a very large Utah server farm."

Fred paused, shook his head, and smiled. "Okay. I understand. Please continue."

"In this case, these were found in an emailed internal document from the candidate's campaign server. The exact language used in the posts originated in an internal campaign document."

"Exactly the same?" Fred crossed.

"Yes sir. I wasn't dredging their files for everything I could pick up. I was looking for something very specific and found it. Yes, the same language. Verbatim." Jimmy confidently answered.

"And do we know who penned the posts?" Fred drilled Jimmy.

"Yes sir. We do." Jimmy added with pride. "I first found the exact language in the strategy document. But with a little more investigation, I found it was originally penned, word for word, by the deputy campaign manager."

"And do you have a name?"

"Yes sir, I do. The person who wrote the original disinformation was Katy Lynn Holloway, who submitted the language via email to her campaign staff."

Chapter 44

Cam Barr, The Managing Editor of the *Washington Post* asked Jimmy Olsen a simple question. "Do we have the names who Katy Lynn Holloway sent her email?"

"Yes sir. We have a digital file of the email and the metadata of all recipients."

"And were there any responding emails questioning the false content of the campaign language?"

"Never thought to look. Help me out sir, why do you ask?"

"Jimmy, your computer investigation is impressive. Quite impressive. And it has led us to an incredible story. But there is nothing quite like a quoted source who gives us on-the-record information. It gets us away from having to report we obtained the information by hacking confidential GOP campaign files—however legal it may or may not be—despite the fact we found something completely nefarious and potentially illegal."

Geoffrey Wines picked up on Cam's thought. "Jimmy, if we are able to get all the recipient names, then we can track them down. We can question them in the context of Reverend Brook's congregants, a Metro Story, not a political story."

"That would solve a lot of my concerns with the story as we now have it." Fred added. "At POLITICO, we tried to hang people with their own rope. The electronic snooping, as valuable as it is, could turn into a firestorm and court fights stretching far past the election. Getting folks to reveal they knew the stories were false is a good starting point. Then we can merely establish a 'chain of evidence.'"

"Right." Marty smiled. "If they are forthcoming, then we have an easy story to report. If they deny they coined the disinformation, then it is our task to disprove their statement and then, we can use the email surveillance as the evidence."

Wines turned toward Jimmy. "Could we track down the entire email chain? I suspect there may have been some responses we could use to determine who felt uncomfortable with the misinformation and strategy being suggested. A perfect way to start a story."

"I can Geoff. But it also means I will be directly entering their system. I won't be able to use WikiLeaks or Snowden as the fall-guy. Unless Wiki, or someone else, downloaded the entire stream. I can check it out tonight."

Fred then spoke up. "Guys, I want to be very clear on something. And I know you're not going to like what I am going to say. But unless we can track down the lead, in person, as Cam and Geoff are suggesting, I am not sure we have a printable story. Not yet anyway."

"In what way Fred? Seems pretty clear to me." Marty interjected.

"Let's break this down. And it is pretty much circumstantial and unlike Watergate and The Pentagon Papers, the perps in our story are not elected officials in office. At this moment, they are private citizens. Hell, we can't use or even reference Geoff's confidential source that something is afoot, and the election may be rigged. Second, unless we can connect the Denver Guardian or Washington Liberator, or even 4chan to the GOP campaign, we still have nothing but some wild right-wing radicals spreading untruths. And we sure as hell are not going to assist the Russians in spreading this false news!"

Jimmy started to say something, but Fred's expression stopped him cold.

"And the entire Pee video—while the connection is unsavory, certainly titillating, and possibly embarrassing to the candidate—no laws were broken in Moscow, nor the USA. Plus, we have not been able to prove a direct connection between the campaign and the Russian bots, other than some elevator hearsay by Geoff's other confidential source."

"But . . ." Marty started to refute Fred's take.

"Marty, I would love nothing more than to publish stories about all of this. But with our current leads, we shouldn't . . . we can't . . . and we're not! Do each of you understand?"

A silent pause fell across the room as each journalist wrestled with the legal constraints Fred outlined.

Jimmy then stood up. "I want to say something to all of you. I hope you listen and understand what I want to tell you. Please!"

Marty looked over toward Jimmy. Then to Fred and back to Jimmy.

"Jimmy, I believe you have earned our attention. Please." The Executive Editor said waving his hand for Jimmy to proceed.

"Gentlemen, I am your New Media Correspondent. Like a foreign correspondent, I reside inside my beat. Observe what is going on because I live and breathe inside the web. Being a lot younger than each of you, I also understand how people in their twenties, thirties and forties consume media. Older readers too. We're lazy news consumers. We like it fed to us. And for many, only the stuff we like to read. And the stuff our friends like.

"The smorgasbord of local daily newspapers, well sir, their days are numbered. Gannett, McClatchy, and Tribune are all floundering. We're lucky. We got a rich sugar-daddy in Beez. But the *Times* has been scrambling. Even the *Wall Street Journal* has changed ownership in the past ten or so years. Plus, network viewership, coffers and news staffs are declining.

"Facebook, Twitter, and YouTube are becoming the major purveyor of news in this country. They are not like a newspaper you open—exposing news you're not looking for. They only feed you what you want to read based on what you have already read. And there is an information vacuum being filled by charlatans like 4chan, Redditt, and fake papers like The Denver Guardian, The Washington Liberator, The Herd, and literally thousands of self-appointed and totally unqualified purveyors of information."

The seasoned men in the room could only agree. They have all lived through circulation drops, budget cuts, and publishing a paper that is often just digital air."

Jimmy continued. "Now, we have another villain even worse than no information. *IT IS DISINFORMATION!* Why settle on funding a few swift boat comrades denying someone earned a Silver Star when you can fabricate an entire child trafficking story? Why accurately report the miracle of the latest HPV vaccine when you can take anti-vax to a whole new level with saying it will cause autism? Why present real facts when you can make up and report alternative facts? And if the political use of disinformation spreads, as we are seeing in this election, then God help us!"

Jimmy then emulating Fred Ryan's lawyerly dissertation provided his summation. "Gentlemen, we're on a trajectory where people won't be able to tell the difference between well-vetted, factual journalism versus the off-the-wall ravings of someone with a Facebook or YouTube account. We're on the ground floor of *industrialized, mechanized disinformation campaigns*. Right now. It is escalating every single day. And we MUST find a way to stop it. Mark my words, it will consume all of us. And our democracy simply will not survive."

Jimmy took his seat. Exhausted. Defeated. Head bowed. Hands shaking.

Finally, Jimmy looked up with an embarrassed smile.

"Jimmy." Fred started. "I don't believe there is one person in this room—at this newspaper, or in the whole industry—who disagrees with you. I started POLITICO because I felt political truth needed a full-time watch dog. And yes, our job is to find a way to report 'this disinformation' without spreading it; without adding credibility to it; and . . . *and without getting sued."*

Chapter 45

"Jimmy, hold in here for a moment, I need to ask you something very important." The brass had left the conference room, leaving the 'two stars of the show' alone.

Geoffrey Wines closed the door and turned to face Jimmy.

"Sure, what's up?" Jimmy responded, reading Geoffrey's face. "You look concerned."

"I am. Very concerned. During this meeting you said something like the Russian on the elevator must have had his Bluetooth on and that enabled you to track down the Russian's phone. Is that correct?"

"Yes. Every phone's Bluetooth that is turned on will recognize a Bluetooth signal from another phone with its Bluetooth on. I keep mine off for exactly that reason. Usually, the data never goes anywhere unless someone like me wants to track it down. Why?"

"Jimmy, oh shit, Jimmy. Is it possible our cyber-Russian would know, could know, who Jacob Washington is, using the same type of tools you used to track down the two of them?"

Jimmy Olsen paused, looking past Geoff as he considered his question.

Finally, Jimmy looked at Geoff and sat down in the nearest chair, motioning to Geoff to do the same.

With a concerned smile, Jimmy looked at Geoff and started. "We may have an even bigger problem than our cyber-Russian knowing Jacob's identity. To directly answer your question, yes, our cyber-Russian could very easily know Jacob's identity because Jacob had his Bluetooth on as well. And know Emmett's identity too for that matter."

"And so . . ." Geoff started, but Jimmy continued.

"Not only can our cyber-Russian penetrate Jacob's phone as I did, but if there were others in the meeting with the candidate's son who had their Bluetooth on, as most people do, then he could potentially penetrate all their phones as well."

"And so, we can only assume this Russian purposely left his on." Geoffrey Wines suggested.

"Yeah, that always puzzled me once I learned the guy's identity. And it might also explain why they took the service elevator instead of the busier main elevators."

"Why's that Jimmy?"

"Less traffic on his phone. Ability to isolate a few important phone numbers instead of all of New York City on a busy elevator."

"So, you are suggesting our cyber-Russian was on a fishing expedition as well as screening a video."

"Very possibly. Geoff. Very possibly."

Geoff hesitated for a moment, thinking about how the cyber-Russian could not only know the identity of Jacob—he could also have a gateway into the person Osbourne said would win the presidency, his family, and his staff.

As he stood up and started to leave, Jimmy stopped him and added the following advice: "Oh, one more thing Geoff. You might let Emmett and Jacob know they should immediately destroy their phones, cancel their joint account, and open separate new accounts with another carrier. Tell them to keep their Bluetooth turned off and to change their iTunes accounts too."

Chapter 46

Geoffrey Wines took the stairs down to his desk in the city newsroom. He immediately checked to see if the Bluetooth on his phone was off. He thought it was. But after hearing Jimmy's explanation, he just wanted to be sure. Yes, it's off. Which means it had been off for some time.

Whew.
Dodged a bullet.

He then looked up Emmett Washington's office phone number, wanting to ensure he by-passed his cell phone.

"TIME Magazine, Emmett Washington's line" answered Emmett's assistant.

"Good morning, Geoffrey Wines with the *Washington Post*. Is Emmett in?"

"Yes sir, Mr. Wines. Let me put you through. He has been expecting your call."

Of course.
He shares a block-buster lead, and I don't call.
What's a former intern to do?

"Emmett Washington here."

"Emmett, Geoffrey Wines."

"Hi Geoff. Good to hear your voice. Did my brother Jacob get a hold of you?"

"He did, almost two weeks ago." Geoff answered with just a bit of guilt for not calling Emmett sooner.

"And . . ." Emmett responded wanting his mentor to talk first.

"Well Emmett." Geoff answered with a smile, knowing this technique very well. "Yes, indeed and you would not believe where it led us."

"Oh . . ."

"Let me just say it opened the door on a lot of stuff we are trying to get to the bottom of. And yes, thank you for passing Jacob on to us."

"Certainly Geoff. I just felt the resources of the *Washington Post* would be better suited to investigating the story. We are so pressed here—money and resources are tight. Plus, I in no way wanted to jeopardize Jacob's job. He is getting his life back together, or I should say re-started, after a life on the wrong side."

"I figured that Emmett—once I saw the photo and understood the location."

"Yeah Geoff. I recognized the woman—she's been around the political circuit for a couple of years. But who is the man?"

"Emmett, that is why I am calling you. And this is extremely confidential. Okay?"

"Of course, Geoff."

"The man is a Russian cyber expert. Close confidant to Putin. And that's why I am calling you."

"A lead?"

"I wish. No. Your personal security."

"Whoa Geoff. Personal security?"

"Afraid so. Let me tell you what I know. As we were investigating the photo, we used some sophisticated tools that enabled us to enter the cyber-expert's cell phone. We were able to identify it because these same tools enabled us to read Jacob's phone."

"You hacked my brother's phone? What the hell Geoff!"

"Trust me, no worries. But since Jacob had his Bluetooth on and took a time-stamped photo, it enabled us to track the Russian's phone. We are worried the cyber-expert from Russia may have been fishing in the high-rise that day and may also have access to Jacob's phone. And through extension, your phone too, if they choose to look."

Geoff heard a long sigh from the other end of the phone.

"Sorry Emmett, but I have more thoughts from our WaPo cyber expert."

"Can't wait Geoff."

"Since the editor of TIME Magazine would be such a ripe target, you should immediately destroy yours and Jacob's phones. Completely destroy them. Smash and drown as they say. You should cancel your friends and family cell phone account with Jacob and open separate accounts with another carrier. And, close, delete and change both of your individual iTunes accounts."

"No good deed goes undone. Huh Geoff?"

"Sorry man. Afraid the damage could have been done the moment the Russians got off the service elevator. And God knows what havoc this could cause the next president."

"Next president? Geoff, did you say next president?
Shit!

"I meant presidential candidate." Wines responded as evenly as he could.

"Right Geoff. Any other good news you would like to share?"

"Nope."

Thanks Geoff. We'll take care of the phones tonight. And I won't use mine until then."

"Good move Emmett. And please thank Jacob and tell him we are sorry."

"Not your fault Geoff. Not your fault. Bye now."

"Bye Emmett. Be safe."

Interesting.
Emmett was glad I called.
But in a big hurry to get off the phone too.

Chapter 47

As soon as Geoffrey Wines hung up, he called Jimmy Olsen's desk. "Olsen" the line was answered.

"Excuse me, I am looking for James Olsen" Geoffrey teased.

"Yeah, yeah, yeah. Now that the cat is out of the bag, how can I answer to "James" around here?"

"Jimmy don't worry about it. The brass isn't going to spread around your birth certificate name. You made a real impact on those guys today. They were intrigued and impressed. Can't believe Fred didn't know your background."

"Me too. Guess Marty holds things close to the vest."

"Comes with years in the business. CEO's and Publishers come and go."

"What's up Geoff?"

"I called Emmett about their phones. He will handle it tonight with Jacob."

"Okay . . ."

There goes that pregnant pause.

"Okay, Jimmy, we need to meet tonight." Seems we have been holding out on each other."

"Sorry about . . ."

"Not here Jimmy. Let's talk tonight. Meet same place downstairs?

"See you then Geoff."

Chapter 48

When the meeting broke, Marty Baron followed Fred Ryan, his boss, upstairs to the executive floor of the *Washington Post* and into the Publisher's suite. The budget meeting had been held on the newsroom floor, closer to many of the editors. The metro reporters shared the next floor down.

"Fred, we need to talk."

"You think?" Fred replied sarcastically.

"Listen, this is a huge story. It should be breaking right now. We need to give the public a heads up on what is happening."

"I absolutely agree. Seriously, I agree one hundred percent. These are the kind of stories a political journalist only dreams about. We got a candidate who is bullet proof for some inexplicable reason. We got his campaign staff initiating totally bogus stories about the other candidates. We got some Russian operatives who could be blackmailing the candidate with a porn video the candidate himself seems to be directing. And this isn't even the important part of the story. The bigger story is this entire election is somehow being fixed by someone only Geoffrey Wines can help identify."

"So, you heard everything being said in there?" Marty stated.

"Don't mess with me Marty. I'm not some corporate flunky. I successfully started the premier political news organization in the country. I spent years inside the White House and later assisting a former president. My journalistic chops are strong, maybe not as strong as yours, but more than most in the C-Suite. But I am also a lawyer who absolutely knows his shit and if this newspaper proceeds the way I think *you* want to, we will be stepping in more of it than we could ever imagine. Can't you understand that? Don't you see that?"

Marty sat down—to signal to his Publisher he was backing off and wanted to hear what he had to say.

"Please shoot Fred. Lay it out."

"Good. Thanks, Marty. I will." Fred walked over to his desk and picked up his notes from the meeting.

"My problem is virtually all our facts are coming from what will be called "personal account hacking." The pee video, though delivered to us, its background and the direct tie to the candidate's son is through phone hacking. The source of the spread of disinformation to black DC residents was derived through hacking. The charge that the deputy campaign manager for the GOP candidate for president was via deep hacking of her email and the campaign's computer server. Currently hacking into someone's system is considered breaking and entering—and invasion of privacy. It doesn't matter what we found; we will be hung by how we got it. And it will expose a major capability of this newspaper—though I didn't know that until today."

"Sorry about that Fred."

"Sorry? Shit Marty. I didn't even know his name is 'Jimmy.' Though I should have looked at the backgrounds of each of our reporters. That's on me. But today I learn he has a facility that rivals the best out there? And you're sorry?"

Marty paused for a bit. Though Fred was new to the paper, Beez appointed him publisher—and his boss.

"So, Fred, what do we need to do?" Marty accepting and respecting his boss's instincts, legal expertise and realizing the blowback from revealing the *Post's* electronic information gathering would create a whirlwind that would 'out-news' the story itself.

"Get direct human sources to begin with. Best case, sources talking on the record. But I would even settle for off-the-record confirmations to move forward. And trust me on this, the campaign staffers working under Katy Lynn Holloway aren't going to say a word on or off the record. Political operatives at that level just do not talk, until the elections are over." Fred then added, his expression changing from a scowl to a toothy grin, "then, Mr. Baron, we'll get an earful."

"And where does that leave us. Again, in your mind?"

"Best case, we track down how, who and why the election is being thrown. Somehow exposing the source of Geoffrey's confidential source. Or we find a leak in the FBI or a slip of the tongue by one of the candidate's family members."

"Whoa there Fred! FBI? Family? Are you delusional?"

"Hey, the number two person in the FBI fed Bernstein and Woodward inside info. And the Unabomber's brother led to his capture. It happens. Hell, we might be able to get the candidate himself to brag about it, if we handle his ego correctly." Fred answered, but truly did not believe they would be so lucky. After all, no one was getting killed and most FBI agents knew after four years Richard Nixon could not be trusted to do the right thing. "If we can't get him now, he will get himself once he is in office."

"Should we assign a separate team to this?" Marty suggested.

"What do you think?"

"Fred. I would not replace Geoff and Jimmy at all. Geoff is one of our single best reporters and Jimmy seems to be learning from the best." Marty spoke as he thought it through. "But maybe we coordinate them with Jeff Leen in Investigations. Jeff worked on the 9-11 investigations; getting the Dick Cheney Iraq War story out; and with Jimmy when Snowden broke, so he knows all about his capabilities. And I believe he and Wines respect each other's work."

"Great. Geoff. Jeff. And Jimmy. It will be an interesting group." Fred quipped. "And I think we should keep the political reporters away from this story as well."

"Why would we do that?" Marty responded with an edge of indignation.

"Marty, we need to keep our Capitol staff completely clean here. We are walking a very fine line. And my gut says all of this is going to get increasingly political before it is all out. Our political reporters have sources throughout Washington, and we just cannot take a chance of them getting tied up into this and no one talking to them."

Marty considered this for a moment. Fred is right on this. We forget Watergate's Woodward and Bernstein were just metro reporters following up on a break-in.

"Yeah, I agree Fred. Let's pray we can beat the clock and print this story before it's too late."

"I agree Marty. I agree one hundred percent."

Chapter 49

Geoffrey Wines was running a bit late and met Jimmy at their usual place inside the parking garage. While waiting, Jimmy scrolled through his phone, catching up on the latest trending stuff on Facebook, Twitter, and YouTube. The feeds are all in real time, unlike published newspapers or news programs.

"Hi Jimmy. Sorry about being late. Marty stopped by about 4:30 with a little news for us. The paper wants to move on the stories we discussed this morning and is assigning Jeff Leen to help.

"Jeff Leen? From Investigations?"

"Yip. Marty says you know him and worked with him when you first came on board."

"Right. On Snowden." Jimmy smiled. "My first editor. Taught me a lot about news reporting. I like him. He's good!"

"I do too Jimmy. He's experienced and helpful. Seems to have an uncanny way of asking the right questions too. I'm glad he'll be helping us."

Jimmy then added, "He too wrote a lot about the Drug Cartels. Did you cross paths in writing *The Camp David Conspiracy*?

"No, he came to the paper several years later, but he was part of the reporting pool during the Operation Blueprint trials. I believe he worked with the *Miami Herald*." Geoff remembered. "And incredibly knowledgeable about how the cartels operated. Had even cracked a few sources in South America."

"Well, maybe he can help us crack who is behind all of this."

"Jimmy, that's why I want to meet tonight. I got something I need to show you. But let's talk about it once we're inside your cave."

"Got it Geoff."

• • •

Geoff and Jimmy crossed the threshold into Jimmy's house.

"My gosh Jimmy, do you even live here?" Geoff said looking around the virtually untouched living room. Nothing out of place. Nothing left sitting on the table. The kitchen spotless. No breakfast dishes left out. Toaster and coffee maker always in exactly the same place. Blinds untouched.

Jimmy said with a laugh. "My mother visits me every day."

"Huh?"

"Oh, not literally. But every morning her memory tells me to put everything back in order. But then again, I spend most of my time inside The Planet, and all food is delivered. Only groceries I bring in is a millennial assortment of beers. Want one?"

"Thanks. The usual please."

Jimmy handed Geoff an open beer and they headed through the door and secure hallway leading to Jimmy's computer lab.

Once inside, Geoff sat his beer down away from the workstation and opened his satchel and handed a copy of a fax to Jimmy.

"What's this?" Jimmy asked, then reading the prose out loud.

Weapons defeat armies.
Slings and arrows, the sword.
Missiles, the plane.
Bombs, the bunker.
You will amass the greatest ever witnessed.
Ever conceived.
For all to see.

Your target will perceive defeat.
And fold.
Without ever lifting a sling, an arrow, or stone.
Of their own.

Jimmy looked up and then read it again. "Poetry?"

"You remember the day I came by when I showed you the photo Jacob had taken?"

"Yeah. Sure. You had actually called me to set the meeting before your conversation with Jacob. Is this what you wanted to show me?"

"Yip."

"What is it?"

"Hopefully fodder for your Kryptonite system and the key to our investigation. And this is to be kept highly confidential. Even from Marty, Fred, and Jeff. At least until we get a hit."

"But what is it?" Jimmy asked again.

"This was supposedly written by The Fixer behind this year's election fraud and the man behind the Gulf War in 1991." Wines answered slowly and hesitantly.

If I need Jimmy's tools, I need to fill him in.

"This is from your anonymous source we discussed this morning?" Jimmy asked while once again studying the prose.

Wines slowly nodded—still not sure he was doing the right thing in sharing President Osbourne's evidence.

"Geoff. Is this describing the strategy used in Gulf War I?"

Geoff again nodded.

"And this was sent to your source by the man who arranged the Gulf War to happen?"

Wines again nodded slowly, but he couldn't stop his smile as Jimmy began to put things together.

"The person who received this fax was in the position to do this—amass a great army?"

Another nod.

"Geoff, my guess is this was sent to your old friend President Osbourne. He was president during Gulf War One and your host at Camp David when you investigated Operation Blueprint. Seems things are running full circle. Would you care to corroborate my hunch?"

"Right so far Jimmy." Wines said with a smile thinking he divulged nothing other than the fax.

"Another thing is interesting here, Geoff."

"What's that, Jimmy?"

"In both cases, seems our mystery man recruited prideful men requiring money as his central characters. Saddam and our candidate."

"The GOP candidate is broke?" Wines asked, somewhat incredulously.

"Geoff. The answer is yes. Nearly so. I've seen his returns." Then with a wink, "and a few other things too."

"Well, that explains a lot. I'm not going to ask anything more. We have enough on our plate, but I would keep an eye on his accounts for any large money being moved around. That could take us where we need to go."

"Will do, Geoff. Got anything else I can use to track down our mystery man?"

"The fax number this was sent to—and the time and date stamp on the fax which I am sure would have been completely accurate given its location."

"White House?" Jimmy teased.

"Upstairs." Wines simply retorted.

"Hmmm. Let me set this poem up on the Kryptonite system and see what it finds. It is distinctive. Short. Crisp. A bit of Shakespeare too. Hopefully whoever wrote this is still writing like this. Somewhere. Somewhere on-line."

"Let's hope, Jimmy. We can only hope."

"Geoff, let me see the phone number of the machine that received this fax."

Geoff handed the photocopies he had made of the sheets of paper Pat Hayes had sent him.

Jimmy took the White House fax number and ran it through his system. It instantly dinged. "Still there. Listed as an 'unlisted' US Government number."

He sat down at his terminal and typed in a few more numbers and they both heard the distinct tones of a fax machine trying to engage. Jimmy then disconnected the line. "This might drive them crazy trying to figure who tried to send a telephone fax in this day and age. From an untraceable bogus phone number in Sri Lanka, no less."

Wines just smiled.

Jimmy then paused and looked at the second sheet of paper. "What's this second phone number?"

"Supposedly the phone number Osbourne used to call our mystery man in the first place."

"Hopefully we will be able to track down both numbers through some very old phone records. Then maybe we will be able to link it to someone, somewhere."

"Sounds like a plan Jimmy."

Jimmy waited, then looked up at Geoff.

"Geoffrey, you know I was not keeping the pee video from you. Don't you?"

"Jimmy, if I did, I would not be here right now. I distinctly remember you asking me if I wanted to know what Marty had you working on in the middle of the day. I was in a hurry and left, saying we'll catch it later."

Jimmy smiled. "Thanks Geoff."

Jimmy then turned and faced his keyboard and monitor. "Let me check one other thing here." He then typed in a few more lines. "It appears our Russian cyber expert is still using his same cell phone. No change. Bluetooth still on. He's been moving around New York City. Oh, this is interesting. He even visited TIME Magazine."

Wines moved closer to the monitor. "And Jacob's phone?"

"On-line. But Emmett's appears to be off."

"Is there any way to see the proximity of Jacob and our Russian?"

"Checking . . . Nope. The Russian never came close to Jacob's phone. But it does seem odd the Russian visited TIME headquarters on Liberty Street. Looks like he was there for only 15 minutes."

Then Jimmy looked up at Geoff. "What time did you call Emmett?"

"Around eleven, why?"

"It appears our Russian friend had already played the video."

Chapter 50

WHO BLEW THE WHISTLE?
IS THE CAT OUT OF THE BAG?
THE PRESS IS AWAKENING.
THERE IS RUMOR IN THE WIND.
AND TROUBLE AHEAD.

MY RUSSIAN FRIEND IS ACTING
BEYOND OUR COURSE.
IS THIS HIS PROLOGUE TO THE 'OMEN' COMING ON?
'LET THEM CRY 'HAVOC'
AND LET SLIP THE DOGS OF WAR.'

CIVIL RESTRAINT IS LOST.
I NOW COMMAND NOT,
WHAT I HATH WROUGHT.

Chapter 51

The phone was answered on the second ring. "President Osbourne's office. Pat Hayes speaking."

"Good morning, Pat. Geoffrey Wines here."

"Well good morning, Mr. Wines. So good to hear your voice. How are you this hot July day?"

"You're right there, Pat. DC in the summer is hot and muggy."

"What can I do for you today?"

"I need to speak with President Osbourne. Is he available?

"Sorry Geoff, he and the security team went fly fishing near Reno yesterday. Won't be back for three days."

"Okay, that's fine. I need to talk to the president when he returns. Is there any way we could set up a secure call when he gets back? I mean military grade secure."

Pat laughed. "Oh, you want to brag to him about the big fish you're catching."

"Something like that Pat."

"No problem, Mr. Wines. You know former presidents maintain their security clearance. Private calls are nearly daily when he is in town. We can make the arrangements. It will be best from your cell phone. Better yet, go purchase a burner phone and don't use it until we call you. It will probably be Thursday morning though. Is that okay?"

"That will work." Geoff replied, but he detected something in Pat's voice he could not quite discern.

Humor?
A laugh?
Or just trying to lighten the situation?

"Good. Send me the phone number and I'll send you the exact time via my email."

"Thanks Pat."

"My pleasure Mr. Wines. My pleasure."

Chapter 52

"Marty. Wines here. Any chance I can see you and Fred for a quick gut check."

"Something interesting?" The Executive Editor of the *Washington Post* responded with a touch of intrigue in his voice. "It's only been a day since our meeting with Jimmy, Terry and Cam."

"Maybe. Don't know. But I just learned something that seems very odd. Very odd indeed and your thoughts and experience would be helpful."

"How about right before lunch. Say 11:45?"

"Perfect. Thanks."

• • •

Wines took the stairs up two floors to the Publisher's suite. Marty was in Fred's office, the door wide open.

"We meet again. So soon?" Fred ventured.

"Yeah, thanks guys." Geoffrey took a seat in the center of Fred's meeting cluster.

"What's on your mind Mr. Wines." Marty asked.

"Do you think we're being played?" Geoff volunteered straight out.

"In what way?" followed Fred, again taking the lawyerly stance.

"Well, Jimmy continues to track the cyber-Russian's phone. He appears to still be in New York City. But what continually nags me is here is a guy who should know all the hacking and tracking precautions a person should take if they want to be discreet. Wouldn't you think?"

Fred and Marty looked at each other, jaws withdrawn and agreeing.

"Yet, he is roaming the streets of New York, sending signals every place he goes. He keeps his phone turned on, his Bluetooth turned on, and he is visiting some unusual places."

"Like where?" Marty probed.

"Yesterday, Jimmy tracked his cell phone to an office in south Manhattan, where it appears he played the pee video."

"Do you think he is shopping it to other media outlets?" Fred interjected. "Several media companies are down there."

"That's why I'm here. Do you guys have any thoughts or feelings?" Wines probed.

Marty affirmed. "He just sent us the video, confidentially, if in fact it was him. No solicitation. No communication. Just a video on a nice safe flash drive according to Jimmy."

"What else do you know Geoff that you're not telling us?" Fred crossed.

Wines shifted in his seat. "Sir, it's one of my two confidential sources. The one in the elevator who took the photo of the two Russians."

"Go on." Fred coached.

"The person who took the photo is Jacob Washington. Name ring a bell?" Wines answered. He knew Jacob's name never appeared in any of his Operation Blueprint articles. Only in the broader book *"THE CAMP DAVID CONSPIRACY"* that Jimmy had hacked from the WaPo archives.

"Jacob Washington. Jacob Washington." Marty repeated. "Nope, doesn't ring a bell here."

"Same with me. Doesn't sound familiar." Fred confirmed, then asked. "Who does he work for?"

"How about the name 'Emmett Washington?'" Wines added.

Both men stopped in their tracks, instantly putting together the connection.

"Emmett Washington. Managing Editor of TIME Magazine. Is *he* Jacob's brother?" Fred inquired, somewhat bewildered.

Wines nodded. "Our cyber-Russian appears to have visited TIME Magazine's headquarters yesterday. At about the same time the pee-video was again played on his phone."

"Well, why don't you call Emmett and just ask him if he has seen any good movies lately?" Fred quipped with a mischievous smile.

"I could. You know Emmett interned here one summer. Worked directly with me. That is why he had his brother call me with the lead in the first place. Felt the *Post* could better investigate the story. Plus, he wanted to minimize any connection of his brother with the story since Jacob was getting reacquainted with society after a stint at Rikers. That's why I agreed to keep Jacob's name confidential."

"And we will." affirmed Marty.

"But I worry our cyber-Russian could track Jacob the same way Jimmy tracked the two of them."

"Any evidence of that?" Fred interjected.

"Nope. Jimmy said Jacob's phone has not been in proximity to the Russian. But is it just a coincidence the Russian visits TIME Magazine?"

Suddenly Marty's face erupted with a thought. "Was the Russian in proximity to Emmett's phone?"

"Hmmm. Don't know. I had purposely called Emmett on his office line just before to warn him of the cyber-Russian and suggested they destroy their phones and open new accounts."

"What am I missing here, Geoff?" Marty quizzed.

"Sirs, our thinking heretofore has been the Russian bots are being designed to harm the Democratic candidate and help the GOP candidate. Right?"

Both the Executive Editor and Publisher nodded their heads in agreement.

"But what if they really don't care who wins. Maybe all they are after is to disrupt our election and erode our trust with their disinformation."

"That's obvious Geoff." Fred asserted. "But that doesn't get Katy Lynn Holloway off the hook for starting the disinformation to begin with. That is the story I want to publish in *this* newspaper. And if we can prove the Russians are using her strategy to create more havoc, then that is the icing on the cake."

Fred then paused and added one more thought. "Geoff, next time you meet with Jimmy, ask him to look into a website called 'Breitbart.'

The relationship between the campaign and that site seems too close for comfort. Much too close."

Chapter 53

Immediately after meeting with Fred Ryan and Marty Baron, Geoffrey Wines headed down the stairs to his desk. He called Emmett Washington's office line.

The line answered on the first ring. "Emmett Washington."

"Don't New Yorkers ever eat lunch?" Wines teased.

"Good afternoon, Geoffrey. Nope got too many bad guys to chase down. Plus, without my cell, can't leave the office. Sent my assistant to get us something."

"Interesting Emmett. Got to ask you something."

"Sure, what is it Geoff."

"Have you seen any good movies lately?"

Emmett took a long pause, then set the phone down and Geoff could hear his office door close before he returned to the line. Then Emmett answered Geoff's question with just one word. "Yes."

"And was it an American movie or a foreign movie."

"Definitely foreign. And not a genre I typically watch."

"And is the star someone who also has screen credentials on a certain reality show?" Geoffrey teased.

"Enough Geoff. Yes. I saw a video yesterday right before you called. Promoted by none other than the Russian man Jacob photographed in the elevator."

"And did you identify the man?"

"No. And he wouldn't identify himself. He basically played the video and left."

"Was the woman from the elevator with him?"

"No."

Wines paused until Emmett started again.

"Geoff, I wasn't sure how to handle the video until your call. I certainly recognized the face from Jacob's elevator photo, but that was all. Of course, I didn't say anything about that either. But then you call and tell me the guy is some sort of Russian cyber guy, a close associate to Putin and then you let slip that the movie's starring male would be the next president. And that we should destroy our cell phones."

Damn.
Emmett picked up on that.

"Fortunately, Geoff. I never have my cell on while I am in the office. Too many distractions and since the Snowden revelations, poses a huge security risk. In fact, we have a policy that all our reporters and editors keep their phones off while on premises."

"Smart move Emmett. Very smart move."

"But Geoff. You seem to be deeper into this story than us. What am I missing?"

Wines paused, thinking of his young intern from so many years earlier who had been the first to understand the possibility of a cocaine tainting conspiracy.

"More than you could ever imagine, Emmett. Much more."

Chapter 54

"Oh, this is interesting." Jimmy Olsen said to himself as he sat alone in Planet Krypton enjoying a beer before Wong delivered dinner. "Looks like Guccifer just transferred a new tranche of emails to the WikiLeaks server . . . Hmmm, let's see . . . Wow! These are DNC emails . . . Wonder when this will become public?"

The last couple of days had been exhausting for Jimmy; but he was beginning to feel WaPo's management supported him in trying to shed light on the disinformation story. Geoffrey seemed to be working it full time. And the addition of Jeff Leen, Chief Editor of the *Post's* Investigations Unit also showed a mark of trust.

The gong of the front door camera sounded; Jimmy looked over to the Wong Cam to see if dinner had arrived. It wasn't the delivery person. Fred Ryan, Publisher of the *Washington Post*, stood at his front door.

"Guess we got his attention." Jimmy said out loud as he clicked a few keys on the console and turned toward the locking corridor.

Jimmy opened the front door just as Wong stepped onto his front porch.

"Hello Fred." He cheerfully acknowledged his guest, stepping aside so Fred could enter while reaching for his wallet to pay Wong for the delivery.

Fred looked around the living room waiting for Jimmy to place the food containers on the kitchen counter.

"Hi Jimmy. Sorry to come barging in on you with no notice. Geoff said I could probably catch you here tonight. I was in the area and thought I would see our new media correspondent —and investigator I might add—in action."

"Gee Fred, if I knew you were coming, I would have ordered more Szechuan," he said, while shaking the publisher's hand.

"No worries Jimmy. Seriously, since our meeting the other morning, I have been dying to see your set up. May I?" Fred cordially asked, still scanning the room.

"Sure thing Mr. White." Jimmy teased, referencing Perry White, the editor of the *Daily Planet*, the paper where Jimmy Olsen and Clark Kent worked.

"Funny Jimmy. I used to read *Superman* too."

"Beer sir.?" Jimmy offered while reaching in the refrigerator for his second bottle of Lagunitas IPA. "Mostly craft brews, a rather wide assortment."

"Scotch?" Fred countered.

"Nope. No scotch. I do have a bottle of bourbon in here somewhere — 'Something Van Winkle.' Can't vouch for how good it is sir."

"Pappy Van Winkle?" Fred repeated, surprised.

"Yeah, that's it. Got it down here somewhere." Jimmy answered over his shoulder as he kneeled and reached deep into the cabinet next to the refrigerator. "Know something about it, sir?"

"Maybe." Fred responded watching Jimmy dig into the cabinet for what could only be described as a true treasure. Finally, Jimmy stood up and turned around with a dusty bottle of 20-year-old Pappy Van Winkle Family Reserve.

Fred observed the full bottle with the tax stamp still unbroken. "How long have you had it?

Jimmy looked at the bottle in his hands and over to Fred. "Forever. I guess. It was in my dad's cabinet when he passed. I never had the heart to throw it out since he seemed to have held onto it for so long."

"Throw it out? OH GOD! Don't throw it away. Or even give it away." Fred answered with an air of assertiveness that surprised Jimmy. "No, no, you have there one of the finest, and possibly most rare bourbons ever made!"

"Really?" Jimmy reacted, rotating the dusty bottle in his hand as he closely looked at the label. "Humph. Who'd imagined?" Then looking up at his boss and swinging open the refrigerator door. "You want a beer then?"

"Sure Jimmy. I'll drink what you're having. Why don't we save the Pappy's for when we crack open this election story. Maybe we'll have an occasion to enjoy it then."

Jimmy grabbed a second bottle of Lagunitas, removed the cap, and handed it to Fred. He then dished out the food from the carton onto a plate, covered it with a silicone disc, placed the plate in the refrigerator and put the empty carton in the trash can under the sink. "I'll have that later."

He then returned the bottle of Pappy's to the lower cabinet, leaving the counter immaculately clear.

"Sir, would you like to visit Planet Krypton?"

"I would Jimmy."

• • •

Jimmy and his guest passed through the security hallway and once again when the inner door opened, Fred, like Geoffrey, just stood there marveling at the wall of monitors.

"My god Jimmy. Marty wasn't exaggerating." Then Fred added with astonishment. "You built this yourself?"

"Yes sir. Thank you, sir." Jimmy answered with a tinge of pride. "Anything special you want to look at?"

"As a matter of fact, yes. You know I'm a co-founder of POLITICO. We started the news-site to compete with more partisan websites on both the left and right. Seems that during the early Obama years, each side went to their own partisan corners to get the truth out about what our politicians were up to. Our approach was to be even-handed, and I believe the site pretty much fulfilled that objective. I left a little less than two years ago to become publisher of *The Post*."

"So, Mr. Ryan, you want me to analyze POLITICO?"

"Interesting idea Mr. Olsen." Fred howled, wiping his eyes. "Would love to send it over to the editors there. But no, I am thinking you do an analysis of the alt-right news sites and see what they are up to. Maybe turn on that Kryptonite system you described and see how the news they report bounces from one site to the next. And maybe from where it originates."

"You want to give me a clue, Mr. Ryan?" Jimmy probed. "Not sure who you are talking about and what you are looking to find."

"I won't tell you what I am looking for. You need to see if there are any interesting patterns."

Jimmy laughed. "You and Geoffrey Wines. You know what you are looking for but want me to find the evidence to confirm your hunch."

"That's right." Then Fred instructed. "Good reporting is letting the facts lead, not follow."

"Okay then." Jimmy yielded. "Who are these alt-right sites. Fake news sites like 4chan or the Denver Guardian or Washington Liberator?"

"It could include them. But I am thinking news sites like Breitbart, InfoWars, Gateway Pundit, Realclear Politics, Truthfeed, Daily Caller and another one named Ending the Fed."

Jimmy looked up from jotting down the names. "How come I haven't heard of some of these? I know the traditional conservative outlets like Fox News and *The Washington Examiner*? Maybe the *New York Post* too. But these others have escaped me. Do all these sites have a staff of reporters?"

Fred hesitated for a moment, wrestling with whether to answer Jimmy's question.

"See what you can find, Jimmy."

"Okay sir. Anything else?

"Nope." Fred said as he stood, demonstrating his intent to leave. "Jimmy, I have intruded on you enough tonight. And thanks for the beer too. Remember, save that bottle of Pappy's until we publish something meaningful and earth-shattering. I will let Geoffrey, Jeff and Marty know about my request, so we are all on the same page. Review your findings with them."

"Will do sir. You don't want me to brief you on this?"

"No Jimmy. You guys are the reporters and investigators. I am only intervening here because I happen to have a career of experience in this specific area—and I want to ensure it is examined."

Then giving the wall of monitors one last examination, Fred continued. "Plus, it gave me a good excuse to see your Planet Krypton, Jimmy. That is all." Fred then turned toward the door. "Now how do I get out of here?"

Chapter 55

After taking Fred Ryan back through the security hall and out the front door, Jimmy Olsen returned to Planet Krypton with the warmed Szechuan. Sitting away from the console he examined the list of alt-right websites Fred Ryan had given him—Breitbart, InfoWars, Gateway Pundit, Realclear Politics, Truthfeed, Daily Caller and Ending the Fed.

While he ate, he used his iPad and searched each of the sites.

"Wow, some pretty crazy stuff here." Jimmy uttered out loud as he read more breaking news about Obama being born in Africa; Lots of stuff bashing Fox News and calling it an arm of the Democratic Party. A few articles about the Democratic candidate selling weapons to ISIS and asking Christians to deny their faith. Follow ups on Ted Cruz's father being a part of the JFK assassination plot. New details found in the Meteor Pizza-Child Trafficking saga. Exclusive detail on how a former president's foundation is being funded by the Saudi's. Updates about shipping auto factories to Canada. And a chronology of how the US singlehandedly turned China into a superpower.

He also noted other even more elaborate "breaking news stories" coined together using half-truths and far-reaching assumptions to create conspiracies inside the FBI, State Department and even the CDC. "Amazing stuff, apparently written to reduce confidence in those government institutions."

After reviewing each sites' content, he hit the "About" tab to learn who published the site, when it was established, and something about the ownership. He would follow up with the WHOIS info from the metadata and learn the servers each site used.

The pattern was consistent. Most of the sites were started sometime during the Obama-Tea Party movement and proclaimed to be "the source of information for the alt-right" or "What the mainstream media is holding from you."

With this last statement, Jimmy leaned back in his chair and laughed. "Yeah, I got a spicy video and some pretty interesting sources for stories that *we are holding from you*."

Then Jimmy pondered: Wouldn't it be a hoot if I hacked a few of these and put up the 'pee-video'; or maybe the connection of the Russian bots spreading fake news stories; or a breaking news scoop with an accompanying CIA photo identifying two Russian visitors to a certain candidate's offices?

> *Yeah, that would be news their readers would not see anyplace else.*

Jimmy mused as he took another bite of his Szechuan.

Chapter 56

Geoffrey Wines went to a very non-public spot in Washington DC to receive the call from President Osbourne. Older model cars, pickups and more than normal trash occupied the industrial street. There were no storefronts, no residents and no one walking along the sidewalks. His experience in DC crime told him this area was probably free of drug activity, petty theft and therefore no surveillance cameras. His "beater car" fit in nicely with the surroundings as he waited for the burner phone to ring. He had also taken the precaution of turning off his regular cell phone before leaving the office.

The burner-phone rang, exactly at 10:30 a.m. as planned.

"Hello." Wines said simply. No identification.

After a moment of silence and a couple of clicks, he heard the former president's voice.

"Well hello Mr. Wines. President Osbourne here. Am I right in assuming you are in some non-disclosed location taking this call?" Wines heard the amusement in Osbourne's voice. "What's wrong, don't you trust the government's secure lines?"

"Good morning, Mr. President. Wasn't sure of the protocol since I was instructed to use a burner phone for this call."

"No fear Mr. Wines. My line is absolutely secure. Pat was just playing with you. No one can hear what we are saying over the line. You don't need that burner phone. But make sure Boris and Natasha are not near-by listening. Comey either.

Why did Osbourne mention Russian spies?
And an FBI reference too.

"Thank you, Mr. President."

"Are you going to fill me in on your investigation?" Osbourne asked nonchalantly.

Wines thought for a moment before answering. "Well, I am hoping to pick your mind sir."

"Oh, still holding stuff close to the old reporter's vest, huh?" Then added with a laugh, "What's a confidential informant to do?"

Wines started to say something when Osbourne interrupted.

"Oh my, Mr. Wines. No worries. I don't expect you to brief me. Not one bit. Not your place and not my place to evaluate anything you may have found. But you seem to have some questions for me. Am I right?"

Somewhat relieved, Wines answered "Yes sir."

"In which area, Mr. Wines. Iraq or this election?"

"The latter sir. This election?"

"See, I told you it would be much more exciting than chasing down some story from the past," chuckled Osbourne. "What can I help you with?"

Wines hesitated a moment to gather his thoughts. Though he had known for several days what he wanted to discuss with the former president; he just wasn't sure how he wanted to ask the first question. He needed to know if the Russians were truly interested in the election, or just playing with us. He decided to coin the question this way.

"Mr. President. Why would Vladimir Putin want to disrupt our election?"

The line went silent for a moment. Just breathing.

"Mr. President? Are you okay?" Wines probed.

A few moments later President Osbourne answered. "Whew, Mr. Wines. Not beating around the bush, are you? Now I am guessing for you to ask that question, you must have some specific facts that say the Russian leader is. Is disrupting our election. Am I right?

"Mr. President . . ."

"Oh, never mind giving me an answer. You're asking me for my thoughts. Well . . ." Osbourne paused, then quipped, "I guess for the same reason a dog licks his balls."

"Sir?"

"Because he can, Mr. Wines. Because he can. And . . . because he has a willing partner who makes it easy for him to mess with us."

"Willing partner. Who?" Wines asked as he jotted down Osbourne's answers.

"Who? Who? Oh, come-on Mr. Wines." Osbourne retorted quite seriously. "Okay, let me lay this out for you. It's what you want anyway. Right?"

"Thank you, sir. That would be most helpful." Wines responded, knowing Osbourne would have done so anyway.

He wants this to end well as much as we do.

"You know Mr. Wines: I have been in four presidential races. Twice as the candidate for vice president and twice leading the ticket. And though we—the ticket and those working on our behalf—wanted to win, none of us were going to sacrifice our integrity to do so. And I believe every man who has held this office during the past 100 years did not either—except maybe JFK, but that was more his dad and not him. None of us were opportunists. Politicians yes. But not opportunists. We believed in our office. Our country's traditions. Our institutions. We were men who believed our ideas and leadership would be good for America. We believed in debate between the parties. And deep down we felt both perspectives were needed."

"Okay. I'm with you so far." Wines interjected, for no other reason than to let Osbourne know he was listening.

"We were serious men with serious agendas. We did everything we could do to honor the office we were running for. To give it the respect it deserves. After all, why would we run for an office people did not respect. You with me Mr. Wines?"

"Yes sir. I think so."

"But this year is different. We have a leading candidate—representing my party no less—who does not respect the office, the former holders of the office, nor the other candidates running for the office. He talks about penis size from the debate stage; calls the other candidates derogatory names; makes up ridiculous claims; and ridicules the men and women asking the questions—your fellow reporters, Mr. Wines, your fellow reporters. And he spent the last eight years dishonoring the man who currently holds the office with clear lies he knows are not true."

Wines found it hard to keep up as President Osbourne spoke emotionally and significantly faster than usual. And, per their agreement, he could not record the call since this subject was totally off-the-record.

But men, like the former president, should be saying this stuff out loud.

"This candidate has gone out of his way to discredit—not disagree—but discredit his opponents, former office holders, and the mainstream press who have the will and resources to fact check him. And I am sorry to say, too many of his supporters are following along. With his supporters following along, it won't be long before other office holders will board the train."

"Sir?"

"Wait a minute, Mr. Wines, I'm not finished answering your question." Osbourne retorted sternly.

Here it comes.

"Mr. Wines, you are asking me 'why Mr. Putin would mess with our election?' Right?"

"Yes, Mr. President. Why would he?"

"BECAUSE HE CAN!" the president practically yelled into the phone. "He has a willing partner—this candidate—who will assist him in doing so. If a foreign leader had done anything to influence my election, I would have publicly called him out. And I feel strongly the other candidates would have as well. But this one . . ."

Osbourne's voice then trailed off "this . . . this is part of some hare-brained scheme initiated by three former presidents, no less. Though they had no idea it would come to this. Damn! What a mess!"

"Do you think the Democratic Party candidate knows Putin is involved?" Wines inquired, testing the former president's theory.

"Absolutely not! I would bet my life on it. She wouldn't hesitate a moment to sound the alarm. Like McCain telling the woman that

Obama was not a Muslim. Not only does she believe our elections should start and end at our borders, but she also hates Mr. Putin. Doesn't trust him one bit. And called him out as Secretary of State. No, I don't think so. I don't think she would have anything to do with Mr. Putin and the election."

Then Osbourne added, almost whimsically, "But she is not lily-white either. She has committed unnecessary infractions, like her email server. Made disparaging statements at high ticket speeches. Things that are just stupid. Stupid! And plays right into Putin's scheme. Makes it easier for him to stir things up. And for the GOP candidate to call her names."

Osbourne then hesitated, before continuing, "Plus, her cautious nature seems to come off as sneaky and guarded to a lot of people. Too bad, in person she is warm and funny. But from the podium, not trustful. Too guarded."

"What about our mystery man?" Wines followed-up, hoping to get a break—some more info about the guy who helped Osbourne win the Cold War and who consorted with the three former presidents to convince Americans that elections are important.

"Fishing again, Mr. Wines? I gave you everything I have about 'Elvis'—yours and my mystery man."

Osbourne then paused and asked. "How sure are you our mystery man is behind this? This opportunist candidate? I know. I told you he is. The three former presidents believe he is because they hired him. But have you found anything to corroborate his role Mr. Wines?"

Wines thought long before answering. The rush of things he and Jimmy had uncovered flashed through his mind. The video. Putin's associate's visit to the candidate's headquarters and then to see Emmett at TIME Magazine. The false news stories on fake-news sites. Russian bots. The links between the campaign and the misinformation circulating the web. But nothing that directly tied someone to everything they had uncovered so far.

Then Osbourne spoke again.

"You don't need to answer that Mr. Wines. But please hurry and start reporting on what *is* happening here. I believe if this man gets elected, he could literally tear this country apart. And all our future elections could become null and void."

Chapter 57

"Oh my gosh. I found it!" Jimmy exclaimed out loud, though he was the only one inside Planet Krypton. "How did I miss it before?"

After meeting with Fred Ryan and given the names of several alt-right news outlets, he set up his Kryptonite System to roam through each of the sites to extract stories, compare content, isolate specific language, and any overlap between the sites. The system also roamed the entire web searching for similar stories and language. All of this in real time.

His system essentially did what Google's search engine does millions of times a day. Except his algorithms were able to retain, cross-reference and analyze the results of each search. He had programmed his system to isolate everything and highlight those things that were common across multiple sites. He also added WikiLeaks as well as documents and emails his crawlers had uncovered, including those from inside the Republican campaign and Katy Lynn Holloway's computer.

Anticipating the findings would be complex and sprawling, he added a graphing system to display clusters of common elements and links between the sites.

And as a last area of analysis, he applied what he had learned from Reverend Brook's congregants to determine the profiles of Twitter and Facebook users who clicked on the sites or Liked or Retweeted material from any or all of them.

Jimmy stepped back from the largest monitor where the results were displayed. The findings were unbelievable; factual; and except for the GOP document links, totally legal.

He immediately returned to his console and typed in a code and rang Wines' desk phone.

Geoffrey Wines answered. "Who from Sri Lanka is calling me today?"

Jimmy ignored Geoffrey's smart-ass greeting. "Geoffrey, this is Jimmy. Calling from Planet Krypton. You need to see this. Fred and Marty need to see this. Jeff and Terry too. Holy Moly Geoffrey, we just hit the Motherload."

"What is it, Jimmy?"

"Can't tell you Geoff. Better for you guys to see it. It may be exactly what we're looking for!" Jimmy answered, almost breathless.

"Okay. Okay, Jimmy. How should I contact you since you are in the cave?"

"Just text my cell phone. I'll be intercepting texts."

Wines understood Jimmy's protocol. No traceable electronics were allowed inside the Planet. Besides, none would work due to its RF shield.

• • •

Fifteen minutes later, Jimmy received a text from Geoff letting him know he and Fred Ryan would be there in about thirty minutes. Marty and Jeff were tied up.

Jimmy prepared Planet Krypton for the two guests. He rolled in his cart with a large pitcher of ice water, a full ice bucket, pint beer glasses, coffee mugs and added fresh water into the Keurig machine. No beer for this mid-afternoon meeting. He also turned the AC down a couple of degrees to ensure the room would not get stuffy.

The Wong Cam gonged when Geoff's car pulled up in front of the house.

Jimmy met them at the door and the three passed—*tightly*—through the security lock into Jimmy's "Bat Cave."

• • •

Jimmy had arranged his guests to sit against the back wall since he would be filling the largest screen with several images. He moved his console chair away from the monitors and rotated so he could see both the screen and his guests. A wireless keyboard sat on his lap.

"What do you have, Jimmy?" Fred asked, eager to begin.

"Well sir, my dad use to say, 'if enough dogs are barking, there must be something out there.' And sir, there are lots of dogs barking. However, what is out there is not real. They are all barking because one big dog is barking. And I think this 'circle-bark' is absolutely worth reporting."

"Jimmy, let's have it." Fred said, leaning back in the swivel office chair, preparing himself for the show.

"Okay sir. Last week, during your visit, you gave the names of several alt-right web news sites. For Geoff's benefit, they were Breitbart, InfoWars, Gateway Pundit, Realclear Politics, Truthfeed, Daily Caller and another one named Ending the Fed."

"Right Jimmy." Wines added to reassure Jimmy he knew Fred's request. "Fred told me he had asked you to look into Breitbart and other sites. Before that, he had even asked me to ask you. Anyway, here we are, all in the loop."

Jimmy looked at both Fred and Geoff, wondering if there was some issue he didn't know about.

"So, I launched my Kryptonite system to scan these sites for similar language. I looked at each site's data to see who is clicking on what stories and whether that same person clicked on similar stories on other sites. And I examined the clickers' Facebook and Twitter profiles to see who they are," Jimmy explained, and then added with a smile, "of course, I will be more than happy to take you through the technical details of how I accomplished this."

Both Fred and Geoff shook their heads. But then Fred spoke up. "Jimmy, is there anything you did in the 'shady area'" he said using finger quotes "that we discussed the other morning."

"No sir. Not yet sir. I'll explain when we get to it. But since you bring up the other morning, let me add that the sudden activity of the Russian bots did on one hand bring to life what is going on . . . and on the other hand, required an extra layer of investigation to see whose voice is really talking."

Both men had a blank look, so Jimmy explained. "When all the dogs are barking in the neighborhood, it is hard to determine which dog barked first. That is because dogs don't leave a digital track. But if they barked via a computer, with some extra scrubbing of the data we can determine which dog barked first with a story. And what I found really surprised me!"

"And . . ." Fred spoke up, spinning his hands for Jimmy to get to it.

"And I found the big dog. The lead dog. The first dog to bark with each new story. *With each new story.* Got that?" Jimmy stepped toward the screen as a large red circle with the name 'Breitbart' written in it appeared. "Pretty stunning actually." Jimmy turned to face Fred directly, "This may be what you suspected. On story after story, Breitbart started the story and then all these other sites picked them up."

Jimmy continued, "Starting here" the Breitbart circle lit up, "to here" the right side of the screen then filled with smaller sizes of red circles with the names "Info Wars" - "End the Fed" - "Gateway Pundit" - "Daily Caller" - "Realclear Politics" - "Truthfeed."

"Oh," Jimmy said, waving his hand across the names, "the size of these circles indicates the amount of traffic each site has for a given story." Jimmy then clicked again, and lines and arrows formed between the sites. "And these lines show the interaction between sites."

Wines asked. "What are we talking about here? How many clicks? You know, circulation."

"Here is a story, mostly untrue I might add, about immigration." It started on Breitbart and then picked up by the others over the course of a couple of days and its combined clicks totaled over six hundred thousand unique viewers. Here is another citing Fox News as an extension of the Democratic Party. It totaled over one million. And here is a story about the Meteor Pizza Child Trafficking scandal. It has accumulated nearly two million total clicks."

"Lots of dogs barking." Geoff emphasized.

"Right Geoff. Now let me add another twist to this. I constructed a similar analysis of the *Washington Post* and the mainstream media." A large blue circle appeared on the left side of the screen tagged 'WaPo.' Then popped 'NYT' a slightly larger blue circle. Then smaller circles with 'CBS', 'NBC', 'CNN', LA TIMES', 'HUFF', 'MSNBC', 'VOX', 'CNBC.'

Jimmy motioned his hand in a circle around these outlets. "This is an aggregate of all the stories we and our brethren have run. The lines show the interaction between the sites." And then the red circles on the right hand of the screen shifted. "And this is an aggregate of all the stories that have run on these alt-right sites. And again, the lines show the interaction between the sites. Notice anything?"

"Yeah." Fred stood up excited. "We're the big dog! Along with our friends in New York."

"Jimmy, got a question." Geoff spoke up. "How come there are no lines between the left blue side and the red right side?"

"Ah ha, Mr. Wines. Because there aren't any. Or let's say, very few. Very, very few. While our universe is certainly larger overall, there is a significant portion of the population who get virtually all their news from these sites" Jimmy explained pointing to the red circles "and no place else."

"That's scary." Geoff lamented.

"Yeah" Jimmy added, "I believe these sites through Facebook and Twitter links have filled the void left by local papers who have gone under. The big metro papers are still publishing, but the smaller market papers who regularly picked up our stories are struggling or have ceased publication."

Geoff examined the two clusters again. "So, Jimmy, are you saying there is no fake news or fake news web sites on the left as you are showing on the right?"

"Good observation Geoff." Fred answered abruptly. "There are a few—a very few I have seen over the years—sites that purport the liberal point of view, sometimes to exaggeration—but none that just make up stuff. Solon, VOX, Slate, Mother Earth News, Daily Beast and Huff Post certainly tout the liberal point of view, even more than CNN or MSNBC, but I have not seen the out and out lies and made-up crap as those alt-right sites shown in red on the right side of the screen."

Jimmy jumped in. "Mostly right sir. I tracked down stories and using some verification tools, I identified about one hundred totally false stories about the Democratic candidate and about fifteen about the GOP candidate." He then added with a laugh, "But three of those fifteen were comedy sketches from *Saturday Night Live* or from the *Comedy Channel* on YouTube."

Turning more serious, Jimmy then added "But there were also a few doozies: One site called *HotGlobalNews* falsely claimed the GOP candidate called the current president the 'N-word' at a public forum. Incidentally, this site also claimed Justin Trudeau was going to star in the next *Star Wars* movie. Other sites claim to have the GOP candidate's rejection letter from Harvard. Why Harvard? Pretty mild stuff compared to the alt-right claims of child trafficking; a former president's foundation sending millions to ISIS; or Florida Dems unanimously voting to replace US Law with Sharia Law."

Fred nodded his head in agreement.

Jimmy continued, "But mostly, we see the media users on the left tend to read and pass along news stories from what we call the mainstream media. And a significant portion of GOP voters only viewing and passing along information from these alt-right sites. I would like to think our reporting is vastly more accurate and forthright than the alt-right sites."

"So," Geoff observed, "even if we published an exposé about all of this, the folks who probably should see it, probably won't."

"Mostly" answered Jimmy.

Geoff just shook his head. "They make stuff up, post it, and get a million clicks. Un-effing believable. But who pays them? How do these operations survive—financially?"

"Well sir, a few got sugar-daddies just like us. Breitbart has a hedge-fund family supporting them, run by a woman named Rebekah

Mercer, who has been dubbed 'the Queen of the Alt-right.' But they also make huge amounts via Google-clicks. Because they are strictly digital—Facebook and Google driven—ads are placed on the viewers' screens who would be interested in the product based on the reader profile and previous activity. These sites are paid small amounts for this exposure. As we can see, millions of 'small amounts.' And when they click to buy something, Google pays them a small commission as well. It all adds up to significant income, particularly when a site has curated a large, loyal following."

"That is why so many of these sites run such bizarre stories. It attracts viewers." Fred added. "We get click cash for Google Ads on our digital sites too" Fred admitted "but I dare say we use click-bait headlines to draw readers like these other sites do."

"Yes sir, but there is one other twist to this I probably would not have found—unless you had asked me to look into these specific sites" Jimmy offered. "It's around who owns what. And how certain disinformation is generated."

Both Geoff and Fred leaned forward.

Jimmy continued, "And let me say, it gets interesting. Very interesting indeed."

Chapter 58

Jimmy Olsen sat down in his chair and rolled it closer to where Fred Ryan, Publisher of the *Washington Post* and Geoffrey Wines, Metro Reporter and Pulitzer Prize winner were sitting along the back wall of Planet Krypton. He had a fresh glass of ice water in his hand.

"This is where it gets interesting." Jimmy began. "When we met a few weeks ago, I had told you I had tracked certain stories and language to internal memos and emails inside the GOP Presidential Election Committee. Many of these memos seem to have been initiated by the deputy campaign chairperson Katy Lynn Holloway. These were the stories about child trafficking inside Meteor Pizza, banning of campfires in the mid-west, and moving auto plants to Canada."

"Yes, I remember." Fred acknowledged. "And I know about Katy Lynn. She has the reputation as a superb pollster in her ability to translate polling data into insightful and hugely effective campaign strategies. Though it doesn't seem she was successful with Ted Cruz. But he did last longer than all the others."

"Exactly sir. I guess you can't make a silk purse out of a sow's ear" Jimmy responded with a laugh.

Fred reached for his handkerchief to dab his eyes. "Funny, Mr. Olsen."

Fred and Jimmy have created quite a bond.

"Anyway," Jimmy continued "I did a little investigative work, simply because I am intrigued and maybe impressed with how Katy Lynn isolated three stories that seemed to travel so rapidly across the web. How did she come to her strategy of dissuading voters versus getting voters? And which stories to push?"

"I spoke to Reverend Brooks the other morning. Seems his congregants are still getting Facebook feeds about the Meteor and now other stories about the former president's foundation." Wines interjected.

"I did a little fact-checking into that too. Connected some dots. What I found was incestuous." Jimmy offered, then turning to Fred, "Sir, are you aware of something called 'Cambridge Analytica?'"

"Nope." The former executive and co-founder of POLITICO answered.

"How about Rebekah Mercer?"

"Certainly." Fred retorted.

Now Jimmy is cross-examining his Publisher.

"And I guess you also know who Ted Cruz, Breitbart and a man called Steve Bannon are? Am I right?" Jimmy questioned, awaiting Fred's confirmation.

Fred simply nodded.

"Now sir, what is the connection?" Jimmy continued with his cross. "And what does all of this have to do with something called 'Cambridge Analytica?'"

"Not a clue Jimmy. Please inform us." Fred answered tartly.

Oops. Jimmy may have just crossed the line.

Jimmy paused for a moment, took a sip of his ice water, and then leaned toward his boss.

"Sir, this is all fruit from the same tree" Jimmy said answering his own question. "Let me explain. Like you, I was not aware of Cambridge Analytica. They are a research company that uses Facebook data—illegally and under false pretense—to segment people and voters into psychological and demographic clusters for designing better messaging. This segmentation breaks out fears, passions, affiliations, and types of stories each person has read—then segments them into hundreds of clusters for messaging."

"Polling data." Fred retorted, still on edge.

"Yes, polling data. But polling data on steroids. More like personality profiling, enlisting: fears, joys, affiliations, interests, and a whole lot more personal data obtained and generated by asking folks to fill out a survey—with the guarantee the results would be kept confidential and only used for academic purposes. Cambridge

Analytica then illegally sold this confidential data to our candidate's campaign after Cruz lost. I guessed is through some Bannon connection. But I am getting slightly ahead of myself."

"Jimmy." Fred said sternly. "Get going. Please get to it!"

"Yes sir." Jimmy said, increasing the speed of his delivery. "Katy Lynn evidently discovered it when she joined her current candidate's campaign. And now it appears to be powering Katy Lynn's incredibly successful strategy."

> *I better get into the middle of this to give Fred a break. He seems pissed.*

"Jimmy," Geoffrey spoke up, "how did you find out Katy Lynn Holloway utilized the Cambridge data? And what's wrong if she did?"

"Nothing, if breaking a law to break another law is okay. Cambridge Analytica broke two laws. Three really. First, they issued an invitation to Facebook users to take a special personality survey saying the data would only be used for academic purposes. Two, they are using the data in this election. I don't think an election is an academic exercise. And three, it appears every person who agreed to complete the survey also opened all their Facebook friends to analysis and inclusion into the Cambridge Analytica data. Essentially creating a humongous database. Then by using Facebook's own tools, the campaign can reach these individuals on nearly a one-on-one basis. This means the messages—like the one's Reverend Brooks' congregants received—no one else can see."

"So, what's the circle – the connection?" Geoffrey probed, keeping Jimmy's attention on him, and not Fred.

"Mercer. She is in the center of all of it. Rebekah Mercer is a significant investor of Cambridge Analytica and sits on their board. Steve Bannon does too. Mercer is also the money behind Breitbart; owns a significant portion of the company; sits on their board; and is Steve Bannon's boss. Mercer was also a major backer of Cruz's run for president and is now a full backer of the party's soon-to-be nominee."

Fred Ryan then leaned forward in his seat, "And as you pointed out, Breitbart—with its publisher, Steve Bannon, which is owned by Rebekah Mercer and her dad—is the primary source of much of the disinformation spreading across the web via all these alt-right sites." Fred summed up with a tone of resignation in his voice.

"Yes sir, that's right. And sir, using the tools you may object to, I also found a direct communication link between Katy Lynn Holloway and Steve Bannon."

"The subject?" Fred responded, his expression turning more somber.

"The initial stories we have been talking about" Jimmy answered without emotion "and others."

"So, to be clear, you're saying you have the direct link between the campaign and Breitbart?" Fred asked to confirm the last stunning tidbit Jimmy communicated.

"Right sir." Jimmy acknowledged, taking another sip of his water, and patiently waiting for someone else to speak.

The space inside Planet Krypton became silent of human voice. Only the quiet hum of god-knows-how-much processing power and the movement of air from the air conditioning system could be heard.

Sensing he still was not out of the woods with the paper's boss, Jimmy then quietly added "And sir, if I may add context, Cambridge Analytica—with Mercer's board agreement—was used to actively support Brexit, a move Breitbart also reported and supported."

"Tearing down everything." Fred uttered, mostly to himself.

"Sir?" Geoff asked, purposely so Jimmy would not.

Fred raised his head and looked at the two reporters. "Since day one, this GOP candidate has been knocking down American institutions. Sowing distrust. Slamming all the past presidents. The FBI, the CIA. The Supreme Court. The EPA, the CDC. Hell, the GOP itself! Not to mention NATO, the European Union, and the United Nations. The press too. Even decorated vets. And the Russians seem to be helping him. It almost seems orchestrated."

Just as Osbourne described.

Fred stood and headed toward the door.

"Gentlemen. If you will excuse me, I have a few things I need to do. Must do. Now!" Then looking over to Geoff he added, "Mr. Wines, no worries about a ride. I'll walk to the Metro."

Geoffrey stayed inside Planet Krypton as Jimmy escorted a rather pissed-off publisher of the *Washington Post* out the front door.

• • •

Jimmy returned to his lab.

Wines was seated in the back row, reexamining the graphic depiction of various news sites still displayed on the largest monitor.

"What was that about Geoff?" Jimmy asked, with more than just a little concern in his voice.

"Not sure Jimmy. But if I ventured to guess, I would say Fred Ryan is deeply concerned. He has spent his life in politics and political media. He knows its power. And when he sees powerful tools being used to generate out and out lies—campaign propaganda, if you will—and the citizens who are reading this stuff have been convinced to disrespect the working press and not expose themselves to an opposing viewpoint, then I think he is sensing something America has not seen in a very long time."

"How so?" Jimmy asked.

"Fred worked at Ronald Reagan's side in the White House during the bad old days of the Cold War. Cold War propaganda was an incredibly effective tool. It held the Soviet Union together until it didn't and kept Europe divided for decades. This situation must be raising some alarm as he is learning how it is unfolding. And who is making it up. Fred knows distrust; then civil unrest, and finally revolutions were started when these conditions existed."

"What should we do Geoff?"

"Get evidence we can print. *And fast.*"

Chapter 59

Will I succeed or not succeed?
That is the question.
Is it better to fulfill my contracted deed?
Or doom it for a greater good.

My task is my path.
There is nothing to stop it now.
But I must realize some cupids kill with an arrow
Some with traps.

Here I am,
Caught.
Ensnared.
And looking for an exit.

Chapter 60

Geoffrey Wines had sources all over Washington from his years of reporting crime, drugs, bribery, influence peddling, extortion, and the myriad of misdeeds humans commit every day.

The evidence he and Jimmy had uncovered clearly indicated crimes were taking place, from both outside foreign governments and inside political operatives. The brass at the paper was reluctant to report on any of it; yet they truly wanted the story to get out.

It needs to get out!

Should I give my FBI friends a heads up?
Or maybe disclose it to President Osbourne?
He must have contacts throughout the FBI and CIA who would be interested.

Or maybe Emmett at TIME as well.
We could both work the story.
One prodding the other forward.

Or perhaps just let Jimmy loose and "place" some of our findings across the web.
He even joked he could do that with the pee vid.
Would that be yellow journalism?

• • •

Jimmy Olsen had similar thoughts.

All he needed to do was hack into Breitbart or InfoWars and plant the "deer hunter email" or the "Russian video." He laughed. The reaction would probably make the news, even the *Washington Post*. He could see Alex Jones, the face of InfoWars, taking credit for the in-depth reporting.

Or he could pull a Julian Assange "WikiLeaks" and simply dump the information using the moniker "Lex Luthor" or "The Penguin."

That last thought made Jimmy remember something.

Just before Fred Ryan's unexpected visit to Planet Krypton, he remembered seeing a new tranche of emails had been placed onto the WikiLeaks server. Jimmy had been monitoring the server for years, starting with his crude setup when he was just hacking and not reporting. It had been his example of hacking into those files that had impressed Ben Bradlee and led to his recruitment by the *Washington Post* when the demonstration accurately predicted when WikiLeaks would spill a new grouping of data.

Wonder if Marty Barron remembers that day?

And he knew a new batch stood cued and ready to be dumped.

Perhaps I should plant my findings onto the WikiLeaks' trove of documents for the world to see!

But no need. Fred Ryan and Marty Baron had both he and Geoff on a top priority assignment that needed to be completed before the next morning.

Chapter 61

Fred Ryan could not in any way justify the information Jimmy Olsen and Geoffrey Wines had shown him. It troubled him deeply and he knew he had to act.

When he abruptly left Jimmy's house, he immediately returned to the office to set a conference for the next day in New York with the Board of Directors of Nash Holdings LLC, the Jeff Bezos company that owns the *Washington Post*.

He did not call the meeting to ask permission. He stood solely responsible for the actions of the newspaper. However, he wanted the ownership to be aware of his intents—so they would not be blind-sided when the *Post* story broke. He also had a nagging concern that anything the paper did that smacked of high-tech snooping could and would probably blow back and impact Amazon and Bezos, the paper's ultimate benefactors. He also knew Amazon Web Services hosted WikiLeaks and many of the alt-right sites.

To this end, he asked Marty Baron, the paper's Executive Editor to have Wines and Olsen write the first installment of the *Post's* series on what he now framed as "Cyber-Intrusion into the Presidential Election." He asked the reporting to not hold-back in detailing its sources, the findings, and the operatives behind the disinformation being waged in this year's election. The guys worked all night writing the story and emailed it to him in New York.

To Fred, this represented a "Democracy Dies in Darkness" moment for the paper—embodying the new slogan he contemplated for the *Post's* masthead.

If we don't report this, then what should we be reporting?

His plan would be to distribute Wines and Olsen's story to the Board members, and Bezos, for discussion later this morning. He figured this would be the best way to communicate the stakes. Distributing the fully executed news story prior to the discussion also kept with Jeff Bezos' decision-making operandi he used so successfully in his other ventures. No vagueness. Just the facts of the story—and its sources.

The facts didn't concern him. He believed them to be forthright and accurate. But the way the paper uncovered the facts—its sources—continued to tug at his conscience. In a way, asking the Board's perspective would provide a gut check.

Ryan fully understood his sudden request to write the first installment put the reporters on a very tight deadline. But he also knew Baron, Wines and Olsen were motivated to get the story out and would work to meet the deadline. With their job done, it was now his responsibility to pave the way forward toward publication.

Fred re-read the sixteen-hundred-word story several times to ensure it was fresh in his mind for the meeting. Yes, it's lengthy. Comprehensive. Explosive. Given the facts, also even-handed. But it still lacked something. Maybe he would catch it this time.

• • •

Presidential Election Manipulated by Disinformation

Part One of The Washington Post Investigation of Cyber Intrusion into the Presidential Election

By: Geoffrey Wines, Washington Post Metro Reporter and
James Olsen, Washington Post New Media Correspondent

The integrity of this year's Presidential Election is under attack by outside foreign governments and inside political operatives working in tandem to spread disinformation. The

Washington Post has uncovered multiple examples and willing parties whose purpose appears to be to spread mistrust and blatantly false news stories about the Democratic candidate for president and a compromising video about the Republican candidate. Both could disrupt the integrity of this year's election for President of the United States of America.

It is this paper's belief these are direct assaults on our democratic process and should be fully reported and understood by all Americans. This series of documented stories will describe the disinformation being spread and the cyber-steps used to ensure its dissemination to both broad and micro-segments of voters.

TWO STORIES – TWO TARGETS – ONE SOURCE – ONE PATH

Many false news stories have circulated on the web, creeped into mainstream reporting, and become "fact" to many citizens who tend to get their news from non-traditional news sites. We are using two stories to illustrate the way misinformation has been conceived, disseminated, and permeates our election discourse.

One story involves the notion that a certain pizza and game restaurant in Washington DC imprisons children who have been kidnapped and trafficked by members of the Democratic Party. Our investigation reveals this story was originally conceived by campaign manager Katy Lynn Holloway in a position paper circulated inside the election committee of the presumptive candidate for the Republican Party.

THE FIXER

According to the position paper reviewed by this newspaper, this child-trafficking story's purpose is to dissuade Black urban voters in many key areas such as DC, Philadelphia, Detroit, Cleveland, and Milwaukee—who are traditionally supporters of the Democratic party—to withhold their vote for president. The paper predicts these people will not vote at all rather than shift to the Republican candidate, thereby diminishing a large block of Democratic voters, and potentially resulting in a small margin of victory in each of those states and ultimately the Electoral College.

Another false story is outlined in the same strategy document to dissuade upper-Midwest men who are union members and often deer hunters from supporting Democratic candidates. These blue-collar men, who are also typically Democratic party voters—living in Wisconsin, Michigan, and Pennsylvania—were told in the name of globalization, the Democratic party was pressing for US auto plants to be relocated across the border into Canada. Also, for environmental reasons, Democratic regulators were introducing policies to ban all campfires and BBQ grills. And lastly, ammunition for their hunting rifles would soon be outlawed to extend the Democratic Party's gun-control agenda.

The *Washington Post* has extensively examined the veracity of these stories and found absolutely nothing to substantiate the child trafficking claims and found no formal legislation to move US auto plants to Canada; halt the sale of ammunition; or ban campfires and BBQ grills. Though, in the case of the latter, some Democratic candidates are pushing for a ban on open burning of brush, farmland, and forests to limit carbon emissions.

Our source describes how these stories were originated inside the GOP's presumptive candidate's campaign headquarters, then passed along via email to the editors of one partisan website – Breitbart – who then reported the stories as fact. These stories were then picked up by other right-wing identifying news-sites and spread via Facebook to citizens who match the demographic and psychographic profiles outlined above.

Corporate filings show the Breitbart site is owned by Texas billionaire Rebekah Mercer, a former supporter of Ted Cruz's campaign for president and who sits on the board of Cambridge Analytica, a consulting group that specializes in analyzing Facebook data for political campaigns. While this type of company is perfectly legal, sources inside Facebook have told the *Washington Post* the group used illegal practices to gather key data from Facebook subscribers to develop their recommendations. The GOP campaign strategy documents reviewed by the *Post* mention Cambridge Analytica as the source and inspiration for the negative campaign communications cited above. We should note, Katy Lynn Holloway, now the associate campaign manager for the GOP presumptive candidate managed Ted Cruz's campaign before his loss in the primaries.

The *Washington Post* has found the major driver of this negative campaign is an exceptionally large number of Russian internet

"BOTS" that suddenly came to life to spread these stories across the web.

"BOTS" are computer driven accounts that read and pass along specific stories to specific profiles of Facebook and Twitter accounts. By artificially increasing the readership of a story, Facebook algorithms move the story further up the chain and feed it with more stories like it to Facebook users who match the "profile" of the bot. This causes multiple stories on the same subject to feed into a given person's account, thus giving the false impression the story is widespread and presumably true.

This sudden Russian bot activity coincides with another series of events designed to disrupt the candidacy of the Republican front-runner while also impacting the presumptive Democratic candidate for president.

RUSSIAN INTERFERENCE

The *Washington Post* received from an anonymous source a computer file containing a video showing the presumptive GOP candidate for president watching two young women in a Moscow hotel room having sex. During this video, the candidate directs one of the women to urinate on the other, while the candidate watches intently. When done, the candidate simply gets up and leaves the scene.

This video appears to coincide with the candidate's reported business trip to Moscow and the room décor corresponds with the hotel where the future candidate stayed.

To the best of this paper's ability, the legitimacy of the video has been verified, though the computer file the *Washington Post* received consisted of a video recording taken by a smart phone aimed at a large flat screen monitor displaying the video.

The presence and actions on the part of the GOP candidate are not illegal in Russia or the United States. This paper surmises this video's intent was to create what in Russia is called "kompromat" (Russian: компромат)—short for "compromising material"—developed and used as damaging information about a politician, a businessperson, or other public figures in order to create negative publicity, extortion, blackmail, or exert influence. Kompromat is typically acquired from various Russian security services—or outright forged—and then publicized. Kompromat is typically used inside Russian politics and other post-Soviet states. To the best of our knowledge, this is the first time "kompromat material" has been used in a US presidential election.

Through a confidential source, the *Washington Post* later learned the video had been played for the son of the GOP candidate in their New York headquarters by a man we identified as a close cyber associate to Vladimir Putin. We have proof the candidate's son expressed a willingness to cooperate with the unnamed Russian's request.

While this paper does not know the Russian's request, or the real reason the video was shown to the candidate's son, we surmise its presence could create a problem for the candidate's strong religious values voters and support by conservative Christians.

What this paper does know is one day after the cyber-expert showed the video inside the campaign headquarters, the Russian bots identified above began spreading the child trafficking, hunting ammunition, and campfire / BBQ stories cited above along with multiple other stories defaming the Democratic candidate for president.

Further, the *Washington Post* has learned the same Russian cyber-expert shopped the video to another major news organization based in New York City. Neither the *Washington Post*, nor the other news outlet, have revealed or played the actual video in their newsfeeds.

TWO WORLDS OF NEWS

Earlier in this article, we reported the alt-right news site—Breitbart—had been fed the disinformation directly from the GOP candidate's campaign headquarters. To understand the spread of disinformation, this paper conducted a cyber-review of the flow of partisan news by Breitbart and other alt-right sites including InfoWars, Gateway Pundit, Realclear Politics, Truthfeed, Daily Caller and Ending the Fed.

The *Washington Post* found in almost every instance a story that touts disinformation about the Democratic candidate for president originated from Breitbart and then spread to the other alt-right sites. In some cases, the stories then migrated over to more traditional news organizations, including the *Washington Examiner*, *New York Post*, and Fox News. In fact, the traffic on the Breitbart site is higher than any of the above reported outlets, including Fox News.

We should also point out three additional sites generate significant traffic of disinformation and false news stories. One is called "The Washington Liberator" – once an abolitionist newspaper that doesn't exist except to pass along disinformation, mostly to urban Blacks. Another is called "The Denver Guardian" that purports to be Denver's oldest newspaper. This paper does not exist, except on the web, where it only passes along the disinformation generated by these alt-right sites. A third fake news site, called "The Herd" feeds to upper-Midwest hunters with the stories pertaining to the ban of ammunition, globalization, moving US auto plants, and ecological restraints on campfires and BBQ grills.

During this analysis, we also found there are two worlds where citizens get their news and seldom do the two worlds connect.

Our analysis shows there is a large block of people, approximately twenty-five percent of the electorate, who only get their news from the alt-right sites outlined above. They do not consume news from mainstream media—*Washington Post*, *New York Times*, *USA Today*, or their local market newspapers; nor from network news—NBC, CBS, or ABC television. And conversely, most users of mainstream news media do not visit the alt-right sites for their news.

This paper believes this "two-worlds of facts and information" is very dangerous for the American public. Without a common set of

```
substantiated  and  vetted  data,  a  world  of
"alternative  facts"  will  prevail,  leaving  our
democracy in tatters.
```

Fred closed the article on his phone.

His first thought was the image of Katy Lynn Holloway clawing the eyeballs from the faces of her staffers as she tried to determine who leaked her brilliant strategy documents to the *Washington Post*.

> *Oh well . . .*
> *If she chooses to live by the web,*
> *Then she must be prepared to die by the web.*

But this image also revealed the source of his concern with the way the paper's investigation is described in this draft article. Geoff and Jimmy had done an excellent job in not mentioning how Katy Lynn's documents and emails were sourced; nor the heads-up given by Geoff's confidential source that the GOP candidate would win by some mysterious means. Certainly not any mention the *Post* hacked the cyber-Russian's phone to reveal his showing of the video at the GOP's candidate's New York headquarters. And later at TIME Magazine.

> *Yet . . .*
> *Every news organization had reported widely on the Snowden NSA files.*
> *Hacked.*
>
> *Every news organization reported Julian Assange's WikiLeaks documents.*
> *Hacked.*
>
> *Even Sara Palin's private emails just two weeks before the 2008 election.*
> *Also hacked by Assange.*
>
> *Does it matter who does the hacking?*
> *Is hacking the new form of journalistic investigation?*

Fred Ryan, Publisher of the *Washington Post*, wondered whether the paper should just bite the bullet and report some of the sources were via hacks of private emails, computers, and phone files by a *Washington Post* staffer?

Maybe he was coming around to his Executive Editor's point of view – "the free press is entitled to ferret out wrongdoing by any means possible." And while this type of investigation cannot be used in a court of law, "it is fair game for a reporter and the news media."

The lawyer in him made him realize they were protected by the Supreme Court precedent—established in *New York Times v. Sullivan*—if they were wrong? Not to mention the protections of the First Amendment. After all, their reporting is all vetted, therefore factual, and true. Unlike the disinformation being indiscriminately spread by unworthy competitors who would not report any of their false stories if they took one second to investigate.

Nope, this is the right decision for the *Washington Post*. The paper will move forward in publishing their findings.

With his clear conscience, he had one other thought: Jimmy claims to have all the Democratic candidate's private server emails to analyze and release.

Chapter 62

Katy Lynn Holloway's plan seemed to be working. Her stories were travelling across the web, and some were even being picked up by the mainstream media.

Her polling indicated a softening of Democratic voters in some key urban and upper-Midwest markets, though the national polls were still showing the Democratic candidate with a sizable lead.

It will be a stretch, but things were beginning to lean in the right direction. Barely!

But hey,
The Cubs won this year's World Series.
Being down three games to one.
Anything is possible!

She and Breitbart were becoming quite the team. She had picked Breitbart to be her major conduit after watching how his site had devastated Fox News during the early primary. Fox had hated her current boss. But Breitbart was ruthless in their lies and twisting of facts to diminish the news network. She specifically remembered being awed the way Breitbart created the illusion Fox News somehow supported immigration, terrorism, Muslims, and corruption. Since Ted was her man at the time, she appreciated their efforts with totally untrue stories purporting Fox funneled money to open borders groups; colluded with Rubio to give amnesty to illegal aliens; and recruited a Hitler-citing Muslim advocate to join their next GOP debate team. All fabrications.

Now, Katy Lynn wrote it, and Breitbart spread it. They had even turned Fox into a major friend of her new boss. A complete one-eighty from their anti-candidate stance during the primaries. As a result, their strategy for the dissemination of certain stories now resulted in considerable play on cable television's number one news outlet.

"I love it. Fox is now the 'Anti-Immigration Network'" she said to herself as she examined a listing of the news stories Fox repeated as they picked up on the themes Breitbart had so skillfully curated via their click-bait headlines: "Six Diseases Return to US on World Refuge Day"; "347,000 Convicted Criminal Immigrants at Large in US"; and her favorite of all time, "Social Security Administration Confirms Illegal Immigrants Will Begin Collecting Benefits in 2017." These headlines drew clicks and Fox had read the popularity of the clicks and turned their editorial stance to capitalize on these anti-immigration themes. *So much for never this guy. Money and guaranteed ratings talk.*

Now she had to ensure her communications strategy destroyed her boss' current Democratic opponent. Katy Lynn hoped for this outcome—rather than the old man running against her. "He just doesn't take the bait the way she does. And will!" she laughed to herself as she jotted down the next themes of the campaign. All of these will cause pause to even the most loyal of Democratic Party supporters if they see it.

"Oh, they'll see it!" she said to herself as she thought about her Facebook targeting strategy. "They'll certainly see it." On her pad she wrote:

Private Email Server → Laws and Procedures Don't Apply
Private Email Server → What's She Hiding?
Family Foundation → A Source for International Bribes
Family Foundation → Funneling money to Saudi Arabia
Benghazi → Dereliction of Duty to Country
Benghazi → Worst Sec of State ever!

"We'll hammer these themes in the media and I'll have the boss repeat it over and over during his rallies. I'll get Breitbart to headline this stuff and it will spread from there."

She mused as she started composing her next Breitbart email, with the key points that play directly to the fears the Cambridge study had highlighted.

Yep. Maybe the Cubs will win two in a row.

Chapter 63

Fred Ryan returned from New York after his meeting with the Board of Nash Holdings LLC, the company that owned the *Washington Post*.

Marty Baron practically met him at the front door, eager to hear what had occurred.

"Well Marty. They have owned this newspaper for about three years. Beez said he would be hands-off, and I guess he truly means it."

"In what way?"

"You know the way they operate. Everyone sits around a conference room table and silently read a position paper on a topic. Then they discuss. No presentations. Just reading."

"Okay, got the scene Fred. Go on."

So, they read the story Geoff and Jimmy wrote. When it was time to discuss, each one of them looked up and said something to the effect 'this will be interesting.'"

"And???" Marty said, his voice rising as he moved physically closer to Fred.

"And . . ." Fred laughed, not moving. "And . . . they said . . ." Fred paused, dragging out the drama. "They said . . . 'Fred, you're the Publisher. Just do what you think a major newspaper should do.'"

"That was it?" Marty whispered, hoping for more.

"Yep." Fred sighed with a somewhat sheepish look on his face. "Yep, that was all. Then we went to lunch and didn't talk one iota about the story or the paper either." Then Fred added with a laugh, "But I did learn we also owned a commercial shipping logistics terminal in Virginia."

Marty looked at Fred skeptically.

Fred returned Marty's disbelief with a nod. "Yeah, I know. I guess Beez was serious when he said he would be hands off. And he ensures the Board practices it."

"So, the decision is ours?" Marty said with relief.

"Guess so Marty." Fred answered with a huge smile across his face. "And Marty, we're going to man the torpedoes. Full speed ahead. We're going to save this country."

"Yes sir!" Marty returned with an exaggerated salute. Then added with a grin, "Any specific orders sir?"

"Yes! Please tell Jimmy and Geoff I want to see all of Katy Lynn's emails and Hillary's too. Every single one of them! We're going to shine a big bright shiny light on the use of disinformation for political gain!"

• • •

Jimmy Olsen, Geoffrey Wines and Jeff Leen, Chief Editor of Investigations were given the green light by Marty Baron and Fred Ryan to use whatever means they had to secure, document, and report on the use of disinformation in the presidential election. This included computer hacking or other sources their team could mount.

Fred specifically asked that Jimmy's download of Hillary's email server be thoroughly analyzed for any confidential or high security documents. This was not to be a one-way investigation against the GOP. If they found wrongdoing on the Democratic side, they would report it too. If they could expose all the contents of her server, then no one could speculate. It would be out there for all to see.

"This paper's mission is not to help one candidate get elected over another." Fred instructed the investigations team. "It is to help ensure disinformation will never be used in any political campaign again. And the way to end disinformation is with facts. And if we can harness Facebook too, then all the better. Period."

Wines had noted during the meetings Fred and Marty were connected at the hip. Both were heavily involved and seemed in total lockstep. Whatever conflict going on between them earlier was now gone. Marty took professional pleasure in the paper going to war with true investigative reporting. And since the meeting in New York, Fred felt they had the corporate support of the paper's ownership.

Chapter 64

Jimmy Olsen had sucked in and archived all the contents of the former secretary of state's private email server when the *New York Times* reported its existence during the lead up to the June 2015 Republican House investigation of Benghazi. The "Benghazi event" occurred on September 11, 2012, when a street mob attacked the US Consulate in Benghazi Libya—the US Ambassador and four security guards were killed.

The Democratic nominee had served as Secretary of State until February 2013, when she left due to some health concerns that were leaving her fatigued and unable to travel.

The server had been physically installed in the nominee's household and maintained by an outside contractor. She and her husband—a former president—used the server for their personal and business correspondence. This included the nominee's official State Department emails which should have been handled through the official State Department server for security and archival purposes. Hence, the brouhaha regarding her emails in this election.

When Jimmy had downloaded the data, he remembered being surprised how two people could have had that much personal email in only five years. At the time, he wasn't interested in looking at their personal stuff and quite frankly, he still wasn't. But now Fred Ryan and Marty Baron had asked him to open it up and catalogue its contents.

Given the interest in State Department correspondence, he set his tools to highlight and extract any email chains that were initiated from a State Department address or sent to a State Department address. These were placed in a separate file since they represented official government emails, whether they contained personal information or not. He then extracted any other email strings initiated inside that were sent to any government address—foreign and domestic. Again, official government use.

The remainder of the emails were organized by recipient and sender with a count showing the number by year. He hoped this would highlight activity levels. And through a special cross-referencing tool, he had his system seek out information on each of the addresses to render a short bio on the sender or recipient. If a "person unknown" came up on any of these, he had other tools for determining who they were, and if need be, specifically other emails the person had sent or received outside of this server.

For instance, there were a considerable number of emails to and from her daughter, usually with attachments containing photos of their new grandchild. These, of course, had come in after she left office. Also, numerous bursts of emails from the couple's doctors, usually clustered around the date of an office visit or tests. A quick scan of these showed the former president had been sicker than reported, hence explaining his huge loss of weight. And there were diagnosis and test results of the candidate's illness when she left office.

There were also a few Foundation-related emails, but not many as the Foundation had its own .ORG server address. The former president had also received emails from other former presidents, usually setting dates for lunch, golf, or some other social occasion. Jimmy made a special note of these since he knew of Geoff's relationship with the former president, Robert Osbourne.

These first steps did not take long once he had set the parameters. Computers could efficiently sort and catalogue addresses in literally seconds. All 70,000 emails had taken less than half an hour to sort. Then another couple of hours to seek out and provide the top-line bio information of each sender and recipient. All easily accomplished.

Next came the manual labor. Since he didn't work the political beat, he wasn't sure what to look for in the State Department emails. Fred Ryan had told him there would be endless emails announcing meetings, State Department functions, and birthdays in which Madam Secretary would be copied to keep her in the loop. He explained he would probably not see long position papers, attached documents or anything Secret, Top Secret, or Confidential since these were rarely, if ever, transmitted on anything other than paper. This ensured confidentiality and tightly controlled who sees it. He teased Jimmy "that the big rubber TOP SECRET stamp was still used."

Fred continued to tell Jimmy if any document or email contained anything thought to be confidential in nature, there should be a "C" in the subject line of the email or in the body where the information appears—added by the sender to alert the reader of the status of the information. Fred had added with a laugh "a lot of the confidential information is stuff you may have read in the *Washington Post*, *POLITICO*, or other news sources. "People at State—and the DOD for that matter—are 'confidential crazy.' No one wants to be accused of leaking information—though both places are sieves."

Adding a filter to the official government emails to capture all the "C" notations was easy. As a precaution, Jimmy also added it for screening all the emails on the server. And being a nerd, he also added a filter for the copyright symbol, the ©, in case a user's individual system automatically auto keyed the parenthesis letter. Again, all of these "C" emails would include the bio of the sender and the count. And since Fred had said a lot of the "C's" were attached to published stories, Jimmy added a program to seek out if the Confidential information had been published in one of the top five newspapers – the *Washington Post*, the *New York Times*, *Wall Street Journal*, *USA Today*, *Los Angeles Times*. He then added the *New York Post* and *Washington Examiner* to ensure the center-right papers were represented.

Jimmy placed the results and all sorted emails onto a highly secure encrypted server that only Geoffrey Wines, Jeff Leen, Fred Ryan, and Marty Baron could access. He set a log to record all sign-ins by person. It was now up to them to sift through the data and determine what to report.

Chapter 65

Geoffrey Wines opened the secure link Jimmy Olsen sent to Fred, Marty, and Jeff with the democratic candidate's email server contents. He knew Fred and Jeff's investigation team would concentrate on the "confidential" emails to determine if any true state-secrets—worth reporting—had been compromised.

Geoffrey, however, sought something else:

1. Something that might shed some light on President Osbourne's story of the election being fixed and thrown to the presumptive GOP candidate.
2. Something to shine some light on who is orchestrating this year's election and had implemented the Gulf War strategy that ended the Cold War twenty-five years earlier.
3. Something specifically directed to the three former presidents that might foretell a plan.
4. Anything at all from the mystery man "Elvis."

His hope of finding something, anything, would be tight on the timeline—as Jimmy's download took place the day the *New York Times* reported on the existence of the private server. This occurred literally two days before the GOP presumptive candidate announced his candidacy from his New York City building on Park Avenue.

Only two days apart?
Another coincidence?

Geoff pulled up all the correspondence to and from the former president. Instinctively, he looked for a onesie or twosie sender. He assumed Elvis didn't send updates, but maybe a single correspondence outlining his plan—like the fax Osbourne had received twenty-five years earlier.

Additionally, he searched for any correspondence containing the word "Elvis" since the three presidents and Osbourne used it in referring to the mystery man.

He scanned Jimmy's index, listing all senders of emails and the number of emails sent. As expected, there weren't many onesies and twosies. Maybe five hundred in total.

Geoff started his search from the most recent on the server and working chronologically back to the date Osbourne had said the three other presidents had met with their mystery man for the first and only time.

Of the five hundred, one sender name caught Geoff's immediate attention:

"IIAMAMNOTNOTHEREHERE@gmail.com"

Geoff hesitantly clicked on the link, hoping he had hit the jackpot and afraid at the same time.

The email opened. Sent only to the three former presidents. No names. Their personal email addresses only. No sender name either. Just the strange email address.

The email body composed in only a distinctive Times-Roman Small Caps font and centered on the page. It read:

MEN WITH EGOS ARE EASY TO PLAY.
MEN WITH HUGE EGOS ARE EVEN EASIER.
THEY ALL WANT THE SAME THING.
FAME.
MONEY AND POWER.

BROKE MEN WITH HUGE EGOS ARE EASIEST TO MOTIVATE.
THEY WANT IT ALL. NEED IT ALL.

I DIDN'T LOOK FAR FOR MY TARGET.
FOR THE CENTRAL CHARACTER TO MY PLAN.

> A PATSY BEING OFFERED A NOT-SO-PATSY DEAL.
> FEW COULD RESIST.
> EVEN FEWER WOULD EMBRACE IT WITH SUCH ENERGY AND FLAIR.
>
> ONE PRE-PLANNED TRAIN-WRECK IS ABOUT TO HAPPEN.
> WITH THE MOST UNSUSPECTING ACCOMPLICES.

The email contained no greeting or signature. Just the prose.

Geoffrey read it several times. Each time he compared it to the fax President Osbourne had received years prior. They were similar—succinct prose and maybe a very loose Shakespearian quotation—if you were specifically hoping to find one.

But the reference of placing an unqualified man into the race by playing on greed, money, and ego seemed to fit the reality of this situation. And it used the same MO as the Gulf War strategy—recognizing and leveraging Saddam Hussain's similar character traits and needs.

A match?

Perhaps Jimmy could track this down, and they would have their man.

And one hell of a story!

Chapter 66

After Geoff's call, Jimmy just sat and thought about how Geoffrey Wines skillfully put the story together. It took more than just amazing tools to track things down—it took awesome insights, relentless curiosity, and remarkable creativity to connect the dots.

For weeks Jimmy had been trying to get a Kryptonite hit on the mystery man's prose received by Osbourne before the Gulf War. Nothing surfaced. Or at least nothing that seemed to match this project.

Per Geoff's lead, Jimmy found the email from "IIAMAMNOTNOTHEREHERE @ Gmail.com."

Gmail?

This seems simple enough.

He opened the email, then the meta data showing the path the email passed on its way to the former president's personal server.

Jimmy ran his Spidey tools and found the person associated with the Gmail address through the normal registration fields mandated by the Google email service.

Name: JB
Birthdate: 1/1/1901
City: Nowhere New York USA
Phone Backup: 212-555-1212
Email Backup: (none)

Obviously, the contact and registration information were meant to conceal the user of the account.

He searched the email history to see other emails this account may have sent or received. None, except for the one addressed to the three presidents.

"None of the president's even bothered to answer his email. That must have been disappointing." Jimmy mused.
Interesting.
No other emails.

He checked the sending computer's ISP. Nothing traceable. No computer info and just a public wi-fi located in the lobby of a major New York hotel. Totally untraceable.

He then searched for the name IIAMAMNOTNOTHEREHERE on other email providers. Nothing. Unique to Gmail.

The lack of information made any other links void too. As did the phone numbers Osbourne had sent along to Geoffrey Wines, yielded nothing during his search several weeks earlier.

Just for kicks, Jimmy checked the account's DRAFTS folder. This folder would have emails that had been composed, but not sent, and therefore were untraceable when accessing web traffic. Even to his Kryptonite system. These email entries resided on the Gmail server, but never went through the usual path of passing from one server to another—as all emails on the web—when reaching their designated address.

A listing of DRAFT emails instantly appeared on Jimmy's screen; in the same way they would appear if Jimmy used his own Google Mail window for his personal emails.

"Let's see what we have." He said to himself as he opened the first one.

Jimmy's eyes scanned just the first three lines

Jackpot!

ALMOST EVERYONE IN THE COUNTRY KNEW HIS NAME.
KNEW HIS FACE.
WATCHED HIM ON TELEVISION PORTRAYING A SUCCESSFUL BUSINESSMAN.

THE FIXER

AN ENTREPRENEUR.

HE HAD WRITTEN BOOKS.
HAD PLACED HIS NAME ON BUILDINGS.
OPENED CASINOS, RESORTS AND GOLF COURSES.
HIS PUBLIC PERSONA WAS SOLID GOLD.

HIS BANKERS KNEW DIFFERENT.
HIS WEALTH WAS AN ILLUSION.
HIS BUSINESS PRACTICES SUSPECT AND BANKRUPT.

HE WOULD BE THE PERFECT TOOL TO FULFILL MY ASSIGNMENT.
BUT MY STRATEGY WOULD DOOM MY SPONSORS' OWN PLANS.

THIS WILL GET INTERESTING.
AND DIFFICULT.

Jimmy then clicked through and read the other draft emails.

Incredible!
My god.
There are entries describing every step of the plan!

Chapter 67

Geoffrey Wines and Jimmy Olsen alerted the entire team to meet in the executive conference room to discuss the mystery man's DRAFT emails Jimmy had uncovered.

They both felt it would be best for the four other attendees to have read the emails prior to meeting, so Jimmy had compiled and printed them in order; each showing the date and time they were composed. He distributed them about an hour before the meeting.

The two reporters had also decided between themselves to not reveal Osbourne's tip about the three former presidents' involvement; nor the Gulf War memo, since they now had a new tree of evidence.

The entire team were all smiles when they sat down.

"Thoughts?" Wines inquired.

Jeff Leen, the Investigations Editor asked the first question. "Geoff, there are 70,000 emails on that server. Even with Jimmy's indexing, how did you come to select this one single email to the former president?"

Geoffrey Wines answered quite blandly. "Based on the elevator photo; plus, Emmett Washington at TIME magazine being shown the video; plus, the huge number of Russian bots being released when they did; all made me think there just might be something related to Russia on the candidate's server. A phishing email, or something."

"And so, you went looking for an email to the former president?" Leen followed up, somewhat skeptically.

"That's right." Geoff answered simply.

> *Jeff Leen is good.*
> *Asks the right questions.*
> *I will not lie to this team.*
> *But I do need to protect my source.*

Marty Baron, the paper's Executive Editor then jumped in. "Geoff, when this story first broke, and our cyber-Russian friend had visited

TIME Magazine and played the pee video to Emmett Washington, you asked us whether we thought we were being played by the Russians. What do your instincts tell you now?"

Jimmy leaned forward and jumped in before Geoff had a chance to answer. "Marty, let me partially answer this question. Before I started my indexing procedure on the server contents, I carefully scanned all the emails for any evidence of phishing—you know, someone trying to steal a system password and other stuff. The beauty of a private server—when only a handful of people are using it—is phishing is usually unsuccessful and seldom tried. Even with important people like these. Anyway, I found no evidence their system had been compromised in any way."

Jimmy leaned back, then one last thought occurred to him. "Or at least up until the time I archived the server, which was when the *New York Times* reported its existence and just a couple of days before the reality tv star announced his candidacy. I have no idea what has happened on their server since."

Marty nodded to thank Jimmy and then picked back up his train of thought. "Geoff, again, do you think the Russians are playing both sides?"

> *That ended Jeff's question.*
> *Just for now.*
> *He'll be back.*

"Sir, in reading the progression of posts by our mystery writer, I would say our mystery man had somehow recruited Putin's help for the reality tv star's benefit. Putin sent his emissary—the cyber-Russian—to the candidate's headquarters to ensure cooperation." Wines said looking over at Jimmy, "But when I read the last memo, it would appear our mystery man is losing control and things are not going exactly as he had planned."

There was a knock on the closed conference room door. The conversation stopped as Fred Ryan got up and opened the door.

Cam Barr, the paper's Managing Editor entered and looked around at the players. "Got a skunk work operating huh?" Then smiled and looked directly at the Executive Editor. "Marty, there is a major story breaking, you—well all of you, particularly James—should immediately see."

"What is it?" Marty asked.

"Seems a Guccifer 2.0 has leaked a treasure trove of DNC emails. Via WikiLeaks. The political reporters have already begun their reading and analysis."

Jimmy's head snapped up. "Guccifer? They're Russian! Does anyone now question Russia's involvement?" He then volunteered, "A few weeks ago I saw Guccifer had downloaded to the WikiLeaks server a trove of DNC emails and wondered how and when they would announce them."

Marty spun around in his chair. "You didn't tell us?"

Jimmy answered forthrightly. "Sir. At the time you and Mr. Ryan were telling us not to go rifling through private emails."

"WikiLeaks is not private!" Marty injected with an edge.

Both Marty and Fred looked at each other with wry smiles. Then Fred spoke up looking down at his notes and the pages of mystery man emails in front of him. "Jimmy, obviously, that train has passed. If the truth be known, WikiLeaks is exactly the reason I feel comfortable in reading private servers and emails. If Wiki steals emails, then releases them, and we report on the release and the contents of any one of the emails, how is that any different?"

Fred, then added after a pause. "Our mission is to quell disinformation with facts. Got it?"

"Yes sir. Sorry sir. I had seen Guccifer dumping onto the WikiLeaks server right before your visit the evening you gave me the names of the alt-right sites you wanted me to probe. I guess I also got distracted."

Fred addressed Jimmy directly. "Everything you can find online—or under a rock—is on the table. Understood?"

"Yes sir. Completely." Jimmy quickly answered.

Marty then jumped in and smiled. "Cam. Team. Let's break from these emails." He said looking down at the table. "Let's read what WikiLeaks just dumped with an eye on the story we are pursuing. Cam and the pol reporters will handle their side. We need to see how this Guccifer and WikiLeaks disclosure fits into our mystery man, the candidate's email server, Katy Lynn Holloway, Breitbart, and the rain of disinformation in this election."

With that Marty rose from his seat to signify the end of the meeting.

Cam looked around the room. and shook his head. "Gentlemen. Sorry to have disturbed you." Then with a huge smile added, "And I certainly can't wait to see what you guys have cooking!"

Chapter 68

As Marty, Jeff and Cam exited the conference room, Fred signaled Geoffrey and Jimmy to hold back for a moment. He then closed the door.

"Guys, there is something else we need to consider with this latest round of information." Fred said, settling back into his chair.

Geoff and Jimmy did the same.

"What's that?" Geoff asked, not at all sure where this conversation was going.

Fred shifted in his seat, folded his hands in front of him and looked at the two reporters sitting on the other side of the table.

"Gentlemen, we are sitting on information both the FBI and the CIA should have." Fred said quietly.

That is the last thing I thought Fred was going to say.

He then continued. "We know—no make that surmise—the FBI is conducting some sort of investigation into the democratic candidate's email server to determine whether any secure information was compromised. And apparently, if you believe the reporting, some of the emails are missing. Yet Jimmy here has the complete boxed set for all her years at State."

Jimmy looked at Fred, not saying a word, contemplating the thought. Obviously waiting for him to continue.

"In the world of investigations" Fred continued, "we seem to have several pieces of information pointing toward Russian interference with our election. Not just any old Russian, but Vladimir Putin himself. This is CIA and NSA territory."

Fred then looked down at his notes. "Further . . . Jeff Leen's question is still important. Though slightly off, but he would have gotten there if young Jimmy hadn't waylaid his question." Fred added, giving Jimmy a quick smile.

THE FIXER

Don't underestimate Fred's ability to break things down.

Fred then looked directly at Geoffrey Wines and asked, "Why are three former presidents receiving a note from someone who is trying to interfere with the election? Make that, someone who is interfering with his wife's election."

Geoff shifted in his chair. "Fred, have you and Marty discussed this?"

"Not yet, we just learned about this, and he will be heavily involved with the WikiLeaks dump. But quite frankly, I want your thoughts. Both your thoughts—you are the two reporters who have uncovered all of this."

Jimmy spoke up first. "We're still going to report it. Aren't we sir?"

"Jimmy, we most certainly are. All of it. But we also need to ensure we do the right thing as well.

"We are, aren't we?" Jimmy questioned.

"Jimmy, our investigation has learned our election is being meddled with by a foreign government through the mechanized spread of disinformation. This is national security stuff. Bigger than politics. That's bad enough. But then today, by examining the contents of the other candidate's server, we learn that a former president is somehow connected in all of this."

"I guess I was losing sight of the big story." Jimmy admitted.

"We have a responsibility to let the Feds know what we have uncovered. But we need to balance all of this with the fact that bringing them in could also compromise our sources." Fred said, looking directly at Geoff.

"And how we got it." Fred continued, shifting his stare over to Jimmy.

Both reporters returned Fred's stare, not saying a word.

"So, what say you?" Fred finally asked after a very long pause.

Geoffrey Wines answered, speaking directly to the paper's publisher. "Sir, I believe we report the story exactly as we have it. Lay it all out. If the Feds want to know more, then they can contact us, and we will tell them what we are comfortable with sharing. But sir, let me be clear. I will not divulge my original source of this story. And we will not divulge how we obtained the photo of the cyber-Russian on the service elevator at the GOP candidate's campaign headquarters."

Jimmy then added, having listened to Geoff, and seeing no response from Fred. "Sir. I also hope we do not divulge the existence of Planet Krypton. Nor our ability to look into tall buildings."

"Okay, guys. I agree. Write up the story. All of it. And I'll discuss this meeting with Marty."

Fred then added as he stood up and turned toward the door. "And my gut tells me the WikiLeaks dump of DNC emails is not going to be pretty. Party politics can be incredibly petty."

Chapter 69

The Washington Post launched the "Cyber Intrusion into the Presidential Election" series that Sunday as the paper's primary story with placement on the front-page above the fold. The paper also continued the analysis of the Guccifer 2.0 and WikiLeaks dump of the DNC emails.

Leading up to its publication, Fred Ryan, the paper's Publisher was adamant the Cyber-Intrusion series be given utmost importance, and the WikiLeaks news only supported the larger story. "The much more important story is truth-telling in our elections" he told the paper's staff in an all-hands-on-deck meeting the Friday before, "We need to keep the public focused on the disinformation story. These DNC emails are just internal gossip. Important. But gossip being leaked for nefarious reasons. The disinformation being formulated by the alt-right sites will permanently damage our democracy if we allow it to continue."

During the meeting, Geoffrey Wines noted Fred's passion. He also couldn't help to notice the publisher had quoted, almost verbatim, Jimmy Olsen's plea during the original meeting when Geoff and Jimmy had brought the entire disinformation story to Fred, Marty, and Cam's attention.

The Monday after the first story ran, Marty Baron and Fred Ryan officially notified the FBI and Justice Department of the paper's possession of the candidate's emails and shared with them the story that would run in Wednesday's paper.

After reviewing the paper's forthcoming article, the FBI Deputy Director suggested the paper exclude any reference of the email from the mystery man to the three presidents. Though they did not directly say so, Marty and Fred surmised an FBI investigation of the server was underway and this represented new information to their probe they wanted to keep confidential.

In writing the article, Geoff and Jimmy excluded any mention of the DRAFT emails found on the Gmail server from the account

IIAMAMNOTNOTHEREHERE @ gmail.com. They believed an ongoing investigation of this file would eventually reveal more areas to explore.

The FBI Deputy Director expressed thanks to the paper for sharing the article prior to publication. He asked whether the paper would continue to share information with the FBI.

Fred Ryan answered with a simple "Yes indeed. Delivered right to your front porch every morning before 6:00 am."

•••

```
All Missing Emails Found
- Illegal Server Reveals No State Secrets

Part Two of The Washington Post Investigation
of Cyber Intrusion into the Presidential
Election

  By: Geoffrey Wines, Washington Post Metro
Reporter and
  James Olsen, Washington Post New Media
Correspondent

  Through a confidential source, the Washington
Post has in its possession the contents of the
entire former Secretary of State's personal
email server from its setup in 2008 through
March 2015, when the New York Times reported its
existence.
  According to government guidelines and state
department policy and procedures, neither a
Secretary of State, nor any state department
employee, should use a private email account or
private server to handle any official government
correspondence. In this respect, the former
```

THE FIXER

Secretary of State and current Democratic candidate for president broke the law, plain and simple. Her use of a personal email server for State Department business was illegal.

Further, the candidate's less than forthright answers, legal maneuverings, and actions clouding the content of the server—coupled with numerous missing emails from the server—has opened her candidacy to suspicion, distrust and unsubstantiated speculation from her political opponents, the press—including this paper—and numerous websites.

Most of this speculation and misinformation surrounding the server and the missing emails concerns the content of official emails that passed through the server, which could have leaked confidential elements of national security.

To fully understand its contents, the *Washington Post* created a full index, including subject, sender, receiver, and dates. Our reporters paid particular attention to reading and understanding emails that originated from state.gov since this area has driven the most amount of speculation and disinformation across the internet.

We recovered 523 e-mail chains that either originated at state.gov or her personal mail.com and sent to a state.gov address. Many of these emails contained internal meeting announcements, birthdays, congratulatory recognitions, birth of babies and even a few trying to sell household furnishings or sublease apartments.

In no case did we find the emails contained position papers, treaty strategy discussions, security assessments or any other wide ranging policy directions. This is not unusual as State Department protocol calls for the dissemination of this type of information on paper only, usually stamped with a security classification.

However, seventy-three email chains—to or from state.gov—contained the letter "C" which denotes the e-mail contains some form of confidential information. An analysis of these emails revealed most of the information had been previously reported by one or more major news organizations, including this newspaper, the *New York Times*, *Wall Street Journal*, *USA Today* or other large city dailies.

Three email chains contained confidential information that had not been previously reported by one or more major news organization.

Of those three, one referenced a trip by a diplomat to a certain "unfriendly" government; another a reference of an allocation of cash to a shadow government; and the last an expressed desire to establish a backchannel with another unfriendly government. This paper's political and government policy reporters feel these breaches, while unfortunate, are not critical leaks that would compromise the State Department's duties, nor national security.

Similarly, the Secretary had also received direct correspondence from outside associates providing various points-of-view on certain events of the day. The *Washington Post* includes the oft-cited Sidney Blumenthal email updates regarding Benghazi to fall within this area. No security breaches were discovered in the emails sent to the Secretary or sent from the Secretary to Blumenthal, despite the speculation from the Congressional Committee which cited "missing emails."

The contents of the server also included emails sent to and from the former president or the presumptive Democratic Party candidate with their health care providers, friends, relatives, and even former presidents. We found these notes to be personal in nature and this paper will not analyze or report on their content.

The *Washington Post* will make the entire database of all the emails available to the US Department of Justice, the US Attorney General, and the Senate Judiciary Committee for full analysis. Our purpose for releasing this database is to help minimize the speculation and disinformation surrounding these emails by alt-right sites including Breitbart, FBIAnon, InfoWars and incomplete reporting by mainstream outlets including Fox News, certain syndicated radio shows, and some local broadcast properties.

About the Cyber-Intrusion Series

The Washington Post believes the disinformation being spread during this year's election is detrimental to the well-being of citizens, country, and democracy. We believe it is our responsibility to accurately report the facts and are committed to investigating for the truth.

Chapter 70

The Cyber-Intrusion series broke on Sunday. The Democratic party candidate's email server piece was scheduled to run the following Wednesday. On the Tuesday before, the *Washington Post* received a gift. At least they thought so at the time.

From a podium during a campaign stop in Florida, the presumptive GOP presidential candidate publicly requested the Russians to assist in exposing his political opponent:

"Russia, if you're listening, I hope you're able to find the 30,000 emails that are missing, I think you will probably be rewarded mightily by our press."

Upon seeing the pronouncement on the ever-present television monitors positioned throughout the newsroom, then followed by nearly every reporter's cell phone messaging app pinging, Geoffrey Wines immediately started up the stairs to Fred and Marty's offices. He had been expecting some reaction from the candidate regarding the first article in the series that revealed the video, the alt-right disinformation strategy, and the direct link of the campaign to the disinformation content.

Geoff found Fred standing in the doorway to Marty's office. Marty was trapped on the phone, his glances indicating he was trying to find a way to get off the line. Finally, he hung up and looked at Fred and Geoff.

"Sorry guys. That was a disgruntled reader who had somehow managed to get through to the paper's Executive Editor. Not sure I have had that title thrown in my face so many times in a such a short period of time. She told me no responsible *executive editor* would ever allow reporters to write 'those kind of stories' about the GOP's candidate and his campaign staff."

"Did she give you her name?" Geoff asked.

You never know.

Then Marty just began laughing and couldn't stop. "Geoff, I knew you would ask. It was Katy Lynn Holloway."

Fred then added, "Interesting timing. Coincidence? Did you see the latest breaking story?"

"What's that?" Marty answered—intrigued.

"Seems Katy Lynn's candidate, during a public press conference just now, actually requested the Russians to find his opponent's emails and that the press will be richly rewarded."

Fred Ryan immediately responded with a fiendish smile, "I guess *we* will be richly rewarded."

Marty tilted his head to consider the last few days and the anticipated next few days.

"Fred, is this their offensive? We break a story about the video, the candidate's campaign strategy, the Russians visiting their office, their BOTS, and the dissemination of disinformation—all in the same 24-hour news cycle as Guccifer and WikiLeaks release DNC emails. He then makes a pronouncement for the Russians to find all his opponent's emails. That's interesting. No mention of the Russians before this. And he goes out of his way to bring the press into his request too."

Then Marty looked over at Geoff and said in a distant voice, "And, the only people who know about our review of all of the server emails are us, Jimmy, Jeff, probably Cam, and the Deputy Director of the FBI who we gave a heads up to about the server."

"You don't suppose the FBI leaked our email server story, do you?" Fred asked, since it had been his call to bring them into the server loop before publishing the story.

"Fred, I rule nothing out." Marty said.

Then Geoffrey Wines added, "Or is Jimmy somehow being hacked."

Chapter 71

Jimmy Olsen sat in front of his screens inside Planet Krypton. His sense of satisfaction increasing as he saw Fred Ryan and Marty Baron putting the full resources of the *Washington Post* behind his story. Correction. His and Geoffrey Wines' story. It did not escape him that Fred used his quote about the impact of disinformation on democracy during the staff meeting. At this moment, Jimmy felt good—*really good*.

Suddenly a siren inside the Planet sounded and a red light started flashing—the alarm system Jimmy had installed to alert him if someone had entered his home without the proper procedure.

His cell phone also pinged, and the screen notification simply said "BREACH!" He had designed the Planet's alarm loud to wake him in case he ever dozed off while working. He looked at his watch: 1:30 am.

Somehow the Wong Cam had missed the intruder.

He quickly typed a code on his terminal and a series of cameras in his living room activated showing a single person inside his house. The man moved cautiously toward the back of the living room and slowly opened the door to the hallway leading to the Planet, stepped inside, and began to turn toward the inner door. Jimmy could see on the hallway's camera the person's attention went immediately to the control panel and was jolted when the living room door slammed shut behind him.

As designed—ten seconds later—the alarm system activated a deafening barrage of sound inside the hallway and a strobe light started blinking in an erratic patten of pulses—two devices meant to disorient an intruder. Jimmy could see on his monitor the person immediately trying to open the door leading into the Planet, then the door back into the house. Both reinforced steel doors were sealed tight and nothing short of a cannon would allow the intruder to escape. The person then alternately covered his eyes, then ears, to avoid the flashing strobe and deafening sound.

Jimmy had installed the system, hoping it would never be used. But he had not considered how to handle an actual situation. If he called the police, then his facility would be exposed. He certainly couldn't just let the person escape for the same reason. And killing the intruder would be completely out of the question.

Jimmy also knew he was safe inside the Planet. But just to make sure, he typed in a few more commands and the CO_2 level inside the hallway increased to the point it would incapacitate the intruder. "Whoever this is will have a headache for days."

Jimmy decided to sit pat. He did not want police cars to come screaming into the neighborhood in the middle of the night.

• • •

Morning came and Jimmy gave Geoffrey Wines a call on his cell phone. He explained the situation.

"Jimmy, as you can imagine, I know a lot of guys on the DC Police force, high ranking detectives who might be able to help. But before I call them, see if you can get the intruder to identify himself."

"I'll give it a try, Geoff. I'll need to let some fresh air into the hallway to wake him first."

"You gassed him?" Geoffrey asked with deep concern.

"Just a little extra carbon dioxide in the air. Idles humans without permanent damage."

"Okay. See if you can determine his or her identity."

Jimmy entered a new code and watched as the intruder started to move. "I'm sure his head is splitting and probably very thirsty as well."

Jimmy then switched on a mic and a deep bass voice filter.

"Who are you?" Jimmy's deep-toned voice filled the hallway from every angle and made the walls vibrate.

The intruder raised his head, revealed his face, and looked around the hallway.

"Who is this?" the intruder asked.

"None of your damn business. Identify yourself at once." Jimmy cringed at the bad script. Then added, "You are trespassing. I have the right to kill you on the spot."

The man reached into his pocket.

"A gun will be of no help." Jimmy's deep voice warned.

"No gun. I am an FBI Special Agent. Agent Charles Noble. Here is my badge." He said, waving his credentials above his head, directing it to no place in particular.

• • •

Jimmy kept the man locked in the hallway until he saw Geoffrey Wines, Fred Ryan and one other man appear on the Wong Cam. Jimmy called Geoff's cell.

"And why is someone from Singapore calling me?" Geoff answered.

"I see you have Fred with you. And is that the Deputy Director of the FBI?"

"Yes sir. According to him, your Agent Charles Noble is in deep shit. When Fred called the Deputy Director to tell him what occurred, he was furious. Said he would join us to ensure Agent Noble is properly processed. Whatever that means."

"Got it. Proceed. Tell Fred I will video record everything that happens just in case we need it later."

"Good thinking Jimmy."

With that, Jimmy entered a code and the door from the hallway to the living room unlocked. Geoff opened the door. The smell of stale air, urine and feces permeated the hallway. A man in his mid-thirties, dressed in black trousers, black shirt and black jacket staggered through the door, rubbing his head. In his other hand he still held his FBI credentials.

Jimmy stayed inside the Planet with the inner door sealed.

The intruder looked up, instantly recognizing the Deputy Director who stood directly in front of the freed intruder, staring a hole through the man.

Fred turned to the Deputy Director. "Is this your agent sir?"

The DD answered with a simple "yes" and a slight nod, not taking his eyes off his man.

"Please tell us the agent's name sir."

"Special Agent Charles Noble."

"And did you or anyone in the FBI authorize Special Agent Charles Noble to invade, search, or enter this property."

Still not shifting his stare, the Deputy Director stated, "No, Mr. Ryan. We did not."

"And did any judge clear the FBI to visit this property?"

"No sir. No judge, nor the FBI, nor any FISA court authorized this break-in."

Fred Ryan, the former attorney then looked at the intruder. "State your name sir."

"Special Agent Charles Noble." He softly said.

"Louder please." Fred commanded.

"Special Agent Charles Noble."

"Is the Deputy Director accurately stating that you had no official authorization to enter this property?"

The agent, soiled, smelling bad, deeply embarrassed, and fearful for his job, answered slowly, yet loud enough for everyone to hear. "Yes. I acted completely on my own."

Fred then asked one more question: "Why did you come to this house?"

The agent answered truthfully. "I knew this is James Olsen's home and I was hoping I would find something pertaining to our investigation of Russian interference in our election."

Chapter 72

The afternoon after rescuing Jimmy Olsen from the FBI intruder, Geoffrey Wines sat at his computer in the newsroom working on the next installment in the series about the election when his cell phone rang. The server story had been put to bed for the next day's paper.

The caller ID showed a South Carolina phone number. Wines instantly knew the caller. "Hello. Geoffrey Wines here."

"Well, well, well, Mr. Wines. That's some story you guys are running" laughed the familiar voice of President Osbourne. "Kinda hit the motherlode, didn't you?"

"Good afternoon, Mr. President." Wines answered, genuinely glad the president had initiated the contact.

"You got more jaw dropping stuff?" Osbourne asked, with a big smile in his voice.

"Sir, let me just put it this way, we're fishing in a stocked pond and there will be many fish we can hook." Wines said, thinking one of these days, he might actually know what he is talking about when it comes to fishing.

"I get the analogy, Mr. Wines. Though I would probably have said 'shooting fish in a barrel.' But I just wanted to call and congratulate you. When we saw Sunday's article, Ms. Hayes and I just looked at each other and smiled. We knew you would get to the bottom of the story. Good job. You and this James Olsen too. Quite a dynamic duo you two."

"Thank you, Mr. President. But I am glad you called because I want to ask you something." Wines said, standing up and peering around the newsroom to see who might be in earshot.

"Why of course, Mr. Wines. Of course."

"Sir, you read Sunday's article. Right?"

"We did. Pretty heady stuff too. And your sources, well sir, it's breakthrough." Osbourne answered with a combination of glee and concern.

Interesting choice of words.

"And may I ask you 'who or what were our sources?'" Wines probed.

"Oh, Mr. Wines. Are you asking me whether I feel it is alright to snoop on someone's emails or hack into personal or private servers? Is that what you are asking?" The former president replied.

This guy is always a step ahead.

"Yes sir. I am."

Former President Osbourne paused for a moment before speaking. "Well, Mr. Wines, in a world where no one talks any more, where we text instead of picking up the phone and email everything: we can't overhear a conversation; wiretap into a telephone line—or like your Watergate burglars—break into an office filing cabinet and steal files. It's all electronics now. Can't even steal a computer. All the data is stored in a god-knows-where server farm somewhere."

Osbourne then hesitated and added with a warning "But hacking should be used judiciously."

"So, you don't approve." Wines asked, cringing inside.

"No sir, Mr. Wines. I did not say that." Osbourne said firmly. "My thought is we shouldn't snoop on our friends. I mean, we shouldn't hack for any personal reasons. Or to steal stuff."

Osbourne continued to explain. "You see, in my mind, there is public and there is private. And only your conscience can tell you where the line is. But when it comes to our elected officials—or I should add in this case, the election of our officials—it's pretty clear to me—it's all public business, open fishing with no limits. An election is not a private enterprise. The political parties are not private organizations. A candidate running for office is no longer a private person. These and they are all public. Public. Answerable to the citizenry. And it is your job, as a journalist, to reveal any wrongdoing. And in this capacity, you should be allowed to judiciously use almost any means available."

"Thank you, sir. I thought you only used our paper for fire-kindling."

Osbourne laughed, then added, "Journalists must deal in facts. To dig out the truth. People who run for office should have the inclination to tell the truth. There should be an imperative by public officials to always tell the truth—to never lie. And the press should be laser focused on ensuring every single public official—or candidate—tells the truth one hundred percent of the time."

Wonder where Operation Blueprint falls on this?

"Mr. Wines. You are probably thinking about the time we first met."

Can he read my mind?

"Yes sir, I am."

"And you are wondering if I told you the truth when we—Clarence and Chuck—met at Camp David to discuss Operation Blueprint."

"Yes sir, that thought did just cross my mind."

"I can honestly say to you we never once lied to you. And we did not obfuscate your investigation either. But we wanted to ensure you had the full truth of what did happen, so we did not get into a pissing match with you, the *Washington Post,* and a White House Press Room full of reporters. We knew you were good enough that you would keep digging, revealing your findings as you uncovered them. We wanted to ensure your preliminary findings did not leave false impressions with the public. Any lasting false impressions would have caused havoc with the FBI, the DEA, and the whole Department of Justice. Half-truths, as well as out-and-out falsehoods are deadly to our national institutions."

"Mr. President, I believe we are mostly on the same page. If we weren't, then I would have written more about our conversation, corroborated with our independent findings."

Wines then hesitated for a moment and decided to ask an additional question.

"Sir, as long as we are talking about rogue FBI agents, we had a situation the other night at the home of James Olsen by what appears to be a rogue special agent." Wines said in setting up his question.

"Yes." Osbourne simply replied.

"Just a few days prior we had shared with the FBI some of the information we had found in our investigation. So, we thought it was, let's say, bad form for them to try to break into a reporter's home."

"Yes."

"Turns out we trapped the special agent and held him captive until the Deputy Director, our Publisher Fred Ryan, and I arrived at the home and released the agent."

"The Deputy Director was with you?"

"Yes sir, he owed us since we shared our Russian findings with the FBI. We're talking national security."

"Okay. You did the right thing. What else?"

"Sir, as we were releasing the agent, we learned two things. One, the agent acted on his own. There were no warrants, permission, FISA or anything to allow this agent to enter our reporter's home."

"Yes. Go on."

"Our publisher essentially interrogated the agent on the spot. He asked the agent what he was doing at this house. The agent confessed, and I quote: "I knew this is James Olsen's home and I was hoping I would find something pertaining to our investigation of Russian interference in our election."

Wines heard a gasp on the other end of the line.

"Whoa!" Osbourne exclaimed. "He said that?"

"With the Deputy Director standing next to him." Wines added.

"Mr. Wines, that is a huge scoop. The FBI does not reveal to anyone, even the subject, when they have an on-going investigation. Much less the press."

"And?" Wines asked, letting the question float in the air.

"Oh my God." Osbourne exclaimed, with a heavy breath. "They could track down the original sponsors of this entire deal."

"Elvis?" Wines asked, more to see what Osbourne would say next.

"Yes. And my brethren. My fellow former presidents. And their whole bonehead scheme—though they had no idea what Elvis' plan would be. And, if they dug deep enough, even to my bonehead scheme that brought down the Soviet Union!"

"Sir. I'm on my regular cell phone. Are we good?"

"No worries there Mr. Wines. As I told you before, my end is secure. And I think the rogue agent's intrusion telegraphed—in spades—they are not tapping your lines for information."

Wines decided he would give this former president a heads up. He could choose to use it however he liked.

"Sir, we found an email version of your mystery man's fax, addressed to the three presidents. Explaining his plan to their objective."

"And."

Wines sensed a touch of a laugh in Osbourne's one word reply.

He's playing with me.

"Sir, it's obscure, like the note he sent to you. Only meaningful if you're in on the deal."

"I can see that. May I ask where you found the email? The email sent to the three presidents."

"Sir, with all due respect, not at this time."

"OK, then you know the identity of Elvis? From the email address? Tracking it down. Doing all that cyber-research stuff young James Olsen is so good at."

"Unfortunately, we don't. Not yet anyway. The Gmail account has only been used the one time. To send the note. And all the back-end data is elusive."

"So, you found Elvis' strategy note to the three former presidents on the much discussed email server?" Osbourne teased. "I know. I know. Your secret is safe with me."

"How do you . . . ?"

"Oh Mr. Wines. We figured you had all the missing emails. I didn't figure it out. Pat did. She told you she reads the *Washington Post* every single day. And she forgets nothing. She remembered seeing James

Olsen's by-line on some Snowden articles a few years ago, and then his name pops up again, with yours, in this investigation of cyber-intrusion in the election."

He calls us the dynamic duo.
He and Pat are the ultimate dynamic duo.

"Well sir, I can neither confirm nor deny your statement. But I do suggest you read tomorrow morning's paper."

Chapter 73

Katy Lynn Holloway had read the *Washington Post's* story on Sunday. It pointed right to her and the actions she had taken since joining the presumptive candidate's team.

She could not discredit anything in the piece. She knew the facts of the article were true. The candidate wasn't concerned. Which seemed strange. But her buddy at Breitbart had stopped taking her calls and her emails were bounced back.

However, yesterday—whoever was working the other side of the president's campaign—had delivered, as promised, a boatload of internal Democratic National Committee emails hacked from the DNC server by persons who dubbed themselves Guccifer. And WikiLeaks had delivered the news. Right on time. Just before *their* convention.

Like most other campaign documents and emails—except for the ones the *Washington Post* had revealed concerning her campaign strategy—these DNC emails were innocuous. Little bits and pieces of strategy, gossip, arguments about states and weights; and occasionally, something just plain embarrassing, like the DNC's preference of one democratic candidate over another.

Katy Lynn knew she would not need to read through the trove herself. She had umpteen alt-right news sites and a conservative television news network who would comb through the documents finding the most embarrassing stuff to report. But she worried her pipeline through Breitbart was not functional at this time.

Confidently, she knew she now had two sets of emails to use against her boss' opponent. One: fully exposed thanks to WikiLeaks. The other: presumably from the other candidate's personal server—some non-existent or missing—allowing her to flood voters with endless speculation on what they may contain.

• • •

As was her habit, she opened the morning edition of the *Washington Post* during her mid-morning coffee. The lead story's headline jumped right out at her:

```
All Missing Emails Found
- Illegal Server Reveals No State Secrets
```

She guessed the paper was merely putting a partisan spin on the content of the missing emails.

However, the first paragraph stopped her cold—the *Washington Post* claims to be in full possession of all the server emails from the time the private server was first installed to practically the time her boss announced his candidacy. This period included her full stint as Secretary of State.

> *Why did they gather the server's contents before it became a huge political story?*
> *And how?*
> *Are they that good?*

Had they also hacked into her server, extracted key files, and reported on her strategy? Should I let my staffers off the hook?

She also regretted they had correctly analyzed web traffic and found her misinformation's chain of news through Breitbart. Plus, they had a video of her boss watching a sex show. And they had quantified her use of targeted disinformation she had hoped would never be made public. All of this could be problematic for the candidate . . . and her.

> *How can I twist this?*
> *How can I turn their actions to my advantage?*

She considered options. For inspiration, she brought the Cambridge psychological clusters up on her screen. She needed to find an angle that would enrage voters. She ran her finger across the hundreds of clusters on the screen until something clicked.

> *There it is!*

"Privacy. Can we spin these findings into invasion of privacy?"

Into spying?

"Is the mainstream media spying on us?"
Is Jeff Bezos spying on us?

"What about the government?"
Is the FBI spying on us?
Is the Department of Justice spying on us?

"The current president too?"
That's it!

"The Deep State. The Deep State has so much to hide, they are trying to keep us from being elected?" she blurted out loud, marveling at her choice of words."

Rising from her seat, with her arms spread in a Victory V, she whisper-yells to her empty office, "And my candidate will absolutely love it!"

Chapter 74

There is ill a-brewing to my test.
The press knocks
The scheme laid bare
The plan exposed.

Media walls have crumbled
The waters parted.
Now each man sees
Only what they now believe.

My man is on top
Supported by a mysterious base
Who many can't Perceive
Nor even Conceive.

Leaders,
They follow along
With a sigh,
A laugh,
An excuse.

Driven by lies,
Rather than truth.
Thinking none of this is real.

Reputations will be lost,
Dishonor self-inflicted.
For my man
Will test all men's souls.

Chapter 75

Jimmy Olsen had the crazy thought of making friends with the FBI Agent who had trespassed into his home. He figured he had the upper hand. He also had the nagging suspicion Charles Noble would return to The Planet—this time prepared to mitigate the hallway.

President Osbourne's philosophy would be to show the Agent the inside of The Planet. On my terms, not his.

And per Geoffrey Wines, I should also start cultivating a broad array of law enforcement sources whom I have helped.

Both will pay dividends sometime down the road.

Prior to making the move, Jimmy used his tools to find as much as possible about FBI Special Agent Charles Noble. Grew up in Bowling Green, Kentucky; father a physician, stay-at-home mother, both still living. Younger sister, divorced, a virologist at the National Institutes of Health here in DC. He majored in biology with an advanced degree from the University of Kentucky; played center field on the university's baseball team; entered the FBI as a lab tech, specializing in forensics and the emerging use of DNA evidence. After ten years, granted permission to transfer out of the lab to become a special agent. Still single, drives a refurbished 1968 Corvette, and uses AT&T for his personal cell phone. *You never know.*

This was enough and far from thorough. Jimmy knew he could be more exhaustive and find more—much more—but he did not want to risk entering the FBI's data base. Besides, if Charles had been accepted and spent the last twelve years in the FBI, he was probably a solid guy—minimal risk to Planet Krypton—and hopefully not an elusive "Clyde" from Geoffrey Wines' earlier investigations.

Jimmy picked up his office phone and entered Charles' cell number. The caller ID on the other end would show "Washington Post."

"Noble." The line answered with just a slight hesitancy in the voice.

"Special Agent Charles Noble?" Jimmy responded.

"Yes, this is Special Agent Charles Noble."

"Sir, this is James Olsen. We haven't officially met . . ."

• • •

At precisely 7:00 that evening, Charles Noble stepped onto James Olsen's front porch on Steuben Street. He had taken the Metro from FBI headquarters and walked, leaving his Vette in the Hoover Building parking garage. A smart move, for leaving his classic car on any Washington DC street was dangerous. Even for a Fed.

Hesitantly, he pressed the doorbell he had avoided on his last visit. He felt vulnerable just standing there. The panic of the locked hallway reverberated through his mind. And the session with the Deputy Director later that morning was worse. The DD told him he had broken the first law of the FBI: "You embarrassed the Bureau. But since this is your only strike, coupled with what you suffered that night in the hallway, the Bureau will give you a pass without suspension." Noble also figured the DD did not want to lose any momentum on their election interference investigation—nor the lead the Bureau's baseball team had in their summer league.

"In an abundance of caution and to cover his tracks, Noble had informed the DD of his invitation to visit James Olsen's home. The DD approved.

Charles had also re-read the FBI download on Jimmy "James" Olsen. He had learned of his computer credentials and wondered what the security hallway protected.

• • •

Jimmy opened his front door. Charles Noble appeared much bigger than he had noted while watching his video interchange with Fred

Ryan. Broad shoulders, about six-two, maybe close to 200 pounds. Dark hair. Brown eyes. Suit coat and tie.

Definitely a Fed.
And I bet he can pound a baseball too.

"Special Agent Charles Noble, I presume." Jimmy said with a smile.

Noble returned a practiced smile, but his eyes showed he was guarded.

Jimmy decided to play it friendly and warm. He wanted to make Charles a trusted friend, not an adversary. Figured humor would be the best way to go.

"Charles. Sorry about the other night. Please come in." he said as he offered his hand and grinned. "I promise I won't lock you in the hallway."

The agent hesitated, then gave Jimmy a firm handshake.

"Embarrassing, huh?" he responded.

"Please, come in. You off duty?"

"Yeah." Charles noted, with more of a natural smile. "Still employed too."

"Good. Can I get you a beer?" Jimmy said as he motioned Charles to enter.

"Sure, what do you have?"

"Pretty much anything. I order in most of my food, so the fridge is wide open for beer."

"My kind of guy. Northeast IPA?"

"Harpoon?"

"Awesome!"

Jimmy grabbed two Harpoons and two beer glasses and brought them over to the coffee table. He opened a side drawer, removed an opener, and flicked the caps off the bottles, handing one to Charles before sitting down in the chair opposite his guest.

Chapter 76

The three former presidents set up a group call on a secure telephone line. This wasn't unusual, but rather a precaution in case one of them let slip something they may have heard or read in the security briefings they could receive for life. Somewhere along the line, current presidents determined former presidents should be prepared to give them an informed point of view on a matter if asked. Hence, they would receive top security information for as long as they desired, or until they were deemed a security risk.

Today's topic: Elvis and the pieces they had each read in the *Washington Post*.

"Looks like *The Post* is hot on Elvis' trail." The first said with his usual drawl.

"How'd they get the contents of my server? You know, we all three received that note from Elvis giving us a clue to his plan." The second said in his horsey voice.

"We shouldn't worry about it." Suggested the third. "When I first read it, I thought it was just one of those things that circulates the web. Then I got it. Heck, if I didn't, then I don't think the *Washington Post* or even the FBI will get it either."

"Hope you're right." replied the first.

"Well anyway. We trashed it. It should be gone." said the second.

"Gentlemen. We do have a problem." The third added with his deep southern accent. "My fellow churchgoers are crazy about this guy. Would follow him anywhere."

"Even after revealing the pee video?" laughed the second.

"My guess, they don't believe it's real." responded the third.

"Hey, that gives me an idea!" the first jumped in excitedly. "My nephew once told me about one of the times he met the candidate on a production set out west. The candidate spent the whole time talking about how he could kiss women and touch their privates whenever he liked because he was rich."

"That's not going to mean much. Just hearsay." The second added, being a former lawyer.

"That's right. But he told me the network has a video of it. Said his network always tried to find an angle to promote the candidate's reality tv show, so he popped up all over their schedules. Seemed to be good for ratings. Damn he even dominated their Sunday news program without ever getting out of his pajamas. Called it in."

"Literally. Drove my wife crazy." confessed the second.

"My brother too." added the first.

"Gentlemen. We might have something here. What precisely did he say?" mischief coated the president's southern accent.

"My nephew told me he said something like, 'you can grab them by the pussy, and they won't care.' Oh yeah, said he just started kissing one woman and then took her furniture shopping."

"That's funny. Grab 'em then buy 'em furniture. Another video huh? One in Moscow. And another in Hollywood! Guy is starting a box set if you know what I mean."

"Can we get it? Something like that could dry up some of my fellow Christians' enthusiasm." The Sunday school teacher then paused. "Maybe not all of them."

"I'll get on it. My brother's out of the race. Are you guys sure we want to do this?

The Christian president then spoke up, forcefully. "No question. Have you seen him recently on tv? He's vulgar. My wife calls him a 'pig.' He respects no one and no country. Criticizes every institution of our government. Our treaties. Every former president. The current president. And the press too. Dishonors our military veterans. He's a cheat. Even made fun of his opponent during the debate's potty break."

He then hesitated for a moment. "Gentlemen. We started this mess. Our job is to see we fail. Agree?"

"We all agree."

Chapter 77

"Well, that didn't take long." Fred Ryan said to himself as he watched the FBI Director's news conference on the television in his office. "Though a bit unconventional. Making the announcement to close the Bureau's Server-Gate investigation himself. Guess the Attorney General wanted to pass on it."

His phone rang. The caller ID showed Geoffrey Wines was calling from inside the building.

"Fred here."

"Good afternoon, sir. Amazing what a little sunshine will do, huh sir."

The publisher responded, with just a bit of pride in his voice. "It's what we hoped, heh? If the whole contents of the server are made available—then we, as the press report it—then the authorities can research it and decide guilt or innocence. Jimmy was right. His tools for analyzing it made it easy and fast. I feel good. I feel like we are doing the right thing."

"We should Fred. You, Marty, Cam, Jeff, and Jimmy. We all did good on this one. Sunshine is always good. We did our job."

Wines then waited for a moment, before proceeding. "Sir, you were pretty upset that day at Jimmy's house. Stormed out of the Planet. Jimmy thought he had done something wrong. Did he?"

"Lord no, Geoff. Jimmy was just fine." Then the publisher confessed. "The problem *was* me. I *was* hesitant. I built a problem where there *wasn't* one. I *was* frustrated. I thought the new owner of this paper would not want us to do certain things: use new tools to investigate; report on uncomfortable things; potentially create a problem for our owner and his other business enterprises. I thought all these things. And it made me mad!"

Wines remained silent, hoping his publisher would continue.

"I thought about our duty. Yet, I imagined our owner would want us to hold back. I *was* concerned he would think our use of computer hacking would be abhorrent since his fortune is based on cyber-assets. I *was* wrong. The Board didn't blink an eye. Told us to do what a big-time newspaper should do. But, as you clearly know Geoff, we didn't just hack around. We had the same type of information a court of law would use to obtain a warrant."

Wines added, remembering Osbourne's words. "And none of its personal. It's all about public persons working for the public or running for a public office. Same as WikiLeaks, which we reported. Same as Snowden, who we reported. Same as the file drawers stolen at the Watergate, that put this paper on the map."

"So, Geoff, as an old-style reporter who has spent his career cultivating sources, are you good with the use of cyber-investigations?" Fred Ryan, publisher of the *Washington Post* asked his star reporter.

"Yes sir, I am. One hundred percent! I understand this form of investigation is not a replacement for our cultivated human sources. Jimmy would have never downloaded the entire contents of the then-likely candidate's server if the Secretary's use of it for official State Department business had not been reported by the *New York Times*. We would never have been onto this story—the disinformation side—without Reverend Brooks' congregants or the owner of Meteor Pizza. We would not have tapped into Katie Lynn Holloway's emails if we had not found specific language on several sites and discovered her connection with Cambridge Analytica and Breitbart. And we would have never learned of the cyber-Russian if a certain photo had not been forwarded by a human source. Lastly, yet most important, we would never have learned anything was up, unless my confidential informant gave me a lead."

"And to your point Geoff, we learned from Special Agent Charles Noble, the FBI now has an investigation underway into the Russian interference into our election." Fred then added with a laugh. "Though it could be argued we obtained *that* information through torture."

Wines laughed at his publisher's remark and Jimmy's forethought on how such a situation could occur. "Yes, it is an interesting piece of information we shouldn't be privy to."Fred then turned serious. "It does illustrate an interesting dichotomy. You see, we as journalists can investigate any way we like. We have Freedom of the Press and all we do is report what we find. But the FBI has legal constraints. They cannot follow a lead into someone's email, home, or business without first getting a court order to allow it because of the Fourth Amendment. Why? Because their investigations end in a court case based on legally admissible evidence. And ours, just on the front page for everyone to see."

"So, we carry on." Geoff added, as a summation.

Fred bluntly answered. "You bet, Geoff. We will continue to get, then vet, what we discover. The bottom line is we MUST expose the misinformation and disinformation circulating in this election. We will expose it, whether it's some guy with a computer, a wannabe news site, or part of a campaign strategy."

Fred's tone then changed into concern. "But as Jimmy pointed out, the people who are the targets of disinformation don't read our paper, nor any other paper. Just an overabundance of lies on the internet."

Chapter 78

Katy Lynn Holloway pondered the most recent change in management of her campaign. Her old boss, the man responsible for her inflated salary, was now out and her conduit at Breitbart installed as her new boss. She felt okay with the move, particularly since the *Washington Post* had exposed their disinformation pipeline. If he had stayed at Breitbart, he would be open game. But now, as Chairman of the GOP candidate's campaign, he would be off-limits to Federal investigations or the mainstream press.

Good timing too.

Over the past few weeks, her analytics indicated the readership and clicks of the cyber-outlets, including Breitbart, were being replaced by Fox News. Through the efforts of her new boss, Fox now reliably repeated her distorted messaging. In fact, her new boss proudly crowned the network as "The Voice of the Alt-Right."

Fox also completely supported her "Deep State" agenda. All their commentators talk about it. They spend endless shows breaking down how the deep state and unelected career bureaucrats are responsible for everything perceived to be wrong in the country—and answerable to no one. They also report how "the deep state is spying on her candidate's campaign." Of course, the candidate hammers this at every campaign rally and in every interview.

"I control the news cycle! I pushed the "Server-Gate" story until the *Washington Post* revealed its complete contents and the FBI closed the case."

"I conceived the "Deep State Spying Story" and will continue to use immigration, Mexicans, and Muslims as a wedge issue. Christmas too. The Cambridge analysis was correct. It moves people!"

The mainstream media even picks up a lot of it! Her candidate's use of Twitter is nothing more than poking the Dems and getting a reaction. Mainstream reporters love Twitter, and their reactions keep my man's messages alive far longer than they merit.

We're now in the home stretch.
Fox now firmly supports my candidate, and messaging.
The convention was successful and now behind her.
She even had a former three-star general lead the entire convention audience in the "lock her up" chant she scripted.
And now . . .
The Evangelical vote is solid.
Blue collar union numbers growing.
The Dem's Black vote getting shaky, particularly in the large metro areas. "And the Dem candidate's campaign seems to be ignoring the three firewall states where I have targeted special messaging!"

And then, right on cue, WikiLeaks had dumped a boatload of embarrassing DNC emails right before their convention. The convention chairman had to step down due to the brouhaha. Their convention—a dumpster fire—though hers was hit by a hurricane. Given the choice, she would take bad weather every time.
"The email hurricane was much more destructive!"

Now, her polling technique shows her candidate is now even in the Electoral race—though the mainstream polls aren't necessarily showing it. Thank goodness, many of her voters disdain the establishment's polling and either don't answer their phones or just plain lie to the pollsters.

Yes, everything is working out just fine!

Chapter 79

ALAS,
DISORDER
IS ALL I SEE.

BUT WHERE
WHERE?
DOES THIS LEAD?

I TRIED
TO MAKE OUR CITIZENS BELIEVE
BUT FROM THEIR "TRUTHS"
WE NOW MUST FLEE.

HARM
WAS NOT
MY CURE'S GOAL.

YET MINE
IS TAKING
AN UGLY TOLL.

ANY EFFECTIVE CURE
I NOW CHOOSE TO SOW
MUST ADDRESS
OUR VERY SOUL.

Chapter 80

Jimmy Olsen deduced something in the data that disturbed him. Interest in the disinformation continued to grow. Google searches were being conducted by millions of Americans on just the topics Breitbart—the other sites—and now Fox were pushing. And these searches would direct the person to other sites pushing the same story. And since the mainstream media outlets and television networks tended not to report on the disinformation, the search engines revealed no rebuttal.

No rebuttal.

Jimmy's data clearly showed persons supporting the GOP candidate were nearly ten times more likely to see and click on the misinformation.

It is so widespread—
It might as well be broadcast.

But Jimmy knew this meant something the polls were not telling. The election now one month away. The candidate is getting traction. People are interested in his claims and are seeking more information.

Maybe the Fixer's plan is working after all.
Engagement is up.
Way up.

And though this type of Google engagement analysis represented a new way to measure a candidate's likelihood of success, it had been proven correct in a few previous off-year elections.

It wasn't all cyber either. The frenzy at all the GOP candidate's rallies also indicated a growing populist movement. Shirts. Caps. Flags. Long lines waiting to get in.

What is the line from 'Evita?'
Oh, what a circus.
Oh, what a show.

But this isn't over the death of an actress. Nor even the election of one candidate over another.

> *This is about the death of Truth.*
> *This is about the manipulation of the masses.*
> *Via misinformation and disinformation.*

A movement based on lies.

> *Instead of government, we have a stage*
> *Instead of ideas, a prima donna's rage*
> *Instead of help, we are given a crowd*
> *He doesn't say much . . . but he says it loud.*

With a sinking feeling, Jimmy now understood two things:

One, President Osbourne's tip is in fact happening. The candidate will be elected and there will be nothing short of unplugging the entire internet to stop it. The distortion of reality is now woven into the American psyche, as surely as the plaid on his shirt.

We are doing this to ourselves.

And two, one of the mystery man's insights left in the draft file of his email account. It was prophetic. What did it say? . . . Here it is. The mystery man describing the plan and Putin's role.

> E-MAILS, PRIVATE SERVERS, AND LEAKS, OH MY.
> SOME "MISSING."
> OTHERS EXPOSED "EVERYWHERE."
> SOME QUITE DULL.
> OTHERS STUPID AND EMBARRASSING.
> NONE REALLY IMPORTANT.
> BUT THEY CAUSE QUITE A RUCKUS.
> WHO'D THOUGHT?
> MY FRIEND DID.
> MY FRIEND WHO UNDERSTANDS US BETTER THAN WE UNDERSTAND OURSELVES.

That last line: "My friend who understands us better than we understand ourselves." *Is something else going to happen?*

Chapter 81

Newsrooms of major newspapers are noisy places. While the loud staccato sound of typewriters is now replaced by the quieter clicks of computer keyboards, the mere density of humanity feverishly getting out the news is loud. Phones ring. A cacophony of voices talking, and a few expletives being blurted out.

But one thing brings silence to a newsroom. That is the ding of a breaking story. In the old days, the teletype machines would ring with an important story from the Associated Press or United Press International. Today, cell phones will start dinging as the notification of something BIG breaking through a news service or Twitter. And when every cellphone in every reporter's pocket starts to ding at once, everything just stops. And an eerie silence comes over the wide-open newsroom.

• • •

Geoffrey Wines looked at his phone. The President, Director of Homeland Security and the Director of National Intelligence had just issued a statement. The first paragraph read:

> The U.S. Intelligence Community (USIC) is confident that the Russian Government directed the recent compromises of e-mails from US persons and institutions, including from US political organizations. The recent disclosures of alleged hacked e-mails on sites like DCLeaks.com and WikiLeaks and by the Guccifer 2.0 online persona are consistent with the methods and motivations of Russian-directed efforts. These thefts and disclosures are intended to interfere with the US election process. Such activity is not new to Moscow—the

```
Russians   have    used    similar    tactics   and
techniques   across   Europe   and   Eurasia,   for
example,  to  influence  public  opinion  there.  We
believe, based on the scope and sensitivity of
these efforts, that only Russia's senior-most
officials    could    have    authorized    these
activities.
```

Yes!

The moment the *Washington Post* published their first story, Wines and the editors knew it would be just a matter of days or weeks before the security apparatus of the United States of America would conclude and report on their own findings. Though it would be nearly impossible to know for sure, Wines and the others believed Jimmy's research stemming from Jacob Washington's photo provided the missing piece to lock in on Russia's involvement.

Maybe the good President Osbourne could confirm it?

• • •

Almost on cue, Wines' desk phone rang. Greenville, South Carolina, again.

"Geoffrey Wines here."

"Mr. Wines. How are you? Osbourne here." Was the cheerful voice on the other end.

"Good morning, sir. I was just thinking about you." Wines said with a grin.

"I bet you were. Just saw the flash about the Intelligence Community's assessment of Russia and our election. Have you read it?"

"Yes sir. Just now."

"And . . . ?"

"Sir?" Wines answered, wanting to hear what the president said first.

"Mr. Wines. You guys did good. And you guys are good. That James Olsen will probably be headed to the NSA if he keeps it up."

"Prisoner or key position?" Wines quipped in reply.

"Funny, Mr. Wines. But seriously, your work on this is quite amazing. And impressive. I know you guys gave Homeland an important lead." Osbourne replied with a touch of pride in his voice. "And let me just say this is big news, a bold statement by Intelligence. Basically, said Russia is attacking our shores—though its release is somewhat muted. Why a press release? I would have gone on TV, shouted it, and told Mr. Putin to back off. Immediately!"

"My thoughts exactly." Wines confirmed.

"But there is another reason for my call—other than to expand your hat size Mr. Wines."

"What's that, sir?"

"Disinformation. It changes everything. Hell, Mr. Wines, the Russians are the only ones spreading fact. All they are doing is reprinting emails others have written. And those can be embarrassing. And I guess the Russians are making some stuff up themselves, but they are mostly spreading what the GOP candidate is putting out.

"Yes sir Mr. Wines, my former party, they're making stuff up. Or spinning facts into out- and-out lies. And since so many in the party are so guarded—or have such stars in their eyes—they are ignoring the lies. The disinformation. For no other reason than to win an election! It is so goddamn disappointing."

Did Osbourne say, "my former party?"

"Mr. Wines, did you hear what I just said?" Osbourne's voice elevated. "I'm telling you Russia is important: but the big story *is* this election being manipulated; and it is being done via disinformation by one of the parties; one of *our* political parties! And it will only lead to political divisiveness that could ultimately kill us."

"Sir?" Wines interjected.

"That's the story you need to concentrate on, Mr. Wines. That's the story you can expose and hopefully stop. The Russian story is just noise. An excuse. A diversion. But . . . disinformation is the root of our evil. And mark my words Mr. Wines, mark my words: *Once disinformation starts, it will not stop. It will kill our democracy!*"

The former president then concluded. "Today, it's about political candidates. Tomorrow, it could be about life and death! And even War!"

Chapter 82

Cameron Barr, Managing Editor of the *Washington Post* also looked at the Intelligence Community's statement on his cell phone.

No one else in the newsroom knew the paper had another huge story about to break. One of the political reporters was busily tracking down the exact details. It would hit in the afternoon edition—which meant on their web page and then as the headline on the next morning's front page.

When major stories break in the middle of the afternoon, its distribution is immediately touted on Twitter feeds and re-tweeted by numerous other correspondents and followers. This meant the story would be viewed by well over a million persons within minutes of its release.

In this case, the story was another video with the GOP presidential candidate. This time, he was the star. It took place in the United States and featured the candidate with two well-known broadcast personalities. This 2005 video included both the candidate's voice and presence on and off a motor coach that had pulled onto a studio lot, where the candidate was to do a cameo in a popular NBC soap opera.

The video had come to the *Post* via the Entertainment Editor who had immediately called a meeting with Cam and Marty Baron, the paper's Executive Editor. Its source confidential, but its origin was indisputable. Cam assigned a political reporter to run-down and break the story. The reporter contacted the two actors to ensure they were present and get their statement. Due to the certainty and completeness of the video, the paper would not seek a statement from the candidate until after it ran on the *Washington Post* web site.

As soon as the story broke, teams were in place to get responses from other politicians in both parties. The paper's Twitter feed would report each of these reactions as they occurred. Numerous politicians would retweet the story with their take on the video as well. Teams were building the next morning's front-page story with all the feedback. The website's edition would have the links. It will be a busy afternoon.

Cam had also decided to place the Intelligence Community story on the front page—below the fold. He had the paper's Homeland Security reporter chasing down his contacts to expand on the simple press release the department had issued.

Chapter 83

When the Intelligence Community released the Russian interference communiqué, Jimmy Olsen immediately went home to station himself inside Planet Krypton. There, he would have the tools to monitor the situation and cyber-traffic resulting from their statement.

Unaware of the *Post's* other breaking story, he focused his attention on the international cyber-traffic where he had set monitors to track the Russian bots and other activity focused on the election. He also wanted to see if Guccifer or WikiLeaks posted anything; or if the cyber-Russian from Jacob Washington's photo had made any "interesting" calls.

Things were eerily quiet. It seemed as if cyber activity out of Russia came to a halt. The bots went silent. News stories stopped. Retweets vanished.

Jimmy assumed it would be a long night, so he left the house and took a walk. It was a beautiful early October afternoon. Upon returning from a three-mile walk, he called Wong's, ordered dinner, and sat in his living room to wait and have a beer.

Half an hour later dinner arrived. He loaded the Spicy Szechuan Chicken onto the cart, with chop sticks, and a second bottle of IPA.

• • •

As soon as he opened the inner door into Planet Krypton, the sound of alarms from his traps were deafening and his screens flashing faster than he could follow. A massive amount of traffic had accelerated across the web.

With a few clicks on his keyboard, he isolated the source of the activity.

Two things were hitting the web simultaneously.

The first—a total surprise. It was a breaking *Washington Post* story about a 2005 video of the GOP candidate making remarks about women's genital parts and their willingness for him to grab them. The jump in internet activity occurred as other media sources spread the story, the video, and reactions to the video.

Wonder why I did not know about this?

The second cause of the activity was a major dump by WikiLeaks of emails from the chairman of the Democratic party's presidential campaign. It had started exactly twenty-seven minutes after his paper broke the video story.

Twenty-seven minutes!

Despite the Intelligence Community's news statement, Russian bots were in full force promoting the WikiLeaks emails around the web.

Wow!
One day—three important stories—so close to the election.

Russia poaching our election.
Grabbing pussies.
And Partisan emails.

"Wonder which will grasp the public's attention?" Jimmy said to himself as he reached for his phone, punched in a code, and dialed Geoffrey Wines' cell phone.

Chapter 84

Geoffrey Wines stood in Fred Ryan's office when his cell phone showed a call from Singapore. Fred signaled him to take Jimmy's call, amused at the caller location.

"Wines."

"Geoff, are you seeing what is happening on the web at this moment."

"Yeah, we just broke a story. A blockbuster."

"No Geoff. I'm talking about another huge dump by WikiLeaks. All from John Podesta's e-mail account. And the Russian bots have gone crazy promoting them."

Wines looked over to Fred. "Jimmy's saying WikiLeaks just dumped a bunch of emails from John Podesta's account."

"Put him on speaker, Geoff."

Wines put Jimmy on speaker and set his cell on the small conference table. "Go ahead Jimmy. What are you seeing?"

"I was monitoring my Russian bots to see how they were handling the Intelligence Community release. They were totally silent, so I went for a walk. Came back and all hell was breaking loose. Seems WikiLeaks dropped a trove of emails from the Dem campaign chairman. And then almost immediately, the bots started to promote the more embarrassing emails across the entire internet. Same thing we saw with the DNC WikiLeak drop a few months ago,"

"Continue, Jimmy." Fred said. "What caught your eye?"

"Well sir, the drop occurred exactly twenty-seven minutes after we broke the 'Access Hollywood' video. All was silent, then BAM. With everything we know, the timing seems more than coincidental."

"Wait a minute, Jimmy." Fred said as he walked over and closed the door. "Is this line secure Jimmy?"

"Totally sir. Why?"

Fred then looked directly at Geoffrey Wines and didn't take his eyes off him. "Because I don't think we know the whole story. I believe you guys are holding back on us regarding this entire election story."

Wines returned his publisher's gaze. "What do you mean?"

"Jeff Leen's question the other day. Seems odd that out of 70,000 emails, you dig out a single email addressed to three former presidents. Why three? Why not four? Why was President Osbourne not on the list? And why did the three presidents receive the email in the first place? What's their role in this whole thing?"

Fred Ryan then stopped, looked down at the phone, then back up at his star reporter. "Geoff, is President Osbourne your source? Are the other three presidents somehow involved in this whole election thing?"

Chapter 85

"Did you see today's news, oh boy?" The former president asked the two other former presidents on the phone.

"Yep. The boy came through." proudly answered the second.

"Can't believe men talk like that on an open mike" pontificated the third. "Think it. Maybe lust it. But in the name of the Lord, don't say it."

"This should slow him down." calculated the first. "Those religious types will find it impossible to support him now. Believe me, I know."

"Don't be so sure." quipped the third. "The president of the Family Research Council defended him. Said something like, 'My personal support of the candidate has never been based upon shared values.' What does that mean? 'Save the sinner'—maybe. But isn't belief in all religions based on 'shared values?'"

"No sir." added the second. "Some just like to talk the talk. Few actually walk the walk."

"Faced that my whole life, gentlemen. The good Lord wants us to do good every single day and when we sin: admit it, fix it, and live a righteous life. Not sure this candidate understands that—he is mean spirited, selfish, not honorable, and any moral man should see that."

"Well, I guess Sunday morning sermons will have a new subject. Not to mention the Sunday news shows!" joked the first.

"Hopefully, this will work. And not destroy my boy's career."

"It will take a lot to counter it and move it out of the news cycle." disputed the first. "Trust me, I know. I am sure I will somehow get dragged into this too. Plus, the story about the Russian meddling will move to the backburner. There is too much juicy stuff—genitals and political emails—believe me, that will be all we will hear until election day."

The three former presidents started to say good-bye.

"Oh, one more thing." inserted the first. "Did Geoffrey Wines, the reporter for the *Washington Post* contact you about Elvis' email?"

Chapter 86

"I love WikiLeaks." the candidate extolled from the podium at a large rally. The audience went wild. Katy Lynn Holloway stood on the side of the stage, glancing at her candidate, but mainly studying the mood of the audience.

Are people here—just to be here?
Nope.
They are here because they genuinely love my candidate.

They ate it up. Their eyes said it all—they loved her man.

She had directed the event director to select certain well-dressed white women, a few black men, a black woman, a Mexican and an Asian to sprinkle in behind the podium where they would be on camera throughout the rally. They were asked to be extra enthusiastic and given t-shirts and red hats with the candidate's autograph. Who could resist?

"It's quite remarkable" she said to herself, "how are so many people bamboozled by all this man's bullshit?" Of course, she had penned a lot of it. The cheer lines: "Lock her up." "Show us the emails?" "Enemy of the people." "The Deep State." She had even suggested the press be confined to one area—a way to say, 'these people are not one of you.'

She knew when she got home her husband would caution her about *her* campaign. He would say, "are you sure you want to build up so much distrust in our government. So much hate for the other candidate. So little regard for certain people, other governments, and the world-wide order. And so much praise for our adversaries? There's too much distrust, honey. This is not going to end well for any of us."

She never answered. Couldn't answer. The man who hired her was now gone, but her paycheck remained the same and quite frankly, this is what she had signed up for.

Besides, maybe the mainstream polls were right. His opponent would win.

But her polls indicated something different. Her man would win by winning three states where she had concentrated her disinformation strategy.

Chapter 87

Fred Ryan had a hunch, and he was going to run with it. He picked up his desk phone and dialed a South Carolina phone number.

"Good morning. President Osbourne's office. This is Pat Hayes."

Good morning Ms. Hayes, this is Fred Ryan, publisher of the *Washington Post*. Do you remember me?

"Well, good morning Mr. Ryan. I certainly do. You were in the White House when President Osbourne was vice-president." Pat then added with a laugh, "And I read the *Washington Post* every single day! Seems like the paper hasn't missed a step from the old management. Still getting the story out."

"Thank you, Ms. Hayes. We're trying. Is the president available?"

"He sure is. You're lucky. It's raining and the president cancelled fishing this morning."

"He's still fishing?"

"Every chance he gets. Just loves it. And the lake here is his old fishing hole from when he was just a boy. Hold on one minute and let me see if he is available."

Pat placed the caller on hold and personally went into her lifemate's office.

"Mr. President, seems Fred Ryan is on the line for you."

Osbourne laughed. "Put him through, Pat. Please, put him through."

Pat returned to her desk. "Mr. Ryan, one moment. Let me put you through to President Osbourne."

After a series of clicks, the former president answered, "Good morning, Fred, my, my, it has been a mighty long time."

"Thank you, sir, and good morning to you as well."

"What do I owe the pleasure of this call, Fred? Oh, and if it is anything confidential, I punched in the secure line, we're good."

The man hasn't changed a bit.

Was probably expecting my call in the first place.

"Thank you, sir. Glad we are secure. I wanted to talk to you about the election."

"Figured that Fred. Was wondering when you were going to play an ace and call me. But I have got to tell you, your team has dug out some mighty powerful stuff. Hell, it's the stuff of an Antim Straus novel. What do you want to know?"

Fred Ryan took a breath and then decided to just speak as frankly as he could—the man would see through any disguise.

"Sir, are you Geoffrey Wines' confidential source on this story?"

Osbourne let out a long, deep laugh. "Fred, are you confidentially calling me to see if your paper's finest reporter confidentially received information from me? Is that right, Fred?"

"I am sir." Fred Ryan earnestly replied, though he did notice the added emphasis the president placed on his first name—Fred.

"What about?" asked the president.

"The election sir. Did you tip off Geoffrey Wines that the election was being rigged for the GOP candidate to win?"

"Well, well, well, Fred. Mr. Wines and I did discuss the primaries during his visit late last Spring. We both were surprised at how one candidate was rising to the top, despite near universal rejection from the rest of his purported party." Osborne then paused and added for emphasis. "Our party, Fred. Our Grand Old Party."

"Let me be direct sir, did the names of the other living presidents come up?"

"Yes sir, they did, as I remember. We were surprised two of the presidents weren't more vocal about some of the claims and statements being made by the candidate. But then again, they also had a dog in this fight and could hardly use their office of the presidency to counter a candidate running for the office. Probably were looking to me to make more noise since I don't have a brother, wife or son running. I chose to remain quiet."

"I see sir. Why?"

"I believe former presidents should stay out of presidential politicking." Osbourne continued. "But that shouldn't get the other active members of the party, men who hold office today, off the hook. The cowards. The presidency and the character of the men who serve as our leader is larger than any party. You know the Shakespeare line: 'If I lose mine honor, I lose myself.'"

Interesting line.
Shakespeare.

"Yes sir."

"You know, The Skipper would have had their head if they acted the way they are acting now. Hiding. Making jokes out of something terribly serious—when they should be calling it out. They have lost all honor. You cannot expect a nation to survive if its leader consistently lies, belittles others, gives little respect to our institutions and allied nations. And then having the party members simply following along. Simply follow along. What a disgrace."

"I see." Fred inserted, just so the president knew he was still listening.

"And the Dems are making it far too easy. They aren't countering the lies with stated facts. Their candidate is coming across as distrustful instead of releasing everything she has. And now, with the latest video, the GOP candidate just reminds voters of her husband's indiscretions. Not related. Or even the same thing. But it makes a great headline and gives everyone cover."

"So, sir, are you saying the three former presidents are not somehow behind this election mess?"

The fourth former president took a long pause before answering.

"Fred, are you asking me whether I, or any of the three other former presidents knew the election would be manipulated back last year. And I will tell you none of us had any reason to believe it would, or in any way caused it to happen."

"Then why would a mystery man send the three other presidents an email—the only email from an account—basically outlining a strategy to influence the election?" Fred Ryan, publisher of the *Washington Post* asked directly.

"Fred, do you want me to answer that question? If so, then we will be off the record. And when I tell you, you will understand why." The former president then continued. "You know me. And trust I am making the right decision? Do we understand each other?"

> *That answers my original question.*
> *Osbourne is Wines' confidential source.*
> *But what exactly did the three presidents do?*
> *Do I commit to not revealing his and the three presidents' roles?*
> *Or leave it open to further investigation?*

"Mr. President, let me ask you one question before I answer."

"Certainly, Fred. What do you want to know?"

"Would The Skipper approve of what you and the three presidents are doing?"

"That is not an easy question to answer, Fred. But I would say he would have been totally on board with the request the three men made to a Fixer. It was noble and humbling that they would feel the need to get outside assistance." Osbourne's voice then cracked. "But Fred, the path that Fixer took, while probably successful, is extremely dangerous. And I don't think any of us had any idea how bad it would be. And will be for the future."

> *Us?*
> *Had any idea how bad it would be?*

"Bringing the Russians in, sir?"

"Unfortunately, the Russians are just an excuse. Someone to blame instead of focusing blame where it belongs." Osbourne answered, regaining strength in his voice.

"Sir. I'm not following you."

"Mr. Ryan. This Fixer is good. You don't know how good he is. You might ask your Mr. Wines how good he is—that is why Wines visited me last Spring. But the problem isn't the Russians—they are just doing what Russians do. They disrupt the status quo. They put people and nations on edge. But for them to do what they naturally do; they need inside help."

"So, Mr. President, what is going on?"

"The best I can figure it, The Fixer made a deal with the man who would be president. A broke man with very few scruples. Gave him lots of money and the world's largest ego boost—an opportunity to be a U.S. President and Leader of the Free World. And someone who would play along or look the other way."

"Okay." Ryan acknowledged as he pulled out his legal pad. He didn't think he would need it for the one word answer he was originally seeking when he called. Now he was getting a whole lot more—maybe?

"The role the Russians are playing is that of a megaphone. The ability to spread the word and create a diversion. But the big headline is disinformation. Am I saying this word loud enough Fred? Disinformation! Out and out lies fabricated against the other candidate. And maybe some the other way too. About the FBI. About our trade agreements. About our pact with NATO. About our efforts to stop global warming. Even about the size of his dick. *And your paper has identified the source and the means of how this disinformation has been generated and spread across this land.* You've identified and traced it. Traced most of it. The most important parts, anyway. Great reporting by the damn *Washington Post*. And Mr. Wines and Mr. Olsen. Just excellent!"

"Thank you, sir. I will tell them you approve."

"Oh, no need. I called Mr. Wines myself to let him know."

Bingo!
Question asked and answered.

"Then Mr. President, what is your take on this week's WikiLeak drop of internal emails from the democratic party's campaign. Russian doing?"

"Yes, Fred. They were behind the drop. Let them cry havoc and let slip the dogs of war."

Interesting choice of words.

Again.

The president continued. "Certainly. Guccifer? Russian to the core. But the timing was orchestrated by the Fixer and his plan."

Fred Ryan looked over his notes and saw one other thing not resolved.

"Sir, *how* are the three former presidents involved?"

"Haven't lost it Fred, have you? That lawyer in you. And your note taking. Never miss a hole. You know Mr. Wines is just like that too. Say one little thing and the next thing you know—he's on it."

With those words, a bulb flashed in Ryan's mind. Sitting alone in his office, he shook his head a couple of times.

Could it be?
Could he be?

The latent reporter chops of the *Washington Post* CEO and Publisher took over. "Mr. President, please don't answer that last question. I do not want to know the answer."

"Okay Fred."

"But I do have one more question for you Mr. President."

"What is that—Fred?"

"Sir, are you somehow, The Fixer?"

Chapter 88

Jimmy Olsen's desk phone in the *Washington Post* newsroom rang. It was Special Agent Charles Noble on the line. "Good afternoon, Charles. What's up?"

"Would it be possible for us to meet this afternoon, at Planet Krypton. I have something you might be able to assist me with."

"Certainly."

"And can we keep this on the QT?"

"If you like."

"3:00 pm?"

"That works."

"Thanks Jimmy."

•••

Katy Lynn Holloway looked up from her desk computer. Distraught. It had been a week since the *Washington Post* "pussy video" story broke and received nearly endless airplay on all the networks. Even her dependable Fox.

The latest polling showed a train wreck ready to happen. A disaster. Her "values-voters" were plunging, as were soccer moms everywhere—though the white-male vote remained steady.

Her candidate reassured her everything would be okay.

But how?

•••

Jimmy Olsen arrived at his home at 2:45 pm. Agent Charles Noble arrived at exactly 2:55 p.m. Five minutes early. Right on time. His tie was off, and he had a solid blue running wind breaker on instead of his suit jacket.

No FBI emblazoned across the back.
But I bet he's packing.
No worries.

We've built a trust.

As they passed through to the living area, Jimmy grabbed two bottles of water from the refrigerator and handed one to Charles. They then passed into the security hallway leading to The Planet. Jimmy noticed each time Charles entered the secure hallway, he closely examined the walls, ceiling, and floor—trying to discover the ports of his torture.

Once they sealed themselves inside the Planet, Charles turned to Jimmy with a confession and a request. An *off-the-record* request.

"Jimmy, we just retained an old laptop computer belonging to the former secretary of state's assistant's ex-husband."

"Weiner?" Jimmy laughed. "More photos?"

"No photos," Charles answered without any humor. "This isn't funny. The Bureau found emails, many emails on it from the candidate's server."

"Okay. You should have seen them with the entire set we sent over to you months ago."

"That's what I am thinking, but it seems the boss is thinking they are unique and has confidentially alerted the leadership in the House of their existence."

"Confidentially?" Jimmy laughed again. "Not for long. Pretty juicy stuff to keep a secret."

"Exactly. Seems weird my boss pursued it in this way before we thoroughly checked it out. Said he had to do it. Had to keep the Bureau out of the mud and full transparency is the only way."

"Interesting." Jimmy answered, his mouth in a tight smile and a slight nod of his head. "What'd you have?"

"I got a flash drive here with the emails. Can we cross reference these with the contents of the server?"

"Sure. Won't take a minute."

Charles handed Jimmy the flash drive. But instead of sticking it into his system, he pulled another computer out of a cabinet, and placed the drive into it and shut the door.

"Sorry Charles. Need to make sure the FBI is not trying to penetrate my system. This will take just a few minutes to ensure the drive and the files are clean."

"Are you sure you're not NSA?" Charles laughed.

I hope I am better.

As promised, Jimmy's system quickly analyzed the contents of the flash drive and compared the contents word for word against his original download of the server contents.

"Charles, you have viewed every one of these emails. And since we both have the original server's metadata, we both have verification the emails were indeed received by this one computer. So, what's up?"

"Like I said Jimmy, the boss has served these up to the Congressional Committee. It will take us about a week to reexamine all of them for any confidential material."

"And during that time, with only eleven days before Election Day, our election becomes even more impacted by confusion and disinformation." Jimmy added.

"But why is the Director so hellbent?" wondered FBI Special Agent Charles Noble.

Jimmy answered. "It does seem orchestrated. Doesn't it?"

"Exactly. And we now have yet another interesting character." Charles answered slowly, putting it all together as he spoke. "In this case, another personal computer . . . this time belonging to the estranged husband of the Democratic candidate's number one assistant . . . himself a discredited high profile Democratic congressman . . . who just happens to be charged with sexting obscene material to an under-aged girl." Then looking up at Jimmy, "who could make this stuff up? The pieces falling together, perfectly."

"Interesting Charles. Perfect timing, too?" Jimmy added. "Just like clockwork."

Chapter 89

For Katy Lynn Holloway, the news out of the congressional subcommittee and the FBI could not have been any better. *A reversal of fortune!* A perv's computer is suspected to contain even more of the missing Democratic candidate's emails. Less than two weeks before Election Day.

What a narrative she could spin!

What a show her candidate could put on.

It is exactly what she and her organization needed to bring out the worst once again in the other candidate, *and her husband.*

The perfect coda to quash the current polling trend, seal the deal, and elect her boss!

• • •

Fred Ryan had a strong hunch—some good evidence—but not a direct confirmation.

President Osbourne's answer to his question was convoluted, but telling: "Fred, you know from your days in the White House, all presidents, past and present, are Fixers. Comes with the office. Never goes away. We use the influence we have—to accomplish what we see is needed. And leading up to this year's election, we were taking our democracy for granted. Our parties overreaching. We are letting petty stuff rise and leaving important stuff undone. Unsaid. We are doing what is needed to just get by. That needs to change."

Osbourne then concluded: "We needed to wake everyone up. We needed to find a cure. Maybe it's the worst equipped person possible who could be elected and then hold the office. But only temporarily."

Why then did Osbourne bring Wines into the story?

• • •

The three former presidents convened another conference call.

"Another surprise from Elvis. This time, it will be fatal. The FBI playing the server card one more time" said the first.

"I thought—with the *Washington Post* release of the data—we were in the clear" added the second.

"Guess not. And we'll be hearing more about you too" whispered the third.

"No one can escape their past. Not in politics" admitted the second.

"Gentlemen, we started this with good, honorable intentions. We humbly requested help," acknowledged the first. "I just can't understand why Elvis took this route. Let's just hope the whole thing doesn't backfire on us."

"I hope you're right." wished the second. "But the election is in just a few days."

Chapter 90

"President Osbourne's office, Pat Hayes speaking."

"Good afternoon, Pat. Geoffrey Wines here. Is President Osbourne in this afternoon?"

"Yes sir. He and the team got a good morning of fishing in, and now he's busy preparing for tomorrow's election. The president goes nuts. Sets up several televisions, has an array of remote controls in his hands, and watches the three networks all night long."

Pat then continued with a bit of humor in her voice, "And this year, he insisted on installing a fourth set, so he can watch Fox's coverage after seeing everything you guys uncovered."

"Well, it's going to be interesting." Wines responded, thinking curious indeed.

"Let me get Mr. President for you. One moment."

After a brief hold, and the usual three clicks of the security system, President Robert Osbourne's voice roared with excitement, "Well good afternoon, Mr. Wines. Checking to see if your number one source skipped town, or to get a last-minute scoop before this pre-planned trainwreck is about to happen."

"Pre-planned trainwreck?"
Another familiar phrase.

Wines pressed forward with the purpose of his call. "Sir, do you think the Fixer will succeed? Will his candidate win tomorrow?"

"Not beating around the bush, are you Mr. Wines." The president then let out a long slow exhale. "Two weeks ago, after the pussy parking lot video came out, our Fixer . . ."

"Our Fixer?"

" . . . seemed to have failed." Osbourne took a long breath. "But then more missing emails seemed to have resurfaced, this time compromised by a most despicable character, turning the tide once again. This Fixer's denouement guarantees only one outcome." Osbourne then added with a laugh, "I could not have written a more Shakespearian ending if I tried."

> *"If I tried?"*
> *Shakespearian?*

"The Fixer twisted the fate of each character. He created both protagonists and antagonists. And bystanders too, like you Mr. Wines. And James Olsen too." Osbourne enthused, "His plotline is flawless. Or at least till it be morrow."

> *"Till it be morrow?"*
> *Another Shakespearian quote.*

With that last statement, Geoffrey Wines' gut antenna pointed straight to the president, with the whole story flashing through his mind: Osbourne's original tip; Meteor Pizza; Reverend Brooks; Jimmy's on-line discoveries; political talking points culminating in false Facebook stories; Russian bots; politicians stepping aside and letting things happen; and finally, after valuable time lost, convincing the paper's management to run the stories.

Superseding all these events stood the former president's uncanny way of anticipating *everything*. Had he, Jimmy, Fred, and *The Washington Post* been witnessing—and reporting—a performance. Osbourne's performance?

> *Are we the victims of stagecraft?*
> *Is this a theatrical production on the world's largest stage?*

Bracing himself, Geoffrey decided to follow his intuition. "Sir, I have a question."

"What is that?"

"How did you pull this one off, sir?" Geoffrey asked with a sinking sense of regret, fearing his reporter's position had been compromised, and used for an ulterior motive.

The president said nothing for several seconds. Only his breathing could be heard. Wines sat pat, not saying a word. He did not want to give Osbourne any chance to change the subject.

Finally, the former president spoke. "Mr. Wines. Are you asking me if I am The Fixer? And that it is I who fixed this election?" His voice ice cold.

"Yes sir." Wines answered, stomach churning and mind racing.

> *Had he, and Pat, enticed me with the Gulf War story?*
> *Only to set me up for this performance?*
>
> *I haven't been able to confirm an outsider's role.*
> *No evidence of an actual Fixer,*
> *Nor knowing if the war sequence did, indeed, lead to the fall of the Soviet Union.*

Only silence once again emanated from the other end of the line. Finally, for what seemed an eternity, the president spoke.

"No sir, Mr. Wines. I am not." The president said with a sharp authoritarian edge Geoff had never experienced before. "And you can tell your damn publisher that too, though something tells me he won't believe you."

"Then who is?" Wines probed, straight up—not believing the president.

"I do not know" the president answered slowly and quietly, then adding, his voice now humble and sad. "I really don't. But please hurry and find out. This election is all but over. We'll know what happens tomorrow night. But regardless of the outcome, *this Fixer must be stopped!*"

"And what about the Russian interference?" Wines added, knowing so much that fed the events leading into the election came from Russia: The Bots; Guccifer and WikiLeak drops; the Pee Video;

the man photographed in the elevator, whom Jimmy identified as a "Cyber-Russian."

Again, the president took another long pause. Geoffrey Wines, Pulitzer Prize winning journalist held tight, said nothing, waiting for President Osbourne to continue.

Finally, Osbourne spoke. "Mr. Wines," the president's voice foreboding, "You may not believe me, but I have one last warning for you."

Warning?

"Warning? What is that sir?" Geoff answered, his words precise.

"This election—no matter who wins tomorrow—is certainly not about the Russians. *It's about us.* It's about disinformation. It's about our leaders telling the truth. Wanting the truth. It's about our collective ability to dismiss false narratives . . . and valuing the truth."

Osbourne's voice then deepened and became even more ominous, "And Mr. Wines, if we can't trust in what our leaders say, then our great country is simply ruined. Ruined! And our powerful democracy will be doomed."

Geoffrey Wines then heard a click, as Former President Robert S. Osbourne, Jr. ended the call.

—THE END—
(But The Fixer's story is not over)

THE FIXER RETURNS
Book Three in the Geoffrey Wines Series

The ominous specter of The Fixer returns when Jimmy Olsen receives an ambiguous missive that portends a world-wide disaster. It is now a race against the clock to find The Fixer and stop whatever he is planning.

Geoffrey Wines, Jimmy Olsen, and a new character, Dana Lyons, a witty scientist, begin their quest to fully understand the danger and warn the world.

As they dig deeper, they find more disturbing facts about The Fixer's enigmatic past and reasons to believe he is serious and fully capable in delivering on his cryptic warning.

Author's Note

Since 2016, our presidential elections have become ground zero for the mechanized, industrialized, social media driven disinformation campaigns now permeating every facet of our lives.

As a result, many Americans cannot discriminate between what is real and what is purely fabricated. Politicians use it to fund campaigns. News organizations repeat and create their own false narratives, ones they know to be false—simply to increase viewership / readership and profits. Hence, the press has become the tip of the spear to either defend or eviscerate the truth, leaving their much needed credibility in shreds.

The courts via Special Counsels, Multi-Million Dollar Lawsuits, Litigation Trials, Court Judgements, and a multitude of DOJ Investigations have also attempted to unwind truth from falsehoods.

The place where we get our news remains divided; and is even vaster today than described in this book. This has created two (or more) competing sets of facts—leading to confusion; distrust in our fellow citizens and national institutions; and leaving our nation even more vulnerable to foreign manipulation. We, as Americans can clearly see how "bad guy" foreign governments use disinformation; but we do not (or refuse to) see it when the same falsehoods target us—*by us*.

Bizarrely, the Fixer's entire strategy of installing an unqualified man into the presidency has fulfilled the three former presidents' goal of *"re-engaging Americans into the voting and civic processes."* Voter turnout has skyrocketed across all elected offices, and we have learned more about the brilliance—and limits—of our Constitution than these three former presidents could have imagined.

While this broader engagement is a good thing, my belief is most Americans truly do not understand how they are being individually manipulated. The objective of this book is to somehow convey—using a fictional format based on thorough research—how disinformation is started, fed, made credible, and perpetuated. How responsible news organizations wrestle with repeating and exposing the falsehoods for fear of spreading them.

With this greater awareness and understanding, it is my hope we will not be permanent victims of its grasp.

Want to know how Geoffrey Wines and President Osbourne's relationship began?

(And what Jimmy Olsen discovered when sifting through *The Washington Post's* trash).

The CAMP DAVID CONSPIRACY
The Original Geoffrey Wines Novel

America is losing the War on Drugs. It's simple to understand why. Too many citizens enjoy using unlawful drugs; and too much money can be made producing, distributing, and selling them.

For President Robert S. Osbourne, a solution is at hand, and he must decide whether to take it. His administration has a legal strategy, but one other person has an illegal plan — that is working.

Can Washington Post metro reporter Geoffrey Wines connect the dots to reveal the most brazen plot he could ever imagine? No one will know until the gripping last page of this political thriller.

THE CAMP DAVID CONSPIRACY will keep you spellbound.

Antim Straus spent a career in new food product development and lives in Missouri with his wife of over 40 years.

Straus holds two U.S. Patents and is the author of the *Geoffrey Wines Series*. He also wrote *How Mrs. God and I Created the Universe — A Humorous Retelling* and co-edited the trade book *An Integrated Approach to New Food Product Development*.

Please visit Antim at AntimStraus.com to order books, be placed on his mailing list, and learn of new projects.

> *If you enjoyed this book,*
> *please leave a review*
> *and share a copy with a friend.*
> *Thank you so much.*

Made in United States
North Haven, CT
16 August 2025